THE RISING

A BADLANDS NOVEL

MORGAN BRICE

CONTENTS

eBook ISBN: 978-1-939704-86-3
Print ISBN: 978-1-939704-87-0
Badlands: Copyright © 2019 by Gail Z. Martin.

Cover art by Natania Barron
Darkwind Press is an imprint of DreamSpinner Communications, LLC

THE RISING

A BADLANDS NOVEL

By Morgan Brice

1

SIMON

"We need more pirates. Pirates sell."

Simon Kincaide, owner of Grand Strand Ghost Tours, looked up with a chuckle. "Especially dead pirates. Or should I say 'dread' pirates?"

Pete King, Simon's assistant store manager and part-time tour guide, rolled his eyes. "Both. I'm just saying, we could switch up the scripts and add more pirates to the ghost tours. Especially with the new wrecks the hurricane exposed. That's all everyone seems to be talking about these days."

Simon nodded. "I think you're on to something. I have some good pirate ghost stories, but they're pretty well known. Why don't you do some research and see if you can come up with some that aren't as familiar?" He grinned. "Let me guess—you're itching to try out a new pirate costume?"

"Guilty as charged," Pete replied. "You know the tourists love that stuff."

"Oh, believe me. I know!" Simon used to do all the tours himself, but during the past year, business had grown enough for him to promote Pete and bring him in to expand the number and types of tours offered. Pete did his tours in full costume and made it more of a performance, fitting since he was finishing up a degree in drama. Simon had been a folklore professor before coming to Myrtle Beach, so his tours stuck to the facts and history. Both types of tours were popular.

"People say that the new wreck was a pirate corsair, pretty notorious in its day," Pete went on, obviously thrilled with his topic.

"Don't get your hopes up too much—around here, everything is a pirate ship until proven otherwise," Simon joked. "Seriously, the last time a good wreck washed in, everyone was sure it was Bluebeard's ship until it turned out to be a garbage scow!"

"Shh!" Pete teased. "Leave me my fragile illusions!" he added, throwing an arm across his face and pretending to swoon.

Ten in the morning on a late January Monday meant Myrtle Beach was quiet. The snowbird tourists were likely still sleeping or enjoying breakfast. Not like the summer when walkers and joggers practically crowded the beach and boardwalk at dawn. And with a storm forecast, it was likely to stay quiet.

"I'll go pick up some coffee," Simon offered. "Somehow, I don't think you'll get overwhelmed with customers while I'm gone."

Simon wandered down to the railing and looked out over the Atlantic. Wind blew his shoulder-length brown hair and stung his hazel eyes as he looked out over the whitecaps and the rough surf. He loved the ocean like this, wild and powerful. Simon took a deep breath of salty air and listened to the pounding waves.

Tourists might not be on the boardwalk, but the weather never stopped its resident ghosts. Simon watched two children in old-fashioned clothes skip several yards, then vanish. A translucent old man on a bicycle laden with possessions rode past, giving a ghostly jingle of his bell. On the steps to the beach access, a dreadlocked young man leaned on his elbows and stared out at the water that took his life, in no hurry to move on.

Most people couldn't see the ghosts, but Simon could.

Grand Strand Ghost Tours didn't just arise from Simon's passion for myth, legend, and folklore; it was rooted in his abilities as a psychic medium. Sure, the ghost tours were largely entertainment, but Simon also gave private psychic readings and conducted séances by appointment. Along with the books he wrote about ghosts and the speaking engagements he provided for local organizations, Simon had managed to create a thriving business. He leaned against the railing, enjoying a moment of contentment.

Or maybe, the calm before the storm, a little voice in the back of his mind warned.

His phone buzzed, and Simon pulled it from his pocket and smiled. "Hey. Miss me?"

"Always." Homicide lieutenant Vic D'Amato's voice was a husky rumble. "I just wanted to check what time you finish up tonight. Figured it was my turn to pick up dinner." The tone in Vic's voice promised far more than food, and Simon felt the anticipation go right to his dick.

"I should be finished around seven. It's off-season, so no tours on Mondays. You have a busy day lined up?" Simon asked as he started walking toward his favorite coffee shop.

"Not yet, and I'm hoping it stays that way," Vic replied. "It's never a good thing when we're busy."

"Let me know if you hear anything official about the storm. I've heard six different forecasts, and I haven't even gotten coffee yet."

"Sure thing—but don't expect anything dependable yet. We're too far out."

Simon knew how changeable forecasts could be so close to the ocean. Still, Myrtle Beach had barely gotten back on its feet after the last hurricane, so the news of another severe winter storm—hurricane or not—had everyone on edge.

"Be careful out there," Simon said, letting his voice drop to a growl. "I love you."

"Love you, too. Stay out of trouble."

Despite the forecasts, Simon couldn't help feeling a spring in his step after talking with Vic. They'd been together for less than a year, but Simon was finding it more and more difficult to remember what life was like before meeting his handsome homicide cop. Vic had officially moved into Simon's retro blue bungalow after the holidays, and while they were still working out their new living situation, Simon had never been happier.

The boardwalk might not be busy, but Le Mizzenmast, Simon's favorite coffee shop, was always bustling. The locals called it Le Miz, not to be confused with the musical. The building had previously been a pirate-themed attraction, and when Tracey Cullen took over, she couldn't afford to remodel, so she just incorporated the pirate decor into her theme and went with it.

"Hi, Simon!" Tracey called with a wave from behind the register. "You want the usual?" When Simon nodded, Tracey turned to her barista. "One Dread Pirate Roberts and a mocha please!"

Simon took his place in line, remembering how he and Vic had met right here, waiting for coffee. Simon had taken one look at Vic's muscled body, his dark brown eyes, and the ink on his arms and felt an instant attraction. After all these months and several hair-raising adventures, the magnetism had only gotten stronger. Being in love felt wonderful, and Simon resolved to enjoy every minute of it.

"You must be thinking about Vic. You look like a smitten puppy," Tracey said when Simon made it to the front of the line. Tracey's dark skin glowed with a slight sheen from the warmth of the espresso maker's steam. Her long braids rocked blue tips for winter, after red for Christmas and orange for Halloween.

"Nothing wrong with that," Simon returned. "You're exactly the same when Shayna's around."

"Yep. I won't argue that," Tracey agreed. Tracey was Simon's best friend, a connection he'd made not long after he moved to Myrtle Beach from Columbia three years ago. Shayna, Tracey's girlfriend, was an emergency room nurse, and the four of them often double-dated.

The line ended with Simon for a moment, though he had no doubt more customers desperate for good java would crowd in soon.

"You hear anything new about that wreck offshore?" Tracey asked as she rang him up.

"Why? Are you going to name a drink after it?" Simon teased.

"Maybe. Only if it's got a cool story behind it. I mean, no one wants a boring pirate, right?"

"Are there such things? I figured all the swashbuckling and looting and pillaging was exciting, by definition."

"More for the pirates than the townspeople, I'm sure," Tracey said as she counted his change. "A lot less fun than that Disney ride makes it look. Although it would have been awesome if the town ladies really had chased off the pirates with frying pans!"

Simon moved down to wait for his Dread Pirate Roberts latte, and his attention drifted to the TV in the corner. Even without the volume turned up, he could see the weather map and read the crawl at the bottom of the screen. The green, rotating CGI graphic of the storm looked ominous, and several arrows showed the possible course. Some projected it hitting Myrtle Beach head on, while others showed the storm veering northward, or stalling off-shore. Despite all the forecasting tech and weather satellites, no one ever really knew what was going to happen until the last minute.

"You think they'll have to take the SkyWheel apart again?" Samir, the barista, asked.

The huge Ferris wheel was a Grand Strand icon, visible for miles with its neon lights. Last fall, when the hurricane was on its way, Simon and the other boardwalk merchants had watched the wheel get disassembled to ride out the storm. That might have been months ago, but it felt like days.

"I hope not," Simon replied, taking his drink and Pete's mocha from the counter. "We're out of hurricane season. This is just a winter storm."

Samir raised an eyebrow. "Just? You've been here long enough to know a storm is bad news, no matter what they call it. Between what it blows down and what it washes up, they're nothing but trouble."

Simon nodded. The insurance premium on his shop reminded him of that every time he got the bill. Storm damage and flooding were two of the hazards that went with living at the beach. To Simon, the benefits far outweighed the dangers.

Melancholy settled deep as Simon walked back to his shop. Normally, looking out at the ocean lifted his spirits, but today, he felt a strange foreboding. The Atlantic was beautiful, but it could be deadly. Every year, drowning deaths reminded residents and tourists that the ocean wasn't a wave pool.

Farther out, beyond where swimmers and jet skis ranged, a graveyard of ships held the remains of sailors from centuries past. Like the wreck people were talking about that had been exposed and washed closer to shore by the last big storm. Everyone else conjured up fantastical stories about the doomed ship, like something out of *Treasure Island*. But Simon couldn't shake the feeling that this particular wreck was trouble waiting to happen.

Simon had learned long ago to listen to his intuition, even if it fell short of a full-on vision or premonition. He lifted his face to the wind and let it rush past him, taking his breath away and tangling his hair. While Myrtle Beach in January might be warm compared to other places, it was still cold enough to deter even the most stout-hearted snowbirds from taking a dip.

He ducked into Grand Strand Ghost Tours and handed off Pete's mocha. One woman lingered in the back looking at t-shirts, while another studied the rack with Simon's ghost books. A solidly build man in khaki pants and a contractor-logo polo shirt read their tour brochures as if he were waiting for something. He looked up when Simon walked in.

"Are you Simon Kincaide? The ghost hunter?"

Simon stifled a sigh. "I'm a psychic medium, not really a ghost hunter." He tried not to let wording bother him. Most people only knew what they saw on television. Simon didn't need to go on ghost hunts—the ghosts usually came to him. And unlike the paranormal investigators on television, Simon's gift was solid enough to earn him consulting status with the Myrtle Beach Police Department, thanks to Vic and his boss.

"Sorry," the man said, coloring a bit with embarrassment. He had sandy blond hair and blue eyes, with a tan that said he spent a lot of time outdoors. Not surprising, if he did construction for a living like the shirt suggested. "I've been watching too much *Long Island Medium*."

"It's okay," Simon replied. "I get it all the time. How can I help you?"

"I'm Trevor Nichols," the man said, extending his hand. His

grip was dry and firm. "I'm the general contractor on the renovations for Socastee Manor."

Simon frowned, trying to place the name. "The old plantation on the coast below Murrells Inlet?"

Trevor nodded. "Yes. It's being sold to a developer who wants to bring it back to its former glory. Which, given decades of neglect, is going to take some doing. That's my job. But as you may know, the house has a…history. That's where I'm hoping you come in."

Simon leaned against the counter and took a sip of his coffee. "So, it's haunted?"

"I think so. As far as I can tell—and I've looked hard—no one's pranking us. Frankly, the incidents have been dangerous enough that they'd be criminal, not a joke."

"Tell me." Simon gestured for Trevor to follow him over to the table and chairs that sat in the back corner of the shop. It was where Simon did his psychic readings.

Trevor settled into a chair and took a deep breath. Simon could tell the man felt uncomfortable. But whether it was asking for help or coming to a psychic that bothered him, Simon couldn't discern. He tried to tune in to Trevor's energy, hoping to get some kind of read but got nothing except worry and exhaustion. A strictly non-magical appraisal told Simon that his visitor hadn't been sleeping well and that he was jittery from nerves and too much caffeine.

"Kalston-Waters is the development company that bought Socastee Manor. Jonah Camden is the developer I work for. He's got a great vision for the house, but a demanding timeline. The hurricane last fall put us behind—some damage, but more of an impact because of material delays and weather too bad to risk having crews there."

"The house is directly on the water?"

Trevor nodded. "It's on a spit of land that practically becomes an island at high tide, and it's often cut off except by boat if the water rises. Which, if the stories are true, served well for smuggling."

Simon struggled to remember what he had heard about the old mansion. The family that built it had been wealthy, but not particularly well-liked. The plantation had been prominent before the Civil War, but like many others, fell into decline afterward. There had been whispers about smuggling, but the family—which had been powerful locally until the 1980s—had ruthlessly squashed anything that might tarnish their reputation.

"What's going on?" Simon asked.

"Tools go missing. Sometimes they're destroyed, other times they just never get found. That's expensive—and causes delays. Materials are fine when we leave for the night, and ruined in the morning. And there've been accidents—cracked boards, scaffolding that gives way, and a fall down the stairs that could have really been bad. The guy who fell said he was pushed, but no one else was in the house at the time. Thank God no one's gotten killed or seriously injured, but it's only a matter of time if this stuff keeps happening."

"Can you rule out malicious tampering?" Simon had run into cases where people tried to cover up their crimes by faking a haunting.

"We put up cameras, and of course the whole place is locked at night. Even set a night watchman. The security guards won't stay— they say there's something weird out there and then they don't come back. The cameras have picked up white flashes and lots of those little light spots—"

"Orbs."

"Yeah. Those."

"Other than the man who fell on the steps, have you or the crews experienced anything strange?"

Trevor hesitated as if he were afraid he might sound crazy.

Simon leaned forward. "It's okay. I've seen a lot of weird things. I'll believe you. I just need to know what's been happening."

Trevor swallowed, then gave a curt nod. "Okay. So…we've had places in the house suddenly get so cold we can see our breath, but the rest of the house—hell, the rest of the room—isn't. Then a minute later, the cold spot's gone. The crew hears footsteps in places there aren't any people, and when they go to look, no one's there, and everybody's accounted for. Tools get moved around, like I said. A couple of my guys said they saw movement and thought one of their buddies was coming up behind them, but when they turned, no one was there. But it *felt* like there was someone in the room." He met Simon's gaze, silently begging to be believed.

"Everything you're telling me is pretty classic," Simon replied. "The malicious pranks worry me. That can go wrong fast. Do you get any sense of who the ghost is or what it wants? Or whether there's more than one?"

Trevor shrugged, turning his palms up. "This is so far out of my league, I got nothin'. I've been alone in a room and knew there was something else in there with me, something I couldn't see. I've heard footsteps and thought I saw someone who wasn't there. So my guys aren't making it up. They're getting paid well, so there's no reason for them to sabotage the job. And we haven't had any controversy, so I can't blame it on protesters."

"I can come out tomorrow to have a look, if that suits your schedule," Simon offered. "That doesn't mean I can fix anything on the spot, but if I get a sense of what the energies feel like, I can see what it will take to stop the problem."

"You really think you can make it stop?" Trevor's expression relaxed with hope. "God, it's been awful. I've been worried about someone getting hurt, the job's falling behind, and my boss is riding my ass over the delays."

"I can't do much about your boss," Simon said, "but if I can figure out how to send your unwanted spirits packing, you might be able to get back on schedule and keep your crew safe. I'll do my best."

"You'll get paid," Trevor assured him. "I have a budget for contingencies. I'd say getting haunted counts."

Simon quoted his rate for an on-site consult, and Trevor agreed without blinking at the amount. "I'll see you at noon, if that suits," Simon replied, and Trevor nodded. "Good. In the meantime, I'll look into the history. If there's a haunting, there's usually unfinished business—or secrets someone doesn't want to have come out." He frowned. "Has your crew found anything hidden, or that seemed like someone didn't want it found?"

Trevor shook his head. "No. I'd know if they had. This crew has been with me for two years—we're pretty tight. They're the ones who brought up the idea of having someone come out and bless the house, or even do an exorcism." He grimaced at that last word. "I know—dramatic, right? But they're scared. All of a sudden, they're wearing saints' medallions and burning sage, and I'm finding salt sprinkled everywhere. So I figured it might make a lot of sense to have someone like you come do what you do, before it gets worse."

"I'm glad you came," Simon said, leaning back in his chair. "And with luck, it's just a ghost problem, not something you'd need an exorcism for." Fuck, he hoped not. Ghosts were trouble enough when they went bad. He had no desire to tangle with demons.

"Thank you," Trevor said. They exchanged phone numbers so Simon could text him. "You don't know how much I appreciate this. I'll meet you at the house tomorrow, and show you around. Most of the crew will be there, so you can meet them and hear their stories."

"I appreciate that. And I might take you up on it—or I might get enough from my own impressions to know how to fix it. One way or another, I'll do my best to un-haunt your house."

During slow times during the afternoon, Simon searched the internet for anything he could find about Socastee Manor or the family that built it. Lord Jamison—Jamie—Dunwood had been granted the land back in 1747 for service to the crown and built a rice plantation that thrived through the Revolution. He died in a Yellow Fever outbreak while visiting Charleston, and was buried far from his beloved manor. When Jamie died, the title passed to his son John, and good fortune remained until the Civil War.

After that, the plantation fell on hard times. Bad decisions and business failures dogged the family. Rumors swirled about gunrunning during the War and rum-running during Prohibition. The Dunwood family seemed to have a talent for prompting the other Lowcountry gentry to challenge them to duels or sue them. The last Dunwood to live in the manor, back in the 1970s, had been an ill-tempered man by the name of Patrick. It seemed that Patrick had a reputation for shady business dealings and appeared to have been universally disliked and feared.

"You know anything about Socastee Manor?" Simon asked Pete

when the shop was quiet.

"The abandoned place down past Murrells Inlet? I mean, I know where it is, but not much else. When I was a kid, everyone called it the 'witch house.'"

Simon raised an eyebrow. "Do you know why?"

Pete shrugged. "It was hella creepy, and no one had lived there for a long time. I heard stories that there used to be a mean old man who chased people off with a shotgun, but that might have been made up. As for the witch part—probably just the kind of thing kids say to dare each other to go in."

"Did anyone you know actually go into the house?"

Pete chuckled. "Are you kidding? Some of the older kids said they did, but I'm pretty sure they lied. We all joked about it, but none of my friends went in. And certainly not me—I hate spiders, and that place looked like it would've been full of them." He gave Simon a look. "Why?"

Simon sighed and closed his laptop, pushing his half-empty cup aside. The coffee he made in the break room was never as good as what he got at Le Miz. "That guy who came in—Trevor—is trying to remodel it, and says they've got ghost problems. I'm going out to have a look tomorrow, and just wondered what I was getting myself into." *From everything I've read—trouble.*

"Try not to almost get killed this time," Pete said, straightening the crystals and candles in the glass case. "I like working here, and I'd hate to have to find a new job."

Simon and Vic had chased down a supernatural serial killer in their first case together, and it had nearly cost Simon his life. They'd caught a second killer with the help of a ghost's testimony around Halloween, and stopped a series of murders with a magical connection right before Christmas. Simon had to admit that Pete wasn't wrong to be concerned.

"No one's gotten killed—and hopefully, no one will be," Simon replied. "It sounds like a poltergeist, or maybe just a ghost that's unhappy people are invading its home. With luck, it'll be easy to fix."

Pete's skeptical snort told Simon what his assistant thought of that.

Simon worried much more about Vic than he did himself. Weeks ago a suspect in one of Vic and Ross's murder cases took a shot at the two detectives. While the suspect's aim went wild and no one was hurt, Simon's nightmares were full of what might have been.

Deep inside, Simon knew his fears were fueled by a high-profile case years before, something that splashed all over the news when he lived in Columbia. Murder and politics often went hand-in-hand in the state capitol, and one big story had featured a state representative whose wealthy wife disappeared under mysterious circumstances. When evidence turned up that the missing heiress had been murdered, the husband had hired a hitman to go after the lead homicide detective on the case. Although the politician was eventually caught and convicted, the hitman made good on the contract, killing the detective in a gangland-style murder.

No matter how much Simon told himself that Myrtle Beach wasn't Columbia, he knew that bad things could happen anywhere, and desperate people took desperate measures.

Simon shivered, trying to force his gloomy thoughts away. Vic and Ross were good at their jobs, and they'd managed to stay mostly safe so far. He knew he had to trust Vic to come home safe at the end of the day. Still, in a battle between what his head knew and what his heart felt, Simon sometimes struggled to look on the bright side. To take his mind off his worry, Simon decided to throw himself into researching new merchandise vendors. A few hours of productivity boosted his mood tremendously.

The afternoon flew, and since it was the off-season and tours only ran on weekends, the shop closed at seven. On nice days, Simon liked to walk to work, but it was cold and windy enough for him to drive. Vic had walked to the precinct instead of riding his Hayabusa motorcycle, but he was a little more used to the cold, coming from Pittsburgh, than Simon who was raised in the South.

The blue bungalow had belonged to Simon's aunt and uncle, who had wintered in Myrtle Beach for years until health problems kept them closer to home. When Simon lost his teaching position at the University of South Carolina and headed to the beach to clear his head, his aunt offered to sell him the house and its contents for an amount that was really a gift. Simon had moved in and then started Grand Strand Ghost Tours three years ago.

All the lights were on, which told Simon Vic had beat him home. He grinned, climbing out of the car and heading up the steps, then paused to shake his long hair out of the man bun he usually wore at the shop. Vic met him in the entranceway as Simon hung up his coat, and pressed up against him from behind.

"You're cold. Let me warm you up." Vic wrapped his arms around Simon, splaying his fingers wide across his chest. He drew Simon close against him, pressing his groin against Simon's ass with a shimmy that sent sparks through every nerve in Simon's body.

"I missed you today." Vic's warm breath on Simon's neck was giving Simon all kinds of delightfully naughty ideas, all of which would result in dinner being late. Simon tilted his head, giving Vic access, and his partner licked and nipped his way from Simon's ear down to his shoulder. Simon brought his hands up to cover Vic's, and couldn't resist bucking back against Vic's very evident hard-on.

"Missed you, too. Always do," Simon said breathlessly. "Do we need to worry about dinner burning?"

Vic's low chuckle made Simon warm all over. "It's in the oven. We have time." He dropped his right hand to unfasten Simon's belt and work his zipper open. Vic's hand slipped inside and his fingers wrapped around Simon's hard cock. Simon groaned and reached back to pull Vic even closer.

"God, you smell so good," Vic murmured, still nibbling at Simon's neck. "I like it when you have your hair down. So sexy." His calloused hand worked Simon's shaft with skill, and Simon knew it wouldn't take long like this to bring him off. A few more strokes and Simon's release spilled over Vic's fist, which continued pumping him until he was completely spent. Then, as Simon turned to face his lover, Vic lifted his come-streaked hand to his mouth and licked his fingers clean.

"Fuck," Simon groaned, thinking that was so damn sexy. He kissed Vic, tasting himself on his lover's lips, and then sank to his knees. "One good turn deserves another," he said, looking up at Vic beneath his lashes.

Shit, Vic looked so amazing standing there, eyes lust-blown, face flushed with arousal, smelling of sex. Simon ran his hands down Vic's muscular thighs, nuzzling against his crotch, mouthing Vic's erection through the denim. His hands moved around to cup Vic's perfect ass and gave the globes a good squeeze.

"You're killing me," Vic panted.

Simon gave him a saucy smile, then flicked the buttons open on his fly and nuzzled the briefs beneath, breathing in a scent that was sweat and musk and all Vic. He licked at the wet spot where pre-come already stained the cotton, then pushed Vic's jeans and underwear down to mid-thigh and swallowed his lover's cock down to the root.

"Oh, fuck, Simon—so good," Vic moaned, steadying himself with one hand on Simon's head, tangling with his dark hair, and bracing against the wall with the other.

Simon worked Vic's cock, licking his way up the shaft and swirling his tongue over the head, tasting the salty bead of pre-come on the slit, then going down on him again until his nose hit Vic's dark, wiry pubes, sucking and humming.

Vic didn't last much longer than Simon had, shooting his load as Simon drank it down, then made eye contact as he licked the last drops from his lips.

"Jesus, what you do to me," Vic said as he pulled Simon to his feet and kissed him, mingling their flavors.

From the kitchen came the *ding* of a timer. "I'd like to do a lot more to you, but I'm hungry, so let's eat first," Simon said, giving Vic's ass a pinch as a promise of sexy times to come.

The smell of lasagna filled the bungalow. Simon followed Vic into the kitchen and poured them each glasses of water while Vic took the pan out of the oven. A bowl with tossed salad sat on the counter.

"What's the occasion?" Simon asked, wracking his brain to see if he had missed something special. Vic's birthday wasn't for another few months, and his own was still weeks away. Their first anniversary was closer to summer. And it definitely wasn't Valentine's Day. Simon was already making plans for that.

"It was a cold, blustery day and I wanted to eat comfort food and then maybe make out on the couch for a while," Vic replied, glancing over his shoulder with a wicked grin. "Something wrong with that?"

"Not at all," Simon assured him, grabbing a bottle of salad dressing from the fridge and putting the bowl on the table. Vic had already set the table, and he pulled a sheet pan with garlic toast out after the lasagna. "Just checking to make sure I didn't miss anything."

While they ate, Vic caught Simon up on what he could about the cases he was working. Simon felt a weird sense of relief that the murders were normal and non-magical, and at the same time, sadness that people didn't need supernatural interference to hurt each other.

"How about you?" Vic asked, as he finished the last bite of the lasagna on his plate and eyed the pan, deciding whether to have a second piece.

"Lots of talk about that wreck the rough waters uncovered," Simon replied. "But right now, no one really knows anything, it's all just rumors."

"Well, the rumor at work is that there's a dive team scheduled to come examine the ship," Vic said, with a grin that told Simon he was happy to have a scoop. "Some kind of historic reclamation specialists—like the guys who found the *Titanic* and the *Hunley*."

"Wow. I hope I get to see them out on their boat. That's so Indiana Jones." Simon knew Vic didn't mind when he got his geek on. He'd already confessed to following the search and recovery saga of the Civil War-era *Hunley* submarine and been down to visit the museum in Charleston the last time he dropped in on his cousin, Cassidy.

"More like Clive Cussler," Vic replied, mentioning the famous author who also was an exploration diver. "Count me out. I can swim okay, but I'm not crazy about being underwater."

"Can't blame you," Simon agreed. He'd never quite gotten up

the nerve to go snorkeling, let alone scuba diving, although both were popular pastimes at the beach.

They cleaned up after eating, then headed into the living room. The new couch was their first major joint purchase, and it had been delivered the week after New Year's when Vic officially moved in. The cushiony leather couch was as wide as a twin bed, so they could easily snuggle and watch movies.

"There are a couple of new shark movies streaming," Vic said. He put two beers on the end table and grabbed the remote as Simon arranged the pillows and reached for a cozy throw. Vic turned on the TV and then pivoted so he was lying down. He spread his legs in open invitation, and Simon slipped between them, lying with his head on Vic's chest, very aware of the semi Vic sported in his jeans.

"Oh good. More ways to die at the beach." Simon's mock-protest got an arched brow in response from Vic.

"You love these movies. Admit it."

"Maybe. In a guilty pleasure sort of way."

"There's a reason there are so many *Sharknado* sequels," Vic said. "They're like potato chips. You can't have just one."

"Are you sure you didn't want to grow up to be the police chief in *Jaws*?" Simon teased.

"Nah. The oceanographer guy got to be the real hero," Vic returned with a grin. "Still epic."

Simon nuzzled into Vic, taking in his scent, listening to his heartbeat. Vic's fingers tangled in Simon's hair, then dug deep to massage his scalp, and Simon nearly purred.

The beer on top of dinner and being wrapped up with Vic put Simon in a comfortable daze. He watched the movies, only paying partial attention, drifting in and out as he struggled to keep his eyes open.

The gallows stood in the park, just beyond the dune overlooking the sea. Three nooses dangled from the crosspiece, and a hooded executioner awaited the condemned men.

A crowd gathered, eager for the spectacle. Sheriff's deputies with muskets accompanied the shackled prisoners—nine in all—while a minister with a white collar read a prayer. Once the praying stopped, the crowd took up with catcalls and jeers. Some threw rocks. The deputies turned a blind eye, and the clergyman walked away, having done his part for their damned souls.

The men looked haggard, dressed in stained, ragged clothing. Their hair was unkempt, and they hadn't shaved in a while—whether from preference or circumstance.

Simon saw the events through someone else's eyes, someone who kept to the back of the crowd, who felt the need to bear witness although the execution sat in his belly like a stone.

Then the sheriff climbed onto the scaffold's platform, and a hush fell over the audience.

"William Beecher, Hastings Anders, Jacob Thornton, Steven Hunt, Thaddeus Green, Michael Bates, Caleb Strong, Benjamin Ross, and Joseph Hardin —you have been tried and found guilty of piracy on the high seas. The verdict is to hang by the neck until dead. So be it."

One of the pirates lunged forward. His hands were bound behind him and his ankles shackled, but he managed to nearly reach the platform before two deputies grabbed him.

"You know who the real pirate is," the man snarled. "You know who paid us and outfitted the ship. You're just too much of a coward to have him hang with us." The guards dragged him back, and the pirate fought them, struggling with all his might.

"Hear me!" he shouted to the crowd. "Jamie Dunwood is our master, and if we hang, he should too, by God!"

Simon sat up, gasping for air. Hands reached for him, and he fought his way free, bolting to the other side of the room and crouching in the corner. The vision had been so real, down to the smell of wood smoke and horse manure, and the creaking of the heavy ropes hanging from the gallows' arm. For crucial seconds, he had no idea where—or when—he was, and blind panic took over.

"Hey, hey. It's all right. You're safe." The familiar voice sounded steady and calming, but Simon was breathing too hard, and his mind was spinning. His whole body was primed for fight or flight.

"Simon? It's me, Vic. You're safe. You're in our house—the blue bungalow, remember?"

"When?" Simon rasped. "What year?"

Vic answered, and Simon shook his head. "That can't be."

"Simon, you're starting to scare me. Come on—wake up. You had a really bad dream."

Simon closed his eyes and took several deep breaths, willing himself to stop shaking, and feeling his heart jackhammer in his chest. When he opened his eyes, he saw Vic standing just out of reach, eyes filled with concern.

"Simon?"

Simon nodded, folding forward to rest his hands on his thighs as he tried to get himself under control. "I'm…okay," he panted.

"Is it all right if I get closer?" Vic's voice had the tempered concern Simon had heard him use with crime victims. Simon looked up and saw a red spot on Vic's cheek.

"Oh my God, did I hit you?" Anxiety and embarrassment gave way to shame.

"I caught your elbow when you bolted," Vic said with a shrug. "I'm fine."

"I'm so sorry." Simon's stomach pitched, and he ran for the bathroom, shouldering past Vic to drop to his knees beside the toilet and heave his guts up.

"Easy," Vic said as if he were talking to a spooked horse. He knelt beside Simon and stroked circles on his back, gathering his hair and keeping it out of the way. "Whatever it is, you're safe, I'm here, and you're okay."

Simon rested his forehead on his arm, still leaning over the toilet. His body shook, and he tasted bile. Vic left his side for a moment and returned with a paper cup of mouthwash. Simon managed a weak smile in thanks, rinsed and spat.

"Come on," Vic said, helping Simon up and steadied him while he brushed his teeth. "Let's get you to bed. I'll make sure everything's locked up."

Simon let Vic take his weight, leaning on him when Vic slipped an arm around his waist. They made it to the bedroom, and Vic lowered him to the mattress.

"I'm sorry," Simon said miserably. "This isn't the kind of end to the evening I had planned."

"Don't worry about it. How many nights have I gotten called out in the middle of things?"

Simon appreciated that Vic was trying to make him feel better, but he still felt shitty about ruining their evening. He reached out for Vic's hand and twined their fingers, then pressed them to his lips. "I love you."

Vic rustled his hair and squeezed his hand. "Love you, too. Stretch out, and I'll be right in."

Simon stripped down to his briefs and got under the covers. He heard Vic moving around the front rooms, turning off lights and the TV, checking the deadbolt. Minutes later, Vic cleaned up in the bathroom, then slid into bed beside Simon, putting his phone on the nightstand.

"It was a vision," Simon said in a voice just above a whisper. "It was real. I saw a hanging a long time ago. Pirates. I was really there."

"Maybe we shouldn't have watched that Johnny Depp movie so many times," Vic teased gently.

Simon shook his head. "No. This was something that really happened."

Vic put his arms around Simon and pulled him close, warm and protective. Simon let himself sink into the strength and security and reached out to trace the infinity symbol that was Vic's newest ink, in the cleft of his hip, done just for him.

"It might be real, but it's not able to hurt you now," Vic murmured. "I'm not going to let anything near you. Tomorrow, maybe you'll have an idea why you saw what you saw."

"I know what I saw. I saw the Gallows Nine. That's…bad."

"Who?"

Simon was glad for the darkness, so he didn't feel as awkward sharing what he'd seen. "Nine pirates, hanged back in 1765. They cursed the crowd before they died, and legend has it that seeing their ghosts is a harbinger, an omen that something awful is about to happen."

Vic kissed the top of his head. "Whatever it is, we'll figure it out. And we'll deal with it—together."

2

VIC

"So how is the cohabitating going?" Ross Hamilton, Vic's police partner, asked as he gave Vic a ride to the precinct. The rainy day was miserable for a walk, and Simon didn't need to go into the shop for hours yet.

"It's going…okay," Vic replied. "Technically, it's not any different than before, because I was always over there. But——"

"But it's still different because now you can't just go home if you need space, and it feels strange," Ross finished for him.

Vic hesitated, then nodded. "Yeah. Did you and Sheila live together before you got married?"

Ross shook his head. "Nope. Her folks were real old fashioned about that. We moved in together after the honeymoon. Let me tell you, that was an adjustment!"

"But you made it," Vic said. "And you've been together how long?"

"Five years." Ross drummed his fingers on the wheel as he waited for the poky driver in front of him to turn right.

"It's nice, living together for real," Vic said after a moment. The distance wasn't very far, but catching the lights wrong could add minutes to the drive. "It feels settled. I've never lived with anyone before. So it's kinda a big deal."

Ross slanted a look his way as he angled the car into the precinct parking lot. "Not even the loser you dated back home?"

Vic sighed. His ex-boyfriend, Nate, had been a fellow cop. When Vic had been involved in an on-duty shooting that had a supernatural cause, Nate pretty much threw him under the bus and refused to move with him. "No. Which is a good thing in hindsight. We were never really that much of a couple, I guess." He could see that now, but Nate's betrayal had hurt like fuck at the time, and for years afterward until Vic met Simon.

"It's an adjustment, for sure," Ross agreed. "All the little things —like the way you hang the toilet paper roll, whether you squeeze or roll the toothpaste, where you leave your towel—they add up."

They were still a few minutes early, so Vic took a chance. "Do you ever just know that Sheila hasn't told you everything on her mind, even when you ask? Simon's worried about something, and he's trying not to let on how much it bothers him. I asked, but he won't say. I don't know why he won't tell me."

Ross chuckled. "You've got to leave cop mode at work."

"What?"

"You heard me." He shifted in his seat. "So after Sheila and I had been married for about two years, we were arguing about a lot of petty stuff. We went for couples counseling. And one of the things the counselor said was that I had to quit interrogating her like a suspect."

"I'm not—" Vic frowned. "Shit. Is that what I'm doing?"

Ross shrugged. "Dunno, but I guess it's pretty common with cops. We're trained to watch body language and look for disparities. But on everyday stuff, it's not usually important. I had to learn that if Sheila needed to think something through, she wasn't 'withholding evidence'—she was just noodling it out." He cocked an eyebrow at Vic, who huffed out a breath.

"Yeah. Maybe. I hadn't thought about it that way," Vic admitted. "I'm just not sure I know how to turn off 'cop mode.'"

"Well you'd better learn. Trust me on this. It'll make it easier on both of you."

They headed inside, and Vic played Ross's words over in his mind. As much as he loved living with Simon, making the commitment also fed his worries. He'd lived alone since he had moved out of his parents' house before the Police Academy. While there had been other dates and hookups before Nate, Vic had rarely brought anyone back to his place. Nate almost never stayed the night, even if Vic invited him—something that made sense in retrospect.

Vic loved falling asleep with Simon and waking up with his lover in his arms. He enjoyed quiet nights on the couch and found that even chores seemed like less work when he had someone to talk to and joke with. Still, insecurity nagged him. *What if Simon decides that I get on his nerves? What if he misses having his own space? What if I miss having my own space, for that matter? What if living together turns out not to be what either of us expected?*

Vic shook his head, trying to clear away the noxious thoughts. Simon had given him no reason to doubt. If anything, Simon seemed even more enthusiastic about their new arrangement than when they were planning the move. Vic knew it was his own anxiety manufacturing worries, but he couldn't entirely squelch the thoughts. *We'll take it one day at a time. And I'll work on trusting Simon to tell me what he needs to say in his own time and try to stop grilling him.* That, Vic knew, might be easier said than done.

Vic headed into the break room for a cup of coffee. As usual, the bitter drink made him grimace. If there were an award for "worst coffee," cop shops would be right up there with hospitals as a contender. Still, it got the job done—partly because of the caffeine and partly because the awful taste assaulted his mouth and stomach into wakefulness.

He sat down at the desk he shared with Ross. "So—anything going on?" he asked as he switched on his computer.

"Got warnings about a winter storm coming in off the ocean," Ross observed. "Too late for hurricane season, but they're saying it could be bad."

"Lovely. We barely got the damage fixed from the last hurricane," Vic muttered.

"Horrey Area Museum reported a break in—someone stole three antique daggers," Ross said, glancing down through the morning's recap.

"Unless someone gets killed with one of them, it's not our gig. Next?"

Ross didn't answer right away, and Vic looked up. "What?"

"We've got a death that the coroner said looked like a suicide, but the family is insisting is a murder."

Vic frowned. "I guess some people might prefer thinking that their loved one didn't have a choice about dying."

"Maybe," Ross agreed. "But the family's filed a formal report, so we have to investigate. Everyone else is already out on cases, so it's ours. C'mon. Maybe we can be done by lunchtime."

Vic and Ross drove out to the victim's condo, a nice high-rise on a quiet street removed from the more touristy areas. Vic scanned the report as they drove. Mike Mitchell, age thirty-five, had a good job with a local bank.

"I don't get it," Vic said. "The guy didn't owe money, and there's no evidence of a drug problem. No history of mental health issues. He's single, divorced—but that was several years ago and amicable. Friends said he had a new girlfriend, and she told the cops everything was good. So…why?"

Ross shrugged. "I imagine that's what made his parents ask for a closer look. But you know as well as I do, there are plenty of times someone's struggling and never lets on until it's too late."

Vic had struggled himself, in those first lonely months after he left Pittsburgh and Nate had dumped him. He'd landed on his feet with a new job, but even sunny Myrtle Beach hadn't been able to boost his mood for quite a while.

"This is his condo? Nice digs," Vic said as they parked. The terra-cotta stucco exterior had plenty of large windows to make the most of a view of the beach in the distance. The condo might not be the most expensive in town, but it certainly lived up to its upscale reputation.

They took the elevator up to the twelfth floor, and Ross led the way to an apartment where the door was still tagged with police tape. Ross had the key, and they ducked under the tape. Both men pulled on latex gloves and put booties over their shoes. The forensics team had already been over the place, but neither of them wanted to accidentally contaminate the scene.

"He must have been making good money to afford this." Vic glanced around. The room wasn't lavish, but the furnishings were nice quality and fairly new. The large flat-screen TV and sound system didn't come cheap. Ross turned on the lights, making it seem a little less gloomy. Still, the condo smelled off—no doubt the after-effects of traumatic death.

The whole place made Vic feel jangly, and he thought about how Simon frequently told him that Vic's intuition was just another type of psychic knowledge. Vic used to shrug the comments off, but when he thought about all the times he'd followed a hunch or gone with his gut and had it pay off, he began to believe Simon might be right.

Vic made a slow circuit of the living area, noting photographs, knick-knacks, and books, taking in everything and hoping his mind spotted connections. The TV remote and an e-reader lay on the couch as if their owner had just stepped away. The kitchen was tidy, but the smell coming from the dishwasher told him it hadn't been run, and a glance inside confirmed as much. Vic poked his head into the bathroom, which was clean but still had a lived-in look. He caught up to Ross in the bedroom, which smelled of shit and piss, the byproducts of death. Until they closed the investigation, the apartment was still a crime scene, so clean-up crews hadn't been in.

Ross stood just inside the doorway, taking in the unmade bed, a few pieces of dirty laundry strewn about, and the odds and ends of an entirely unremarkable room. "The police report said the locks hadn't been forced, and there was no evidence that a second person was in the room. The door was locked."

"Note?"

Ross shook his head. "Not that anyone's found. No indicators on social media that he was having problems. His office got worried when he didn't come into work and called his emergency contact, which was his sister. She's the one who found the body."

Vic cringed at the thought. He'd escorted family members to identify the victims of violent crimes, and it was always utterly awful. Not that he'd expect it to be anything else, but still. Vic couldn't imagine anything worse.

"He did it over there," Ross said with a nod toward a chin-up bar in the closet doorway. "Hanged himself."

"Seriously? From that? How much did he have in his system?" The exercise bar looked sturdy, but it wasn't much more than six feet off the ground. He couldn't imagine how the victim had managed it, since he could have touched down and saved himself at any time.

"That's what the report says," Ross replied. "I don't get it, either. As for whether he was high or drunk, we're waiting on the tox screens."

Vic put his hands on his hips and did a slow turn, looking for something—anything—that might indicate more than a suicide. "I'm not sure what to look for, besides what's already here."

Ross nodded. "Yeah. Me neither."

Vic pulled out his phone. "Something about this isn't right. I'm going to bring Simon in on it." He couldn't keep from smiling despite the situation when Simon answered. "Hey, can you spare some time? We've got a suicide that might be a murder, and I think there's something hinky about it—your kind of hinky." When Simon agreed, Vic gave him the address and promised to wait for him in the lobby. He ended the call and looked up at Ross.

"It's possible that Simon won't pick up on anything—that happens. Apparently, ghosts don't always hang around. But if he can read anything, we might have a short cut in knowing whether to keep treating this as a suicide—or investigate a murder."

"I don't doubt Simon's word, but it won't officially count," Ross pointed out.

"Maybe not, but it gives us a signal of which way to throw our effort." Vic checked the time. "It won't take him long to get here. I'll go meet him and bring him up. You stay with the scene."

Vic headed downstairs, pacing in the empty lobby while he waited for Simon. Myrtle Beach wasn't a big city, so it didn't take Simon long to arrive.

Vic buzzed him in, and Simon took a look around.

"Thanks for coming on short notice. The victim's name is Mike Mitchell. Long and short of it is, the scene looked like a suicide, but the family isn't accepting that. They believe it was a murder, but there's nothing to support that conclusion. So—"

"You're hoping I can find something," Simon finished.

"Yeah. If there's something to find."

Simon was quiet as he followed Vic into the elevator, and they rode up. Vic had learned Simon's silence usually meant a combination of getting himself in the zone and listening for spirits. They reached the apartment, and Simon greeted Ross with a nod as he suited up with gloves and booties. Just inside the doorway, Simon staggered and gasped. Vic reached to steady him.

Simon's eyes were wide with terror, and his entire body went rigid in a way Vic knew meant a powerful vision.

"What's happening?" Ross asked, worried and curious.

"Vision," Vic grated. "I'm guessing Simon's getting a look at how it all went down."

Simon's body jerked, and his hands came up to his throat, clawing at an invisible noose as his breath came in painful wheezes. His eyes bulged, and his face reddened.

"Fuck! Get me some salt from the kitchen. Do it!" Vic ordered.

Ross raced away, and Vic heard the sound of cabinet doors opening and closing. Simon bucked like he was fighting for air, and Vic knew all too well the signs of strangulation.

"Now, dammit!" Vic yelled.

Ross rushed back, handing over a container of kitchen salt. Vic upended it over Simon, dumping it onto his throat and chest. He knew that there would be hell to pay for contaminating a crime scene, but right now, his priority was making sure Simon didn't end up like the dead guy in the bedroom.

As soon as the salt poured over Simon's skin, the vision released him. He dropped onto his back, gasping for breath but no longer straining, although his whole body trembled from the fight.

Ross had also grabbed a bottle of water and handed it to Vic. Vic helped Simon sit up and held the bottle steady for him while Simon drank.

It took Simon a few breaths to recover. His eyes were still wide, and despite the cool day, sweat beaded his brow.

"Give me a minute," Simon breathed.

To Vic's relief, Ross didn't push. Finally, Simon handed back the empty bottle and accepted Vic's help to get to his feet.

"It was a vision—of a psychic attack," Simon added in a shaky voice. "Experienced from Mike Mitchell's dying moments. And I've got your answer on whether it was suicide or murder. It was both."

3

SIMON

"What do you mean, 'both'?" Vic echoed.

Simon blinked away the impressions he'd received through his Gift. "The man who died *did* kill himself. But he was forced into it by something supernatural."

"Come again?" Ross asked. "How?"

Simon shook his head. "I don't know. I didn't speak with his ghost. Maybe I can, later, but he's not here right now."

"So how—" Ross looked confused. Vic waited him out, and Simon appreciated the space.

Simon swallowed hard, trying to still his racing heart from the impressions he had received. "I can sense energy as well as ghosts. Like intuition on steroids. If it's strong enough, I can tell things about the energy. I'm picking up two types—a very frightened person, and something that isn't human. The human tried to fight until the end, but the other entity was stronger. For lack of a better word, it *possessed* him and made him do what he did. At least, that's what I make of it."

Simon hadn't touched anything, and his gloved hands protected from contamination, but he felt tainted as if he should take a shower to wash off the psychic stain from the energy.

Ross groaned. "How the hell are we supposed to prove that?"

"It makes sense," Vic replied. "That would explain the difference between the scene in here, and what the family swears is true."

"I'll keep trying to reach the ghost," Simon promised. "No guarantee."

Vic guided Simon back outside the apartment. Ross locked the door behind them, and they didn't speak until they were in the elevator. "I'll tell Captain Hargrove I brought you in on this," Vic said. "That way, you get your consulting fee, and he knows what's going on. I'm just not sure how to pursue a murder investigation against an…entity."

"Hargrove's gonna love that," Ross mumbled.

"It all depends," Simon replied, feeling better the farther he got from the apartment. "We've run into a creature that used people to do bad things before. I'm not sure whether in this case it's a monster or a spirit, but bottom line is, it's a case of possession."

"Like in *The Exorcist?*" Ross asked with a skeptical expression.

Simon shrugged. "Everyone immediately thinks about demons when that word comes up, but there are a frightening number of energies that can temporarily ride a person and rob them of their will."

"Mitchell's dead, and even if we can't satisfy the family with an explanation, whatever killed him is still out there," Vic added. "We don't know why it targeted him, so we don't know if or where it might strike again."

Simon nodded. "I don't think it's 'if.' Definitely 'when.' So the question is—does it kill to feed, or for entertainment, or for some other reason? And did it pick Mitchell at random, or is there a pattern?"

"Yeah, that's what worries me," Vic said as they stepped into the lobby. He met Simon's gaze. "Will you be okay to get back to the store?"

The psychic residue had been vile, the emotional equivalent of a cross between sewage and rot. Whatever had forced Mike Mitchell to kill himself had not only been malicious, but sadistic. He'd sensed Mitchell's pain and terror, and the entity's enjoyment of his suffering. Simon couldn't keep back a shiver. Vic noticed and slipped an arm around him.

Simon let out a long breath. "I think so. It just hit me hard."

"You wouldn't be the first one to throw up at a murder scene," Ross said with a wry smile. "Vic and I have both done it—most cops have."

"Now imagine if you didn't see the blood—you felt the feelings."

Ross let out a low whistle. "Fuck. I didn't think of it that way."

"How about I drive you back, and then I'll walk up to the station from the shop?" Vic's hand pressed gently on the small of Simon's back, steadying him. Simon decided to forego his pride, since he still felt wobbly.

"I'd appreciate that."

Vic glanced at Ross. "I'll see you back there. We can figure out how to tell Hargrove together."

"Oh, joy." Ross headed for the unmarked police car, while Vic and Simon walked together to Simon's Camry.

"I'm sorry," Vic said when they were both buckled in.

"For what?" Simon frowned, confused. This was exactly the kind of thing he and Vic had hoped to accomplish when they sold Hargrove on the idea of bringing him in as a psychic consultant.

"Sometimes I feel like I'm getting you 'dirty' with my cop business," Vic admitted, not yet putting the car in gear. "It's something that happens with the rookies. You see them come in with these expectations that they're going to fight crime like Batman and Captain America, and make sure that good triumphs over evil. And then, little by little, what they see grinds them down, and the light goes out." He reached for Simon's hand and twined their fingers. "I don't want to be the reason your light goes out."

Simon bent to kiss Vic's knuckles. "I'm a big boy, Vic. I know there are bad things in the world. I see the ghosts, with or without the police piece."

Vic nodded, but his expression looked pained. "I know. But I worry that I'll change you. You have a good soul. I don't want to take that away."

"I'm not sure about the 'good soul' part—"

"I am."

Simon smiled and brushed another kiss over their joined fingers. "But innocence doesn't last long for mediums. We see things—understand things—through the eyes of the ghosts long before our time. At least working with you, with the department, means I can actually do something about what I see. We've caught killers, stopped bad things. That matters."

Vic didn't say anything more as he pulled away from the curb. In minutes, they were back at Grand Strand Ghost Tours. "Are you feeling better?"

Simon leaned over to kiss his cheek. "Yes. You know I'll take any excuse to see you," he added with a tired smile. "So stop worrying. Go fight crime, and I'll go talk to ghosts. If you find out anything about Mitchell, let me know—and I'll do the same."

"You have a quiet afternoon?"

Simon shrugged. "I've got a new client who wants me to go out to Socastee Manor and de-haunt it. We'll see how that goes."

"Be careful. I have all kinds of ideas of how to spend our evening," Vic added. "So try hard to stay in one piece, okay?" His joking tone hid the very serious concern Simon could see in his eyes.

"You, too." Simon stole another quick kiss, then hopped out of the car and took the keys back from Vic. "See you tonight."

When Simon walked into Grand Strand Ghost Tours, he found Pete and Tracey talking at the counter and a hot latte with his name on it waiting for him.

"Pete said you got called out with the cops," Tracey said. "That usually rattles you, so I figured I'd bring you a mocha. Sorry I don't have a liquor license, or I'd have dumped in some Jameson, just for good measure."

"Thank you," Simon said, picking up the cup and taking a long sip. "Much appreciated. It was…awful."

"And, as usual, you can't tell us about it," Tracey replied with a dramatic sigh. "Confidentiality, blah, blah, blah."

"You might not be able to share your scoop, but we've got some of our own," Pete said with a big grin. "Someone's spotted Black-coat Benny."

Simon shook his head. "I get that you're excited about the sighting, but dude, that's an omen that a really bad storm is coming. Like seeing the Gray Man out on Pawley's Island."

"I know," Pete said, although the potential danger didn't dim his smile. "But it's so cool!"

"Okay, fill me in." Simon gave a long-suffering sigh, but couldn't help feeling his spirits rise at Pete's gleeful mood.

"It was all everyone wanted to talk about at Le Miz this morning," Tracey replied. She gave her braids a toss, and Simon noticed that she'd added white and clear beads that shimmered like snowflakes.

"Apparently a couple of guys were fishing down past Surfside Beach. They were out a ways from shore, and when they looked back, they saw a man in an old-fashioned pirate coat, striding up and down on the sand with a lantern. As soon as they saw him, he disappeared."

"How sure are you they aren't making it up?" Simon asked. "Or that someone didn't prank them? Anyone can buy those coats at a Renaissance festival."

"Yeah, but it's hard to just go 'poof' and vanish," Pete put in.

"True. But maybe they just made it up to get a story going. With the storm warnings, it's what people want to hear." Simon really hoped they weren't going to be in for a bad turn.

"Maybe," Tracey allowed. "But the forecasters are upgrading from an alert to a warning. Blackcoat Benny might be right about this one."

Simon tried to clear his head on the drive down to Socastee Manor. Sparse tourist traffic meant he didn't spend much time in the car, but with the radio turned up and the window partway down, Simon felt much better by the time he arrived.

He had brought protective charms and amulets to help fend off dangerous spirits. The blessed silver bracelet Vic had given him was on his left wrist, and he had a gris-gris bag in his pocket that Miss Eppie, a hoodoo root woman, had made for him. A canister of salt bulged in one pocket, and in the other, he had several loose nuggets of onyx and agate, good for dispelling negative energy. Just in case, since he wasn't sure what he'd be facing, Simon had also brought an iron dagger and a small bottle of holy water.

The old house had been grand in its day. It rose two stories tall, with dormer windows and chimneys jutting from its sharply pitched roof. The white-painted, cypress wood walls sat atop a high brick foundation to help protect against flooding. Wide porches on both floors gave the house an antebellum elegance. But in this case, Simon knew, Socastee Manor had been built not just before the Civil War, but before the Revolutionary War.

Recent years had gone hard on the old house. As Simon got out of his car and stepped closer, he saw cracked windows, roof damage, and peeling paint. Cypress wood was strong, but not completely impervious. Neglect had taken a toll. Gravel crunched beneath Simon's feet as he walked up the carriageway. He moved slowly, opening his Gift, alert for danger and trying to sense any spirits who might be present.

The whole place fairly vibrated with restless energy and psychic turmoil. Simon wondered how Trevor and his work crews didn't feel the discord. Or perhaps they did, without realizing the source. Simon circled the house and spotted a cluster of old gravestones around a huge tree some distance away. The graveyard drew him toward it, and Simon approached with caution, ready for an attack.

Sadness, frustration, and longing resonated from the spirits entombed beneath the weathered stones. He'd done a bit more reading on the Dunwood family, and the stories hadn't been happy, despite their wealth and political power. Wives died young in childbirth. Yellow Fever, malaria, and other diseases claimed children. Ships sank, horses threw their riders, and duels went wrong. The Dunwoods were proud and hot-tempered, ruthless in pursuit of their goals, and implacable. They did not go gently to their afterlife or cede control easily.

"Can you tell me about the haunting in the main house? I need to make it stop." Simon waited, but none of the ghosts appeared. He sensed fear and wariness from the faded spirits, but nothing that would help him solve Trevor's problem.

"Your time is over," Simon said quietly, addressing the spirits. None of them had enough energy to cause the kind of problems Trevor had mentioned, but Simon knew from experience that having unhappy ghosts around could still spell trouble. "It's time for you to go."

He felt their pushback: silent outrage, stubborn refusal. Simon hadn't really expected the ghosts to go on their own accord, giving them the opportunity was the polite thing to do. Their refusal meant he needed to move to the next level.

"What's happening now to the house is none of your business," he told the ghosts as he took a canister of salt out of his jacket pocket and began to walk in a circle around the burying ground. He moved quickly, just in case any of the spirits could muster up enough energy to cause harm. When he had finished the circle, he stepped back and regarded the tombstones. Salt repelled ghosts, interfering with their energy. He'd done the psychic equivalent of putting a fence around the cemetery, one ghosts couldn't cross.

"If you won't pass over on your own, then I'm going to make sure that you don't cause trouble. And since new people will be living here, I'll make sure someone comes to send you on." Even though the ghosts were sealed behind the salt line, Simon could sense their agitation. Few people would have dared to deny a Dunwood what they wanted in life, and the ghosts weren't gracious about not getting their way after death.

Still, corralling the spirits with salt meant that they weren't going to add to the problems inside the house. From what Trevor had told him, Simon felt certain that the ghosts of Socastee Manor weren't limited to those in the cemetery. He tuned out the pissed off spirits behind him and focused his Gift on the manor house itself. Before he got closer, he pulled out his phone and sent a quick text to let Trevor know he had arrived.

Houses absorbed impressions of the people who lived there. That explained what some called "stone tape" recordings—the imprint of a spirit's energy that remained in an infinite loop but without sentience. Those ghosts— often referred to as "repeaters"— were like the old man on his bicycle or the man with dreadlocks down on the boardwalk. The ghosts weren't really present to interact, they had just left a remnant of themselves behind.

Many old houses had repeaters. They didn't hurt anyone, and new residents sometimes became fond of them, considering the ghosts to be part of a house's character. Simon sensed more than one repeater at Socastee Manor, which might be an unwelcome surprise to a hapless worker, but not the cause of the kinds of issues Trevor described.

As Simon headed up the steps, he felt a darker energy that stained the house. In his inner Sight, it was just a wisp of smoke, a whiff of garbage. Whatever the entity was, it had an edge of malice that put Simon on the defensive. He wrapped his right hand around the protective silver bracelet. The blessed metal strengthened his resistance, and he felt the tainted presence draw back. It didn't leave, and Simon felt sure it would continue to watch him, but just having it keep its distance felt like a win.

"Simon! I was afraid you might have changed your mind." Trevor opened the door and greeted him with a handshake. "Come in. Let me show you around." He gestured toward the rundown interior. "I'm afraid it's not much to look at now, but if we can ever finish the renovations, it'll be a real showplace." Despite the difficulties the job had caused, Simon heard pride in Trevor's voice and excitement about the possibilities.

"You can see that the house has good bones," Trevor said. A long hallway led from the front door to the back door, with four rooms opening off of the corridor, and a wide wooden stairway leading to the second floor. Water damage and lack of temperature control had stained the pine floorboards and discolored the old wallpaper. But beneath the grime, Simon noted the architectural details that once made Socastee Manor famous for its grandeur.

"The crown moldings and baseboards are hand-carved and so is the balustrade. And we're lucky that the mantles didn't get vandalized or stolen," Trevor went on, leading Simon from room to room. Without furniture and unheated, the house felt forlorn, almost brooding.

Simon kept his psychic shielding high, in no hurry for a repeat of what happened at the murder victim's condo. Even so, the ghostly resonance flared strong enough that he struggled to sift through all the impressions.

So many unhappy, unquiet spirits left an imprint in this place. Simon wondered if any of its residents had truly been happy. If he had to name just one emotion, it would be hunger, an emptiness that could never be satisfied. From what he knew of the Dunwoods, that void encompassed both greed and unfaithfulness, an all-consuming need to have more, which was never enough.

Simon felt the malice of ghosts whose bitterness bound them to this ruin, and the pain of those whose lives were ruined in the never-ending quest for "more." As he sorted through the images and the psychic impressions, he knew something else for certain—murder had been done in this place, more than once.

He moved toward the grand stairway and felt a sudden chill. Someone had died in this spot and hadn't completely left. A glance out the window showed him a landscape from long ago, and he caught sight of slaves going about their business, seeing to the chores of the manor. Their restless ghosts haunted the land just as certainly as the spirits of the Dunwood family who refused to leave their decaying mansion.

Another presence lingered at the edge of Simon's awareness as if it were watching and appraising, trying to size him up. It was strong and angry, remorseless and cruel. Simon had no desire to go up against it now. He reached into his pocket and gripped a mojo bag Miss Eppie had given him and shook his blessed silver bracelet —a gift from Vic—so it lay against his skin.

The baleful ghost vanished, but Simon knew it would be back.

"Simon?" Trevor asked, still standing where Simon had left him when they'd come into the foyer.

"Sorry. Just…getting a read," Simon said with a wan smile. The ghostly presences felt distant, some of them too faint to notice, as if they'd provided a warning and withdrawn. Simon had no doubt that the message was "get out."

"Are there places where the ghost activity has been stronger?" Simon asked, carefully stretching out his senses while keeping his protective charms close.

"We've had incidents all over the house," Trevor told him. "But the most recent ones were here in the parlor, and upstairs in what would have been the master bedroom."

"Show me." Simon followed Trevor into the front room and slowly made a circuit, expecting to find a cold spot or a frisson of energy that marked a ghost's presence.

"Are you getting anything?" Trevor asked.

Simon shook his head. "No. I have a general sense of the house, which has more than its share of negative energy. But I'm not picking up a specific vibe in this room." He looked at Trevor and managed a smile, not wanting to disappoint. "That's not entirely unusual. Ghosts don't just hang around in one spot, waiting for people to walk through them. If they're not repeaters, they come and go as they please."

Trevor headed up the stairs, with Simon close behind. The foreboding he had sensed earlier grew stronger, a prickle at the back of his neck and tightness in his gut that warned him on a primal level to get the hell out. A flicker of motion to one side caught his attention, and he saw a woman in a long dress appear, walk a few feet, turn into a doorway and vanish.

"See something?" Trevor asked.

Simon pointed. "A woman."

"We call her Hallway Hannah," Trevor replied. "She hasn't bothered anyone, but it does give you a start until you get used to her."

"She's one of those repeaters I mentioned. A bit like a projector with a short film that gets stuck playing over and over," Simon said. "She won't hurt you."

Hannah might not be malicious, but as Simon reached the second-floor landing, he felt a darker, more dangerous energy that seemed to be everywhere. "Can you feel it?" he asked, amazed that the work crews had remained on the job.

Trevor frowned. "I'm not sure, but I'm guessing that you mean the way it seems 'off' up here. Like someone's watching, and you're not welcome."

Simon nodded. "I'm picking up anger, the way a room feels tense when people aren't getting along, even if no one says anything."

"Yeah, I get that," Trevor said. "Everyone's edgy on the crew, and tempers are shorter than usual. I think some of the guys cover up being scared with being angry, which just makes everything worse."

The bedroom Hannah claimed had the least negative energy. Two of the rooms felt vaguely creepy, but nothing Simon would have considered dangerous.

"This, we think, was the master bedroom," Trevor said, leading the way inside. "I thought that even if you didn't pick up anything elsewhere, you'd get a reading here. Can you tell who—or what—is causing the problem?"

"Did you find anything in the room that might have been a personal belonging? Maybe something hidden?" Simon asked.

Trevor shook his head. "Not so far. I trust my crew; they would have told me if anything turned up. Do you think that's what's causing the problem?"

Simon hesitated. "I'm not sure. Some ghosts just don't like 'strangers' invading their homes. From the energy I read out in the family cemetery, the Dunwoods weren't a bunch of happy campers."

Trevor looked like he was carefully weighing his response. "I don't know much about the house's history or the people who lived here. But I've been in the remodeling and renovation business since I was a teenager, and I go in and out of a lot of houses. I'm not a psychic, but there's definitely a vibe you get when you walk in a place—even if you're just visiting someone—about whether they're getting along, doing okay. And there are times when everything looks perfect, and in your gut you know something's off." He licked his lips nervously. "This whole house feels off—and angry. I'd be very surprised to find out that the people who lived here were at peace."

Simon felt quite certain that they weren't, even after death. He'd picked up a dark resonance just walking into the room. Violent, headstrong, masculine. Undoubtedly a Dunwood, but which one of the manor's former masters, he wasn't sure.

The room's temperature plummeted, and Simon sensed a sudden shift in the air. "Watch out!" he yelled to Trevor, then jumped in front of the other man as a ghostly force rushed toward them at full speed. Trevor stumbled back, pushed out of the way, but Simon took the full brunt of the hit.

He'd never played football, but Simon had imagined getting tackled would feel something like this. The force caught him square in the torso and lifted him off his feet, sending him flying. Simon slammed into the wall, taking the force of the hit on his shoulders. He knew the ghost would come at him again, and he was already speaking the words of a rote magic protection spell before he got to his feet.

The scrim of protective energy that surrounded him wouldn't hold off a powerful, extended attack, but it would buy him time to recover and drain power from any spirit foolish enough to try to break through. The nearly-invisible barrier brought the ghost up short, and for an instant, as it touched the warding, Simon caught a glimpse of his attacker. He saw a tall man with a dour expression, dressed in a frock coat and tricorn hat from the Revolutionary War period. None other than Jamie Dunwood, Socastee Manor's founder.

Get out and stay out! The ghost roared in Simon's mind. *You have no business here.*

With that, Dunwood's ghost flashed out of Simon's sight, and the oppressive feeling lifted from the room. Trevor had flattened himself against the far wall, eyes wide.

"What just happened?" The contractor's voice shook a little.

Simon dusted himself off and stretched his neck from side to side, deciding that there was no permanent damage, and wondering if he'd have bruises that he'd need to explain to Vic. "That…was Jamie Dunwood. He doesn't like visitors."

"Jamie Dunwood…for real?"

Simon couldn't help chuckling. "Well, I sure didn't throw myself into the wall. Yes. The man himself—or at least, his ghost. Death hasn't improved his temper." He glanced around, sensing that other spirits had watched the altercation from a distance, but they evaded his Sight.

"Come on. Let's get out of here before Dunwood powers up again."

Trevor didn't speak again until they were on the stairs. "I saw you fly across the room, and then there was a…shimmer…around you.

After the impression he'd gotten at the base of the steps, Simon made sure to keep a hand on the railing. "A protection spell," Simon replied. "For situations just like that. It won't keep Dunwood away for long, but it made him back off."

They walked down the stairs and out onto the porch. Simon waited while Trevor locked up. "I think you get the picture. What now?"

Simon weighed his options. "How open-minded is your developer? I have some ideas about what we can do to make this better, but they might weird him out."

"Try me."

Simon gave him a lopsided grin. "I'd like to have someone from the clergy bless the cemetery—ideally, I'd say Last Rites, but I don't know what the owners prefer."

"No idea, but that doesn't sound too weird."

"In here, we can smudge with sage—it's like incense, and it's good for cleansing negative energy," Simon went on. "If your crew isn't already wearing charms or medallions with protective properties, it certainly won't hurt if they do. Jewelry or talismans that people have faith in really do have power. Putting down salt lines around the doors and windows can help, but not if Dunwood's anchor is somewhere in the house."

"Okay. What else?" Trevor asked. Simon thanked his lucky stars that the man took the situation seriously.

"I'm worried about the ghost in the bedroom. I think that's the spirit who's dangerous. I'd like to do a séance and try to find out what's behind all this. Do you have any idea whether the violent haunting is recent, or has it been going on for a while?"

Trevor snorted. "I can't get the developer to admit that there's any kind of haunting—violent or not. That might increase the sales price in New Orleans, but not here. I'm taking a risk coming to you —but I'm really afraid my guys are going to get hurt."

"Okay," Simon replied, not surprised that the developer wasn't really onboard. "Then we have to keep this quiet. I'd like to do a séance, and bring a few friends who also have some abilities—or can have our backs if something goes wrong. We'll do it low key—all we need is a folding table and chairs, and some kind of lights so we're not completely in the dark."

"You want to talk to the ghost?" Trevor looked nervous, and Simon guessed he was weighing the potential shitstorm if the developer found out. "What if he attacks and really hurts you this time?"

"If I don't talk to the ghost that's causing the problem, then I'd at least like to speak with some of the other ghosts," Simon replied. "Aside from Hallway Hannah, I think there are other spirits attached to this house, but they're not around right now. It could be that they don't like the noise and fuss of renovations and they go somewhere else on the property. But ghosts can also be afraid of other spirits. And if the angry ghost has gotten stronger for some reason, they might be hiding."

"Ghosts are afraid of ghosts? What can happen? They're already dead?"

Simon sighed. "You've heard of something being a 'fate worse than death?' There are entities out there that can hurt other spirits, feed off them, and destroy them. Those aren't usually things that started out human, but I've read about very bad people turning into really awful ghosts."

"Huh. I guess I can see that."

Simon felt relieved that Trevor accepted his explanation. Whether or not the man was a true believer in psychic phenomena, he definitely seemed to trust Simon and believe he could help. That made Simon all the more determined to figure out how to fix the problem before anyone got hurt.

"Now that I've been here and seen what's what, I need to do some more research," Simon said as they walked back to the car. "I also need to talk to a few people—in confidence—and get their input. I want to take care of this for you quickly, but if we don't do it right, the spirit could get even angrier."

"We don't want that," Trevor said with a shudder. "And I get doing it right the first time. As we say in my business, 'measure twice, cut once.'"

"I'll give you call in the morning, and we can set up a sage smudging and having the cemetery blessed," Simon said. "It's a good next step."

"Thank you," Trevor replied. "Not just for coming out, but for taking me seriously. A lot of people wouldn't have understood."

"This is definitely not the strangest thing I've seen," Simon assured him. "And I'm going to do everything I can to keep your people safe." But as he drove away, leaving Socastee Manor in his rearview mirror, Simon worried that he might not be able to make good on that promise.

Before Simon made it back to Grand Strand Ghost Tours, his phone buzzed. "What's up?"

"There's a guy here who wants to talk to you," Pete told him. "I said you were going to be out for a while, and he said he'd wait. He's been here over an hour."

"Any idea what he wants? If he needs an appointment, just go ahead and get him set up."

"I tried that. He said he read your books and wants to talk to you about the wreck."

"The ship everyone's talking about?"

"I guess so." Pete kept his voice down, and Simon figured his assistant had gone into the break room. "Are you coming back?"

"I'm on my way. Should be there in a couple of minutes. Keep an eye on him until I can get there."

"Okay. I'll see if he wants coffee. Thanks." Pete disconnected, leaving Simon to wonder how it was that two strangers with ghost issues came looking for him within days.

It took longer to find a parking spot than Simon hoped. He turned off the car and got out. From where he stood, he could see out over the ocean, and he paused for a moment to drink in a deep breath and enjoy the view.

In a heartbeat, the perspective changed. Instead of standing on dry land, looking out at the ocean between modern high-rise buildings, Simon saw two young men aboard a black sailing sloop. The ship flew no colors, meaning it was either a pirate or a privateer. Both men looked to be in their early twenties, in clothing that suggested the Revolutionary War period.

The dark-haired man was clearly the leader. He and the other man worked the sails expertly, skimming fast across the waves in pursuit of another ship, with a distinctive figurehead. Then the leader turned and stared right at Simon, meeting and holding his gaze as if he could see through the centuries.

Simon blinked, and the vision vanished. He put out a hand to steady himself against his car and breathed through his panic. Just seeing a glimpse of the past didn't faze him. But the sense of connection he'd shared in that look from the man on the black ship chilled Simon down to his bones. He'd never had something like that happen. Sure, he'd interacted with plenty of ghosts, some of whom were centuries old. But this was a vision. It should have been like watching a DVD—glimpsing a snippet of time without being able to interact.

But the man's expression seemed to make it clear that he hadn't just looked in Simon's direction—he had seen Simon across a span of more than two hundred and fifty years. What did it mean? What message was Simon to take from that—and did it have anything to do with the haunted mansion or the possessed hanging victims?

When Simon felt his heart rate slow, and he got himself under control, he locked the car and headed for the shop, making a mental note to talk to his witch friend Gabriella about the incident. Pete's nod when he walked into the shop told him that the stranger was still waiting. Simon spotted the customer sitting at the readings table and strode to the back of the store to greet him.

"I'm Simon Kincaide. Pete said you were looking for me?"

The man's grip was sure and firm. He was a few inches taller than Simon with broad shoulders and a bearing that suggested ex-military. His brown hair was cut short, and his green eyes had an appraising glint to them. "Josh Williams. I'm an underwater explorer and maritime historian, sent down by USC to have a look at that wreck everyone's talking about. I've read your ghost books, and I wanted to talk to you about the Gallows Nine."

Oddly, shaking the man's hand didn't give Simon any clue about his energy. While Simon's Gift focused on speaking with the dead, it tended to give him some insight into the living as well. Simon's psychic radar was giving him nothing on Josh. That immediately raised a red flag in his mind, despite the fact that Williams's energy made Simon feel comfortable, as if it were easier to breathe.

"I'm not really an expert on the Nine," Simon said, taking a seat on the other side of the séance table. "I know the lore, of course, but I haven't particularly studied it." Until he knew Williams better, Simon had no intention of mentioning his vision, or the fact that he'd seen the hanging.

"The nine pirates who were hanged were the crew of the *Annabelle*," Williams said. "A fast ship that had been a thorn in the side of the East India Company. Rumor has it that they were scuttled by a privateer—a legal pirate—they'd tangled with before. I've always been fascinated with the Nine, and I did my graduate work on known wrecks off this stretch of coast. There had been rumors that the *Annabelle* was one of them, but no one could find it. Then we had the hurricane, and it shifted enough sand that the currents finally exposed her."

Simon sat forward. "So the wreck that's been in the news—you're sure it's really the *Annabelle*?"

Josh nodded. "I'm sure. But that's not the same as being able to prove it. I've got a dive team with me, and we're doing everything the weather will allow to get a look at the wreck in case this storm that's on its way covers it back up or drags it out to sea."

"That's all really interesting," Simon said, genuinely intrigued by the story. "But I don't know how I can be of help."

"We have permission to bring up artifacts from the site," Williams said. "Of course, it's a tangle of salvage and antiquities law as to who they belong to, but one way or the other, they'll probably end up in a museum. Depending on what we find, I'd love to be able to ask you to take a look at them, see if you can contact the spirits of the pirates."

Simon fought an involuntary shiver, thinking about the vision he'd had the day before. "Why? What would you hope to gain from that, even if I could make a connection? Which, by the way, isn't guaranteed. Spirits move on, or they just don't bother to answer when you call."

Williams leaned forward. "I'm a historian, first and foremost. I'm in it for the story. There are so many versions of what happened to the *Annabelle* and what made the Gallows Nine the most wanted men in their day. They've become a legend, like Bonnie and Clyde or Billy the Kid. I want to find the truth."

Simon still couldn't get more of a read on the guy. That rarely happened, but when it did, it threw him off his game. "You know, the truth has ruined a lot of good legends. Do you really want to go there?"

Williams sighed. "The true story is always the most important one. If it turns out to be different from the legend, it won't really matter. Everybody loves a good pirate story."

Simon couldn't deny that the idea of actually making a connection with the long-lost crew of the *Annabelle* intrigued him. He had been very careful visiting museum exhibits with artifacts from the *Titanic* and the *Hunley* because he knew the tragic story behind them and didn't want to live it through the eyes of any spirits that might have attached themselves to the items. But the *Annabelle* was shrouded in mystery, and even the scholarly theories competed. Simon might have walked away from his job as a folklore professor, but it didn't lessen his love for the subject matter.

"All right," Simon told Williams. "If you bring up anything notable, give me a call, and we'll figure out where and when to get together." He gave him a card with the shop's number.

Williams shook his hand as he rose. "Thank you. I know what I've said sounds crazy, but I really appreciate your help."

Simon watched the man leave, adding yet another odd circumstance to a day that seemed full of them.

"You think he's legit?" Pete asked.

Simon shrugged. "I have a friend from my professor days who handles the permits for salvage dives and archeological digs. I'll check into it. If he's not—I'll report him."

"But if he is, wouldn't it be cool to know more about the Gallows Nine?" Pete's ghost geek was in full swing.

"Be careful what you wish for," Simon cautioned. "Between people saying they've seen Blackcoat Benny and all this talk about the Gallows Nine, it makes me worry about the storm that's heading this way."

Pete shrugged. "We made it through the hurricane, we'll get through this. I'm not going to worry until they take the SkyWheel apart again."

4

VIC

Vic felt pretty sure that the saying "no good deed goes unpunished" was originally said by a cop. He bummed a ride home with Ross rather than walking the few blocks from the station to the blue bungalow, but the lights in the windows when he arrived gave him a second wind.

"Go home to your fella and put everything out of your head," Ross advised. "Tell Simon I said hello. Sheila wants the four of us to go out on another double date when she can get a sitter for the kids."

"That sounds like fun," Vic said. "Just let us know when and where." He'd been lucky to get Ross as a partner. Not only was Ross okay with Vic being gay and out, but he'd been cool with Simon's psychic abilities once he had seen enough to realize they were real. The fact that he'd also accepted Vic as a partner and a friend despite his iffy recommendation from Pittsburgh had sealed Vic's opinion. He tried to make sure he never gave Ross any reason to change his mind.

Ross pulled away as Vic headed up the steps. He and Simon hadn't been together a full year yet, but the blue bungalow had always felt more like home than his old apartment. Now he was living with the man he loved, and Myrtle Beach finally seemed like home.

That made Vic happy deep down. It also scared the shit out of him because he'd never had so much to lose.

"Sorry I'm late," Vic called out as he came inside and hung up his coat.

"Dinner's almost ready," Simon responded from the kitchen.

Vic tried to figure out what was cooking from the aromas that made his stomach rumble with hunger.

He stopped just inside the kitchen doorway and closed his eyes. "Meatloaf…mmmm."

"With roasted carrots and mashed potatoes," Simon said, a hint of pride in his voice. "I timed it later figuring it was better to eat late than have to warm it up or hold it too long."

"You did good," Vic replied. "How long until it's ready?"

Simon glanced at his timer. "About five minutes."

"Perfect." Vic stepped closer to Simon, pulling him in by his belt loops. He slipped his arms around Simon's waist, and Simon slid his around Vic's shoulders. Vic kissed him, a gentle brush of lips at first, but then Simon opened to him, and Vic slid his tongue inside, licking and tasting. Simon arched against him, and Vic's right hand moved down to grip Simon's ass.

"Missed you," Vic growled, pulling back just enough to see the flush in Simon's skin and his blown pupils.

"Glad you're home," Simon murmured. Vic tangled his left hand in Simon's loose, long hair to expose his neck, then kissed and nipped from earlobe to shoulder, pausing to flick his tongue against the shell of his ear and then across his collarbone.

A timer dinged, and Simon pushed back ruefully. "We'd better get cleaned up unless we want dinner to burn."

The meatloaf smelled even better than before, and Vic licked his lips as Simon plated the food, drizzling brown gravy from the meat over the potatoes and adding a side of roasted carrots. A loaf of sliced bread from the bakery and a tub of butter were already on the table, along with two cold beers.

Vic grabbed his plate and sank into his chair with a grateful sigh. Simon joined him a few seconds later. They dug into their food, letting conversation wait until they were nearly finished.

"How did it go out at the old house?" Vic scraped up the last of the meatloaf on his plate and washed it down with a swig of beer.

"Worrisome." Simon leaned back in his chair. "There's plenty of spirit activity—most of it hostile. The contractor's sticking his neck out to bring me in because the developer doesn't believe in ghosts. But at least one ghost is angry enough that someone's going to get hurt. So…I've got to figure out an intervention."

The wording made Vic chuckle. "Jesus, you sound like it's a domestic incident."

Simon shrugged. "It is—just one of the participants is already dead. Can't exactly cuff him and drag him off to jail, so I've got to figure out who's pissed and why, and then how to make the spirit go away for good."

"Just please, be careful. Can't you bring one of your psychic friends network buddies in on this?"

Simon grimaced at the nickname and gave an exaggerated sigh at the long-running joke. "Maybe. I'm going to connect with Miss Eppie and Gabriella tomorrow and see what they advise. Josh—the contractor—is really worried, and I don't want anything worse to happen."

Vic helped Simon clear the table. He loaded the dishwasher while Simon put away leftovers. Then he grabbed two more beers as they headed into the living room. He and Ross had spent the afternoon working another suspicious "suicide," with the same pattern as the one he'd shown to Simon. He just hated to bring it up. As it turned out, he didn't get a choice in the matter.

On the television, the evening news ran footage of a scene Vic recognized all too well, with a crawl that read "North Myrtle man found dead in hotel room."

"Aw, shit," Vic muttered, knowing he needed to tell Simon that he'd been called to that scene. The news segued into the storm forecast, promising that the weather would be getting dangerously nasty. That's when Vic realized Simon had frozen in his tracks, staring at the TV with a blank expression, completely zoned out.

"Simon?"

Simon shook off his trance. "He wants our help."

"Who?"

"Roger Burnside, the man in the hotel room. It wasn't what it looked like."

Vic caught his breath. "We didn't release the victim's name to the press," he said quietly.

"No. He told me. Just now."

"Roger Burnside was here in the living room?" Vic sometimes struggled to keep up with Simon's psychic abilities. He no longer doubted; hell, he'd seen Simon work actual magic a few months ago, so seeing spirits and getting glimpses of the future didn't seem farfetched at all anymore. Still, Vic sometimes felt like a guest at a party where Simon was in the thick of the conversation, and no one talked to him.

Simon frowned. "Not exactly. I don't know where he was—he didn't materialize. I saw the picture of the hotel, and I heard his voice."

"What did he say, exactly?" Vic heard himself go into cop mode, and he winced. *Simon's my lover, not my suspect.*

Simon didn't react to the change in tone for once, still preoccupied and trying to parse out what had just happened. "He said, 'I'm Roger Burnside, and I didn't do it.'"

"Is he still here? Can you ask him what happened?" Vic's voice held the excitement he knew too well came with chasing down a lead. He struggled to walk the fine line between cop and partner.

Simon shook his head. "No. New ghosts usually aren't very strong. I'm surprised he managed that much at a distance. I mean, North Myrtle's miles away. It's not like we're standing over his body."

Vic took Simon's hand and led him to the couch, setting the bottles on the coffee table. "Ross and I spent the afternoon at the hotel. Another hanging. A maid found him. No note, but the door was locked from the inside, and there was no evidence of a break-in. The body's with the coroner, but it's likely to get ruled a suicide, although Captain Hargrove asked us to take a look since Burnside's death has the same pattern as Mitchell's."

Simon sighed as he leaned back and closed his eyes. "I can't feel the ghost now. He probably used all the juice he had with that message. It might be a while before he can muster up anything else, but I'll keep trying to reach him, and Mike Mitchell, too. If you want me to go to the scene tomorrow, I will."

Vic remembered their conversation in the car. Had it only been that morning? Simon might dismiss his fears that chasing murder suspects would change him, but Vic had seen that happen to far too many of his police colleagues. Simon hadn't lost his faith in people, hadn't grown weary of seeing people betray each other in the worst ways, hadn't developed the flat, hard look Vic thought of as "cop eyes" that showed a distrust for everyone and everything.

He wanted to wrap his arms around Simon and protect him not only to keep him safe but to make sure he never grew bitter and disillusioned. Vic knew he couldn't, and shouldn't, do that, knew Simon took on the burden of helping solve murders for a good reason. He had to respect and support that, just as Simon supported him. Vic rarely worried about himself, but he knew Simon lived with a silent fear every day that Vic would get hurt or killed in the line of duty. And Simon rarely voiced his fears, knowing that the risk went along with loving a cop. So Vic knew he had to do the same, but it was so damn hard.

"I love you," Vic said, pulling Simon close. "And I'll take you by the hotel in the morning if you're willing to go." He paused, trying to figure out how to put his fears into words.

"You told me that being a medium means letting a ghost possess you long enough to pass along a message. Could the…entity…take you over and not let go?"

Simon hesitated before answering, which Vic took as a partial reply in itself. "I don't think so," Simon said carefully. "For one thing, I've had experience my whole life dealing with spirits, and I've learned how to shield. I've run into aggressive ghosts and either thrown them out or kept them from trying to get in. And I carry my silver and onyx, which help protect me." He met Vic's gaze. "But you and Ross could be at risk. Do you have the bracelet and the kerchief I gave you?"

At Christmas, Vic had given Simon a silver bracelet with an engraved protective warding and a Kevlar vest. Simon had given Vic two hand-woven items made by a powerful Weaver witch with protective magic sewn into the cloth itself.

Vic held up his left wrist and showed that he had the bracelet, then pulled a corner of the kerchief out of his pocket. "Yep. And I make sure Ross wears his saint's medallion."

Simon nodded. "Good. That's important. I usually have some of the other charms from Miss Eppie and Gabriella on me some-where. When I see them, I'll ask if they can give me some amulets for you and Ross, now that we know what we're up against."

Vic pulled Simon close, wanting nothing more than to kiss away the worry. He didn't want to talk shop; he wanted their time at home to be an oasis from the darkness they both saw all too often outside. That wasn't always possible, but for tonight, Vic was going to do his damnedest to make it happen.

"Let's forget about work for a while," he murmured, licking the rim of Simon's ear and tonguing into the shell in a promise of good things to come. Simon shivered in his arms, and Vic bit lightly at his earlobe, loving the moan it earned in response. He reached out and grabbed the remote, turning off the TV, then went back to slowly, thoroughly, exploring Simon's body with his hands and mouth.

"You're wearing too many clothes." Vic reached for the hem of Simon's t-shirt, then pulled it over his head. He tossed the shirt aside and pressed Simon down onto the couch, then sat back to admire his long, lean body.

"You are so beautiful," Vic said, amazed anew that he'd managed to find a man like Simon and be loved by him in return. Vic ran a hand down Simon's chest, tweaking his pink nipples, trailing down over his firm abs to the trail of chestnut hair that led down to the waistband of his jeans.

"I was thinking the same about you." Simon's smile made Vic's heart do flips. Simon tugged at Vic's shirt, and Vic was quick to lose it, leaving them both bare-chested. Simon ran a finger over the tats on Vic's chest, making him catch his breath.

Vic leaned forward and licked a stripe down the side of Simon's neck with the tip of his tongue, glorying in the way it made Simon's breath hitch and his pulse race. He kissed his way along Simon's collar bone, then moved down to suck each nipple to a hard nub. Simon ground against him, bucking his hips, his cock obviously straining against the fabric of his jeans. Vic just chuckled as he kissed and licked his way down Simon's happy trail. He teased a finger inside the waistband of Simon's jeans, stroking over the sensitive head of his prick that was already leaking enough pre-come to wet the cotton of his briefs.

"Vic—" The need in Simon's voice and the hunger in his eyes stoked Vic's own desire, but he palmed his straining cock, promising himself they'd take this slowly.

"These jeans have to go," Vic rumbled. He worked the buttons this time until Simon grew impatient and batted Vic's hands away to shove his pants and briefs down to his thighs. Vic moved off him just long enough to pull the clothing the rest of the way and drop it onto the floor. Simon's scent just made Vic harder.

"I want to see you," Simon murmured, running his fingers down Vic's chest and working at his belt. Vic lost no time shedding his jeans, and lay down between Simon's spread legs, relishing the feel of skin against skin.

"So good," Vic said and slid down until Simon's hard cock was right in front of him. He took him all the way down in one move, earning a yelp from Simon. Vic worked him up and down, swirling his tongue over the slit and the ridge of his knob, sucking and humming until he had Simon writhing and grabbing at the couch cushions. Vic pulled off with a pop and rose up far enough to get a good look at his lover.

Simon's hair was a chestnut cloud around his head, and with kiss-swollen lips and lust-blown hazel eyes, Simon looked utterly, fabulously debauched. Vic reached for one of the many bottles of lube they kept stashed around the bungalow, making a show of drizzling it onto his hand and slicking up his fingers. Simon watched his every move like Vic was a porn star in his very own fantasy.

Vic leaned forward, lifting Simon's legs and exposing his tight pucker, then he bent down and let the tip of his tongue rim Simon with gentle flicks.

"You're killing me!" Simon groaned. Vic kept up the exquisite torture, gradually growing bolder, alternating between the flat of his tongue and the tip, then adding first one finger and then two, opening Simon and getting him ready. When Simon started fucking himself on those fingers, Vic decided to take pity on both of them.

"Ride me," Vic said, swinging his legs around so that he was sitting up on the couch. He poured more lube into his palm and thrust into the circle of his hand to slick himself up.

Simon stretched, giving Vic a good look at his body, then sat up languorously, as if he weren't aching to be fucked. He stood and moved in front of Vic.

"Like what you see?" he asked, presenting himself.

"You know I do," Vic rasped. He reached for Simon, gripping his hips, and brought him closer to straddle him. "Need to be in you, now."

Simon knelt on the couch, one knee on either side of Vic's thighs, and lowered himself until the head of Vic's cock brushed between his ass cheeks. He let the knob breach him and stilled, letting himself adjust, then took Vic in all the way. Vic moaned, watching as his cock slipped inside Simon's ass.

"Move," Vic managed.

Simon gave a sinful smile, and rose up a few inches, then sank again, resting his forearms on Vic's shoulders. He pulled almost all the way off, then came down, hard, watching for Vic's reaction.

Seeing Simon confident enough to seduce him made Vic all the hungrier. He fought the instinct to grab hold of his lover and pound into him, remembering his promise to take it slow. Simon leaned back, bracing himself on Vic's knees, changing the angle so that Vic's cock hit his sweet spot, and Simon let out a groan of pleasure.

"Simon." Vic couldn't manage more than a couple of syllables, not with Simon's ass clenching around his cock and his body on display. He reached for Simon, pulling him closer, kissing him hard. His hands slipped down to Simon's hips and thrust up, earning a happy moan. They began to move together, matching each other's strokes, setting a rhythm that grew faster with their hunger. Despite the promise to take his time, Vic knew he was too close to last.

"Go ahead," Simon whispered, kissing his ear. "Let go. I want to feel you come."

That did it. Vic felt his orgasm slam through him, whiting out his vision for a second as he filled Simon's ass with his spend. Simon's release followed close after, painting Vic's chest with jizz. Vic wrapped his arms around Simon, kissing him slowly, happily fucked out.

"We're going to stick together," Simon murmured after a few moments of cuddling.

Vic grabbed a box of tissues from the end table and handed a wad to Simon, while he used more to wipe down his chest.

"How about round two in the shower?" Vic asked, with a playfully lascivious grin.

"How about we switch it up?" Simon returned, tugging on his wrist to get Vic up off the couch and moving toward the bathroom.

"Okay by me," Vic answered, feeling his dick twitch at the thought. He'd always preferred to top before he met Simon, but now he found that he liked how they fit together, no matter how they did it. If anyone had told him before that he would sometimes crave the feeling of being filled and owned, he would have laughed, but with Simon that intimacy met a need he never knew he had.

Simon turned, soaping Vic up into a massage beneath the hot water, and despite the rough day at work, Vic felt boneless by the time Simon took him from behind, pumping in and out in a leisurely rhythm that made Vic torn between wanting to speed things up and wanting them to last forever. By the time they finished and cleaned up again, the hot water was nearly spent, and so were they.

Vic and Simon made quick work of closing down for the night and checking the locks before they tumbled into bed. "That was…

awesome," he said as Simon snuggled close to him, resting his head on Vic's chest, still lazily tracing his tats with a finger.

"Uh huh," Simon agreed. "I like this. Us, together. You, living here. This is…good." His voice faded as he drifted off, and Vic knew by the rhythm of his breathing that Simon was asleep.

He lay there, sated and warm, listening to Simon breathe, torn between contentment and terror. Everything about his relationship with Simon felt oh-so-right, not just for now, but if he was honest with himself, forever. That thought didn't frighten Vic the way it might have, once. They weren't quite ready for that step, but Vic felt certain they'd get there. It wasn't the claiming that scared him; it was the possibility of losing someone who meant more to him than his own life. He'd never been this head-over-heels all-in before, and it was wonderful and overwhelming.

Vic stroked Simon's hair, taking in his scent, tightening his hold just a bit as his mind strayed to the murders. Like it or not, Simon was in the thick of things, tied up with the case regardless of his role as a consultant. That meant Vic needed to figure out everything from the police side as quickly as possible, to stop the killings and minimize the danger to Simon.

Vic pressed a kiss to the crown of Simon's head with a silent promise that he would keep him safe. But as sleep took him, Vic was damned if he knew quite how to do that.

***

"You want to explain why you asked for the files on all the suicides in the last six months?" Captain Hargrove crossed his arms and gave Vic a look that said he didn't plan to budge until Vic confessed. Hargrove was a former Marine, six feet tall and built like a tank. His blond hair was just slightly longer than regulation, and he didn't look like he'd lost an ounce of muscle since he'd mustered out.

Ross just gave a traitorous smile and stayed quiet, letting Vic dangle. Vic glared at his partner, who managed a look of complete innocence.

"We think that at least some of the suicides are actually

murders, due to supernatural possession," Vic said. The answer sounded bizarre, even to him.

"You've been binge watching *American Horror Story* again?" the captain asked, raising an eyebrow.

Vic shook his head. "It's the perfect 'locked room' mystery. Simon's been contacted by two of the ghosts so far. They couldn't tell him much, but they did get across the point that something forced them to hang themselves."

"Shit." Hargrove shook his head. "Do you have any hard evidence? Because no matter how much I believe Simon, I can't take that up the chain without proof."

"We're working on it, Cap," Ross said. He gestured to the files spread across the conference room table in the room they'd commandeered.

"Do you have a working theory?"

Vic let out a long breath. "Yeah, but you're not going to like it."

"Try me."

"I think the hurricane in September woke something up, or let it get out of wherever it was holed up—or locked up. The locked room suicides both had dried brine on their clothing, even though they were indoors. It's not much, but we're looking for connections."

"Since one of the families is pushing hard to get the death reclassified, I can let you run with it—up to a point. If you get the families of other victims stirred up, and they complain, I'm going to have to shut you down."

"We're not insensitive assholes," Ross muttered. He looked sideways at Vic. "At least, I'm not."

Vic raised his hands in appeasement. "I'm not planning to stir up shit. But if Simon's theory is right, then we also don't know whether the deaths are random or targeted, and what the killer wants."

Hargrove nodded. "All right. Don't make me regret this. See what you can find out, and keep me in the loop."

By late afternoon, Vic's vision was starting to blur, and the coffee in his stomach felt like acid. He tossed his most recent file onto the table. "Nothing in that one."

Ross consulted his notes. "Not surprising. That was the last of the pre-hurricane suicides."

Vic gestured toward two piles of folders, one larger and one smaller. "Yeah, but there've been a hell of a lot more suicides than I ever knew we got here in Myrtle Beach, and most of them are straight forward, open and shut."

"The first locked room suicide was just three weeks ago. There's been more since then, and they seem to be happening more closely together," Ross pointed out. "So…what happened three weeks ago that changed everything?"

"That's the million dollar question, isn't it?" Despite his sour stomach, Vic swigged down the rest of his now-cold coffee. "Let's look at just the locked-room deaths. We've got four now. They've got to have something in common."

"You don't think it's random?"

Vic frowned. "No. Do you?" When Ross shook his head, Vic went on. "We don't know if it's someone they knew who sent the…entity… after them, or whether they all passed through a location where the thing hunts for food and were unlucky enough to attract attention."

"Or if it picked them for a reason," Ross supplied. "I guess it could be a crime of opportunity, but it seems awfully intentional to me. If something just wanted to kill them, there are a lot of other, easier, ways to do it."

"I'm not the one we've got to convince," Vic said, staring at the folders.

Hargrove stuck his head in the room. "Hey, I need you to give it a rest and go out on a call. There's been a murder out at Socastee Manor, and the Murrell's Inlet cops called us in on it."

Vic's stomach flipped. "Socastee Manor?" he echoed, as his heart rate picked up. "Did they tell you anything else?"

Hargrove gave him an appraising look. "Just that there was a man dead. Why?"

Vic took a deep breath to steady himself. "Because Simon's been asked to help with a nasty haunting, and he intended to be out there today."

Hargrove shook his head. "Sorry. That's all I know. Go on, get out there. I'll lock this room up so no one messes with your mess."

Vic grabbed his gun and jacket, moving on autopilot, worried about Simon. By the time he and Ross were in an unmarked car heading for the old house, Vic had already tried to call Simon twice, but the calls went right to voicemail.

"Damn." Vic stared at the screen as if his scowl would put the call through.

"I'm sure Simon's fine," Ross said, not taking his eyes off the road. "Didn't you say that there was a ghost causing trouble for the workmen? Maybe it finally went too far."

"That's what Simon and the general contractor were worried about," Vic replied. "I just wish I could reach him."

"You know what the signal's like the closer you get to the water," Ross said, and Vic knew his partner was trying to be reassuring. "Don't borrow trouble."

Vic's fingers drummed on the armrest for the entire drive to Socastee Manor. When they arrived, he saw Simon's Toyota in the parking lot. *Hold it together,* he told himself.

A worried man wearing a dress shirt, slacks, and loafers paced at the edge of the gravel parking lot, puffing on a cigarette. When he saw them pull up, he dropped the cig, ground it out with his heel, and strode to meet them.

"You're the cops?" he asked.

Vic sized the man up. Mid-forties, dark hair with a receding hairline, expensive shirt, pricy slacks, designer leather shoes, and a Tag Heuer watch. Vic guessed that the BMW with the dive flag license plate belonged to him.

"Lieutenant Ross Hamilton and this is my partner, Lieutenant Vic D'Amato. Homicide," Ross responded. "What's going on?"

"I'm Jonah Camden, the representative for the development company remodeling the manor." He spoke quickly, in clipped tones, like he really needed another smoke. "We can't afford bad publicity."

"With all due respect, we need to see the body." Ross cut

through the bullshit, keeping his tone crisp and professional and completely sidestepping the douchebro's mangled priorities.

"Yes. Yes, of course," Camden said. "Follow me."

While Ross handled the niceties, Vic scanned the surroundings. He didn't see Simon, which made his chest tighten. The manor was actually in better shape than he had thought, given what Simon had said about it, and with enough money it might shape up into quite a beauty. The location was remote for the area, on a spit of land that likely became an island in bad weather. Then again, Vic thought Simon had said something about smugglers and pirates being part of the house's history. The site was perfect for that, isolated from any other beachfront development.

"Do you know who the victim is?" Ross asked, and Vic's attention returned to the here-and-now.

"Jacob Platz, the man we hired to do the landscaping," Camden replied. Ross jostled Vic's shoulder, making sure he heard the news. Vic let out a breath he didn't realize he had been holding. "My GC found him and called me. Of course, I came at once."

"Who all is on the property?" Ross asked. Vic appreciated his partner taking the lead to let him get his shit together.

"My GC, Trevor Nichols, and a historical consultant whose name I didn't catch. Trevor could tell you which of the workmen were scheduled to be here today. He'd also know if Jacob had anyone working with him."

Camden led Vic and Ross away from the house, across a windswept piece of land that hardly looked like a lawn. Vic didn't know much about landscaping, but he did know that Myrtle Beach's sandy soil made gardening a challenge. Still, someone had cleaned up the weeds and to replace them with plants that thrived in the humid, hot weather—oleander, bougainvillea, and palmettos.

The dead man lay face-down, one arm splayed to the side, with a knife hilt-deep in his back.

"Has anyone else been near the body?" Vic asked, able to breathe again now that he knew Simon wasn't in immediate danger.

"Trevor, of course—he said he came out to ask Jacob a question and found him like this," Camden said. He bit his lip—a nervous tic

—and his gaze seemed to go everywhere except toward the body. Not surprising, Vic thought. Real death wasn't like in the movies.

"Was Trevor alone when he found the body?" Ross asked. Vic hated that Simon might be dragged into this as a suspect, but the questions had to be asked. And he would repeat this and other questions to Trevor later.

"Yes, I believe that's what he said. He and his consultant are waiting up at the house."

"Hey, Vic. Take a look at this." Ross squatted beside the body and gave a nod toward the knife.

One look told Vic it was likely one of the three historic blades reported stolen from the Horry Area Museum. He met Ross's gaze, a silent message passing between them.

"Have you seen this knife before?" Ross questioned.

Camden recoiled, and Vic wondered if the man was afraid he'd somehow stain his expensive clothing. "The knife? No. Is it important? It looks old."

"That's why I ask," Ross replied, giving nothing away.

It seems like an odd choice for a random attack. Vic thought. He looked around at their remote location. *It's difficult to think this was a mugging.* "Do you know of anyone who might have disliked Platz?"

Camden shrugged, regaining some of his composure. "How would I know? He's the landscaper. We didn't swap life stories over a beer at the pub."

"Sometimes details show up during the hiring process," Ross answered.

"I put the job out to bid, and his was the best price. References checked out. You'd have to ask my assistant for details—I didn't do the paperwork myself."

No, of course not, Vic thought. Simon had told him that Camden didn't believe in ghosts and wanted to hush up the incidents with the haunting, even though Trevor worried about his workers getting hurt. Camden looked annoyed to have been called out of his office for something so trivial as the murder of someone he obviously didn't consider to be important. *Asshole.*

"It this going to take long?" Camden asked, practically twitching for another smoke. He finally gave in and shook a cigarette out of a pack in his shirt pocket, and lit up. His fingers trembled as he held up the lighter, but after he'd taken a few drags, he seemed to relax.

"It'll take as long as it takes," Ross said, straightening. He called back to the precinct, requesting the rest of the team. "We need to get forensics out here, and the coroner. Then my partner and I need to take statements from everyone who was here when it happened."

Camden winced. "Can we keep it out of the news? My company is putting a significant amount of money into this project, and bad publicity can kill the real estate values."

"This is private property. You can keep reporters from entering," Ross said, and his tone had grown cold. "But homicide is a matter of public record. The more helpful you and your people can be in telling us everything you know, the sooner we can wrap this up—and the quicker the news cycle moves on to something else." Left unsaid was the fact that Jacob Platz would stay dead, and his friends and family would grieve his loss. Vic didn't have the feeling Camden cared much.

"All right," Camden replied, sounding annoyed. "I can pull some security guards from one of our other projects and put them on the front entrance."

"Just make sure they stay at the front," Ross warned. "We don't need more people tramping around, contaminating the crime scene."

"We always cooperate with the authorities." Camden's voice held a touch of sarcasm.

He turned away, walking back toward the parking lot, with his phone glued to his ear as he barked orders to an underling. Vic and Ross watched him go, and Ross shook his head.

"Well, he's a peach."

"Not exactly the word I had in mind," Vic muttered. Camden might be an asshole, but at least Simon was safe. Vic felt a flicker of guilt at his relief when another man's family would grieve their loss, but only a flicker. He'd never wish misfortune on someone else, but he wasn't above being grateful when the Angel of Death spared him and his.

"Thoughts?" Ross asked, now that Camden was out of earshot.

"I think it's a hell of a coincidence that there's an antique knife sticking out of the guy's back, on the grounds of a house with ghost problems," Vic said. He and Ross stayed well back from the corpse, but both studied the dead man intently, looking for clues.

"Maybe he saw something he wasn't supposed to see—or someone," Ross suggested.

Vic nodded. "Yeah. Or went somewhere he wasn't supposed to go. But there's no indication he was killed elsewhere and moved here."

It took a while for the rest of the team to show up. Ross stayed with the techs and the coroner, while Vic headed up to the house. He found Simon and a man he assumed must be Trevor Nichols sitting on the floor in the front room.

Even though Vic knew Simon was safe, seeing him set his heart at ease. Simon gave him a warning glance, and Vic read it as a clue to play it cool, although everything in him wanted to pull his boyfriend close. Vic decided that could wait for later, in private.

"I'm Lieutenant Vic D'Amato, Homicide" he introduced himself. "I need to take your statements about what happened here." He glanced to Trevor. "I'm told you found the body?"

Trevor swallowed hard and nodded. "I'd gone looking for Jacob to talk over his plans to protect the landscaping he'd already done in case the big storm hit. He didn't answer his phone, and he wasn't in the supply shed. I called out, and then I went to find him. And I did." He looked shaken, and Simon put a hand on the man's shoulder to calm him.

"Did you touch the body?" Vic cut in.

"No."

"Were you with him?" Vic asked Simon.

Simon shook his head. "I got here just as Trevor called the police. Since I was already here, I figured I should stay."

"Is there anyone else on the property?"

Trevor answered. "The crew that was supposed to be here today got delayed because materials shipped late. I'd been trying to get another crew in to work on something else when I found

Jacob and figured it was better not to have any extra people around."

"Good thinking." Vic spent the next two hours taking their statements, finishing up shortly before Ross came to get him.

"The team is finished," Ross said, and Vic saw the ambulance drive away with Platz's body. "You ready to head back?"

Vic nodded. "We're done." He looked from Simon to Trevor. "I'll be in touch if we need anything else." He and Simon shared a look, and Vic couldn't help a slight smile. He knew that Simon would work his end of the case, and if there were any ghostly witnesses, he felt certain Simon would find out everything they knew.

That night, Vic managed to beat Simon home. He brought take-out from Simon's favorite Thai restaurant and managed to have the table set by the time his man came in the door.

"What's all this?" Simon asked, surprised.

Vic pulled him close and kissed him hard. "You scared me today. We got that call about a death at the old house, and I couldn't reach you on your cell—"

Simon kissed him back, then slipped his arms around Vic's waist and rested his head against Vic's shoulder. "Sorry—the reception out there sucks. Trevor used a landline to call in the report."

Vic breathed in Simon's scent, holding him tight. "I was worried about you being in danger from the ghosts, and it turns out we've got a real, live murderer wandering around."

Simon kissed him on the cheek and disentangled himself, moving to hang up his coat and set down his messenger bag. "About that. Trevor and I have no freaking idea why Jacob was killed. And while the ghost possession victims might be manipulated into hanging themselves, I don't think Jacob stabbed himself in the back."

"That developer, Camden. He's a real piece of work," Vic said, setting out the take-out containers and pouring drinks for both of them. "When did he get there?"

"Trevor called him right after he called the police. He'd only just arrived."

"But he managed to get there first. Do you think he could have had anything to do with it?"

Simon raised an eyebrow. "Jonah? He's not that hands-on. And I can't quite imagine him taking out a hit on the gardener."

"The guy was a real asshole," Vic said as he sat down at the table. "He's probably made a ton of professional enemies. Do you think someone might be willing to kill in order to tank the project? I mean, Camden's company would lose a bundle if the house renovation fell through or it didn't sell."

Simon considered the theory as he loaded up his plate with Pad Thai and grabbed a couple of spring rolls. Vic had a plate full of curry chicken, and they split a container of Tom Yum soup. Hot green tea warmed Vic and soothed his nerves.

"Yes, the development company would lose money and get bad publicity, but Platz isn't the guy to kill to make that happen. Trevor's the lynchpin—he's the one coordinating all the work, managing the budget, dealing with the vendors. That's what's got me puzzled. I can't figure out what anyone stood to gain—or was afraid of losing."

Vic knew he would have to talk to Simon at some point about the suicide files he and Ross had gone through today, but right now he felt tired and raw, and very ready to leave work at the office.

"What kind of emergency plans are being talked about for the storm?" Simon asked, finishing his soup.

Vic shrugged. "Not the full hurricane evac but definitely thinking about trying to get people out of the areas prone to the worst flooding." He raised an eyebrow. "Which includes the boardwalk."

Simon groaned. "I know. I've got empty sandbags Pete and I can fill and put around the doors if this storm stays on course. It might veer off. Storms wobble."

"If it's as bad as some of the forecasters think, I'm probably going to get pulled into emergency duty," Vic warned. "Like back in September, with the hurricane. I'm worried about you being at the shop—or here. We're still pretty close to the ocean."

"Figured we'd sandbag the bungalow, too. We were fine with the hurricane. This place has weathered a lot of storms. Gotta give the house credit. Same with the shop. It'll be okay."

"I wish I could get you to go inland, just until it blows over."

Simon leveled a glare. "And go where? I'm not going to visit my folks, that's for damn sure. If the storm's that bad, every hotel north to Columbia and south to Charleston will be filled. I'll do what I did during the hurricane—help out at the crisis shelter."

"I just want to keep you safe." Vic knew he was overreacting. Simon had lived through plenty of hurricanes before they got together. But Vic was Pittsburgh-raised, and ocean storms were still new and strange to him. After the scare at the manor, Vic felt off his game.

"And how do you think I feel?" Simon snapped. "I'll either be here or helping at the shelter. Inside. Safe. You and Ross will be out in the weather, dealing with crazy drivers and truck pile-ups and people getting stuck in flooding. If one of us is going to freak out about safety, I kinda think it should be me."

"I'm not freaking out," Vic muttered.

Simon reached across to take his hand. Vic fought the petty instinct to jerk back, but he still didn't meet Simon's gaze. "Bad word choice. Sorry. But…if I can deal with you being out in the thick of it, I think you can come to terms with me being inside a concrete shelter."

"Maybe." Vic sulked. Jeez, all he wanted to do was keep Simon from getting hurt. He knew he was being a jerk, but he'd kept a hospital vigil for Simon once already, and that was the worst day of his life.

"Hey." Simon squeezed his hand. "We'll be okay. Goes with the territory—for both of us, right?"

Vic let out a long breath and nodded, trying to shake off his mood. "I'm sorry." He managed a wan smile. "This," he gestured between them, "is still an adjustment." His ex had been a cop, and worrying about each other wasn't part of the deal. Everything was different now, reminding Vic that his relationship with Simon wasn't like anything he'd had with anyone else before.

"For both of us," Simon replied. "But thanks for worrying about me."

"Always," Vic said. He got up and cleared the table, trying to shift the mood. "C'mon. There are a couple of new movies streaming." He gave Simon a wicked grin. "How about Netflix and chill?"

5

SIMON

"I hear there are a lot of cancellations," Jay Gutierrez said. Jay owned Boardwalk Ink, a tattoo shop just down from Grand Strand Ghost Tours, and he and Simon had become friends as well as neighboring shop owners.

"Someone told me that the hotels were looking at a twenty-five percent cancellation rate, and we're still a couple of days out," Tracey replied. The fact that she could take a few minutes away from the counter during the early morning rush said volumes about how slow things had gotten as Myrtle Beach hunkered down for the storm.

"We've had to cancel a couple of ghost tours because there just aren't enough people around to sign up," Simon added, taking a sip of his latte.

"Do you think it'll really be as bad as they're saying?" Jay leaned against the counter. On busy days, the line could be out the door, but right now, only two people waited for Tracey to pull their drinks.

"I'm a psychic, not a meteorologist," Simon joked. "I get that the officials want to err on the side of caution so people don't get hurt. But I feel bad for the people who cancel their vacations, and then the whole thing blows over."

Tracey shrugged. "I feel bad for the rest of us, who still have to pay rent when nobody's on the boardwalk. This year's been the worst for storms since I've been here."

"Blame it on climate change," Jay muttered. "On the other hand, the divers that were in my shop last night said that the rough water is churning up all kinds of stuff from the old wrecks out there."

"Anything new about the *Annabelle*?" Simon asked. "One of your diver friends dropped by to see me, hoping I could get an impression off anything he brought up."

"Did he give you anything to ghost-read?" Jay asked, and Tracey paused, intrigued.

Simon shook his head. "Not yet. I have to admit, I'm interested. But I sure wouldn't want to be diving in the surf we've had." The waves were higher and rougher than usual, with a dangerous undertow. Anyone crazy enough to dive under those conditions needed to be a real pro.

"These guys struck me as the diving equivalent of those storm chasers who drive around looking for tornadoes." Jay tipped up his cup and drank the rest of his coffee, finishing with a satisfied sigh. "Hit me again," he said to Tracey, holding out his cup.

"Clearly, you've mistaken me for the bartender at Dock's," she said, naming a popular boardwalk bar. She tossed out his used cup and poured him a fresh coffee, accepting the bills he passed to her in exchange.

"You brew good stuff," he said with a grin. "Keeps the blood pumping."

"So did you guys decide what you're doing if the storm rolls in big?" Simon asked, thinking about his near-argument with Vic from the night before.

"Shayna and I are going up to her mom's place in Conway," Tracey said. "We're due for a visit anyhow."

"I'm staying," Jay declared. "If my place didn't flood too badly during the hurricane, it'll be fine for this. How about you?"

Simon shrugged. "Figured I'd help at the shelter. Vic has to stay, so I'm staying, too."

Tracey gave him a look, and he knew she was reading between the lines. "He wants you to get the hell out of Dodge, doesn't he?"

Simon looked away. "Yeah. Maybe."

She and Jay chuckled. "That is so adorable!" Tracey said. "Don't be mad at him, Simon. He's a cop. Cops protect. They're like German Shepherds, guarding the pack. I think it's sweet that he's looking out for you. Admit it—you don't really mind."

"Yes and no," Simon replied. "I *can* take care of myself. And he's going to be out on emergency duty, so between the two of us, *I'm* the one who should be worried about *him*."

"And he's not used to that," Tracey filled in.

"Family of cops, you know? Nobody admits to worrying about anything," Simon muttered.

Tracey reached across to pat Simon on the arm. "You'll adjust. Both of you. Having someone want to protect you is a good thing. Don't let all that testosterone get in the way."

Simon tried to take Tracey's advice to heart as he headed back to the shop. He was early, and Pete wasn't due in until closer to noon, since the lack of tourists made for slow days. Simon got set up, then pulled out his phone and left messages for both Miss Eppie and Gabriella, letting them know he needed to meet with them. He'd missed two phone calls from hunters—people who chased down supernatural creatures. Given Simon's background with folklore and mythology, he'd become a go-to resource for the hunting community whose questions were often far too detailed to get answered on Google.

Once he had returned those calls, he started down the list of people he thought of as his "Skeleton Crew"—those with low-level psychic gifts that Simon had gathered into a loosely-knit group who traded information and looked out for each other. Many were otherwise on their own since their gifts made them unwelcome in some circles.

"Yeah, it's Simon," he said when Michelle—a telepath who worked for a swanky hotel answered. "Just making sure you've got somewhere to go if the storm gets bad."

"Anyone ever tell you that you're a mother hen?" she asked, but Simon heard fondness beneath the snark.

"I might have been accused of that a time or two," Simon admitted, thinking of Vic. But when it came to his Crew, he knew that most of them had very few people to check on them, and he had promised himself that in exchange for asking them to use their Gifts to help solve cases, he intended to give back as much as he could. "Just want to make sure everyone's safe."

"I've got to work," Michelle replied. "But if it gets bad, they'll let us stay in the hotel. Since the place didn't collapse in the last hurricane, I figure I'll be okay."

"Good," he replied. "Hey, have you picked up anything weird lately, *you know*?" Michelle would understand without him having to say it that he meant through her telepathy.

"Had one of my regular customers end up on the news for all the wrong reasons, if that's what you mean," she replied. "Roger. Nice guy, even if he was a little dweeby. I didn't figure him to end up dead in a hotel room."

"The last time you saw him, how long ago was it?"

"That's the thing," Michelle replied. "I'd just seen him earlier that evening, and I swear to God, he wasn't broadcasting anything about hurting himself. Some guys, they're just radiating gloom, and you know they're in trouble. Roger didn't seem any different than usual. And I know they say people who are gonna do it hide it, but they don't hide it from a person like *me*."

"Thanks," Simon told her. "That's exactly what I needed to know. If you do pick up on anything weird, call me."

"You're the first person I think of when I think of 'weird,'" Michelle said with a snicker. "Take care of yourself, Simon. Don't be a stranger."

Simon put down the phone when he heard someone knocking on the glass. He went to the door and saw Rennie, another one of his Crew, standing outside. *I wasn't even sure she knew where the shop was. This is a first.*

He opened the door and waved her in. "Do you want coffee?"

Despite the puffy faux fur coat and thigh-high boots, Rennie looked cold. She nodded, and Simon went to fix a cup, then brought it out.

"I need your help."

Simon took another look at Rennie and realized that she looked exhausted. Even her flawless, dramatic make-up wasn't quite up to par. "What's going on?" he asked, worried.

"I've got a stalker."

"One of your clients?" Rennie usually worked the corners by the nightclubs and mid-level bars, offering companionship to tourists looking for a good time. She was also the only other medium in Myrtle Beach, and her gift had taken a toll on her. Simon was used to Rennie's fierce independence and sharp sarcasm. Seeing her scared—and admitting she needed help—worried him.

Rennie shook her head, and patted her pockets, like she was looking for a cigarette, then realized she was indoors and gave up with a sigh. "No. A ghost. I think he might have been a sailor. Keeps saying 'Annabelle is coming back' and he won't fucking go away!"

Simon frowned. "Could he have been a pirate?"

Rennie gave Simon an incredulous look. "A pirate?" She thought about it for a moment. "Yeah, maybe."

"Is he threatening you, or could he be passing along a warning?"

Rennie wrapped her arms around herself. Simon noticed she'd bitten her nails to the quick. "He just keeps saying that, and he won't go away. I thought he was trying to scare me, but maybe…I'm the only person he's met who can hear him." She grimaced. "Why the fuck couldn't he have found you instead?"

"Just lucky, I guess," Simon replied with a lopsided grin. "Can you describe him?"

"Straggly kid, maybe eighteen or nineteen, dirty long hair, plain shirt, and baggy, old-fashioned pants. Looked like he'd missed a few meals, and his teeth were bad—I remember that."

"Okay, the next time he shows up, send him to me," Simon said. He dug into the case beneath the counter and came up with a smooth onyx disk, a chunk of agate, and a gris-gris bag. "Take these," he said, pushing the items into Rennie's hands. "They'll make him keep his distance, and think twice if he tries to hurt you."

"I'm low on cash," she said, moving to put the items back on the counter. "I can't pay you."

"You don't have to. It's a gift," he said. "Do you have somewhere safe to ride out the storm that's coming?"

Rennie shrugged and looked away. "I'll find something. I always do."

"I'm going to be down at the storm shelter, helping out," Simon told her. "If you need a place to go."

She snorted. "I'm sure they'd be happy to see me."

"I'd be happy to see you, and I'll make sure it's okay," Simon promised. "Deal?"

She looked away and huffed out a breath. Simon could tell she didn't like accepting help. "Yeah. Sure. But it's not going to be that bad."

"Just in case," Simon said.

"Remember—I'm sending sailor boy your way the next time I see him," Rennie replied, stuffing the charms into her pockets and heading for the door. "Don't say I didn't warn you." She bumped shoulders with Pete on her way out.

"Something going on?" he asked, as he walked past the front counter to the break room to put his lunch in the fridge.

"Just more ghosts acting up," Simon said and sighed. His coffee was cold, but he finished the rest anyhow and chucked the cup in the trash. "There's a fresh pot already made."

"Thank God. For the sunny south, it's damn cold out there," Pete replied, leaving his jacket in the back room, keeping his sweatshirt on.

"Heard any more about the storm?"

Pete ambled back to the front with a steaming cup of coffee. "Yeah. We're all gonna die. It's not gonna happen. It's just rain. Take your pick."

Simon rolled his eyes. "And they say psychics aren't reliable."

"You planning to be at the shelter when the hammer falls?"

"Yeah. Vic has to work, and I'm not leaving without him.

Besides—we rode out the last hurricane. This is just a winter storm."

"I might come help, if that's okay." Pete began straightening up merchandise and looking for what needed to be restocked.

Simon dusted the saint's candles on the shelves behind the counter and wiped off the glass front of the case that held the small charms and amulets.

"The more, the merrier," Simon told him. "It's sort of fun—like a slumber party you throw for the whole city." There was more to it, of course, and people were worried about their homes, friends, and livelihoods, but Simon had always been amazed at how most folks bucked up under pressure and pulled together to make the best of it.

"Sounds like a plan." Pete went to the stock room and returned with an arm full of t-shirts and books. "Meant to ask—what happened at the manor? I saw on TV some guy got killed?"

Simon filled him in, without giving away anything that the police had requested not be disclosed. Pete let out a low whistle when Simon finished.

"Day-um. As if a malicious ghost wasn't bad enough."

"Yeah, well. The murder is Vic's job. I don't see a connection to the haunting, and I'm going to keep my focus on cleansing the mansion."

His phone chirped, and Simon saw an incoming call from Miss Eppie.

"Sebastian." Ephigenia Walker was the only person who called Simon by his given name. "I was wondering when you'd get around to calling me."

"You were? Why?" Even though Simon had initiated the contact, her greeting flummoxed him.

"Because you're in the thick of it again, aren't you? Dead men and bad ghosts. You shouldn't have waited so long."

Simon felt like a kid called to the principal's office. Miss Eppie was at least seventy years old, and she didn't mince words. "It took me this long to put some of the pieces together and know what I'm dealing with."

"Uh huh. You're not usually slow on the uptake," Miss Eppie

replied. "Come on over to the shop at closing. I'll have tea ready. Don't be surprised if Gabriella is here, too. I know you called both of us."

Simon chuckled. "Guilty as charged. I'll be there. And…thanks."

Miss Eppie gave a huff. "Don't thank me yet, Sebastian. Pulling your butt out of the fire is becoming a regular occurrence."

"Sorry."

"Don't you apologize! Nothing wrong with asking for help. You just need to learn to ask sooner, that's all. Now, I'll see you at six. Don't be late. We have work to do."

Simon ended the call and slipped his phone back in his pocket, trying and failing to rid himself of a vague feeling of guilt, like he'd been caught cutting class. Pete glanced at him and chuckled at his expression.

"You're so busted."

Simon flipped him off, but he had to grin. "Yeah. I just take my lumps because she's right—and she and Gabriella together are a force of nature. I'd even bet on them against the storm."

The rest of the day passed unremarkably. Simon had a radio on, tuned to the weather forecast, which grew increasingly dire. The number of pedestrians on the boardwalk had slowed to a trickle, with a cold wind and spitting rain. Hours passed without someone entering the shop, even to browse. Simon finally sent Pete home early, since there was nothing left to do. Maybe tomorrow, if the weather still looked bad, they'd fill those sandbags.

He closed up for the night, checked the alarm, the wardings, and the security camera, and headed over to Miss Eppie's store. Her shop didn't need the visibility of a boardwalk address. People who needed her found her. The sign outside the modest storefront proclaimed: "*Lowcountry Roots*." Simon could feel a shiver of magic as he crossed the threshold, aware of the warding Miss Eppie had placed there.

Inside, the store appeared to be an offbeat gift shop, with a selection of handmade crafts including sweetgrass baskets and woven shawls. The case beneath the counter held boxes of different colored powders, bottles of Four Thieves vinegar, and gnarled clumps of High John the Conqueror root.

Those in the know understood that everything in the store had a connection to hoodoo, and was either an ingredient for a root work spell or had been blessed by Miss Eppie herself. The air smelled of sage and cinnamon. Simon felt the positive magic like a warm blanket, making him feel safe.

Miss Eppie bustled up to the counter from the back room. "Sebastian. I'm glad you're here. Gabriella is on her way. Come into the kitchen. I have tea." Miss Eppie might be in her seventies, but she moved with cat-like grace and preferred jewel tone colors that brought out the golden undertones in her dark skin. Today she wore a deep blue silk scarf over an emerald blouse with practical black jeans and ankle boots. Gold hoop earrings set off her short hair. The semi-precious gems in her rings and bracelets were all known for their protective magic.

Simon followed her to the dated but clean kitchenette that held a table and chairs, small refrigerator, microwave, sink, and coffee maker. A pitcher of iced tea and three glasses sat in the middle of the table.

"Sit. Have something to drink. I can feel your tension." Miss Eppie might not be a mind-reader, but her hoodoo and years of experience made her a sharp observer.

Simon poured a glass for her and for himself. "Thanks. I like the new baskets up front, by the way." The sweet tea was brewed strong and sugary enough to make his fillings ache.

"They are nice, aren't they?" she replied, clearly waiting for Gabriella to come so she could lock up. "A friend of mine down in Charleston—another root woman named Mrs. Teller—sent those up. She does good work. And they've all got a bit of her magic in them."

Gabriella Hernandez showed up a few minutes later, a slightly built woman in a crimson twin-set over dark slacks who looked like she had just come from a business meeting. She defied the stereotype of a caftan-clad *bruja,* and she took a thoroughly modern approach to her magic. "Simon. Eppie." She greeted with a nod.

Where Eppie reminded Simon of a grandmother, Gabriella seemed more like a strict librarian.

"Come on in and have a seat. I'll lock up," Miss Eppie said, shooing Gabriella into the kitchen. She returned and took her place beside Simon, then focused her gaze on him.

"All right. You called and said there was a situation. Fill us in."

The women listened, occasionally interrupting for clarification, as Simon told his story. He left nothing out, starting with his terrifying visions of the Gallows Nine and the men aboard the black ship, to the cryptic messages from the hanged men and the hostile ghosts of Socastee Manor. The few details he omitted were those the police had asked not to be revealed about the Platz murder.

"That's quite a lot," Gabriella said when Simon finished. She tapped a manicured nail against the glass tumbler as she thought. "And you think that somehow, everything is connected?"

Simon let out a long breath. "I do, but I can't prove it. I'm just afraid that it's all coming to a head, and the storm is part of that."

"Storms can magnify power, and increase the energy of spirits," Eppie remarked.

"Do you think someone—or something—has called the storm?" Simon asked.

"No one can fully control the weather," Gabriella replied. "A weather witch can affect a very small area, to protect it or make a storm more violent. It's a rare type of magic. But there have been stories about people and creatures and objects that could influence storms."

"Not just stories," Eppie said. "True tales. Right here in these waters. I remember when I was a girl, hearing an old story about a man with a cursed set of bagpipes who sank a smuggling ship off the coast of Bermuda."

Her comment sent a chill down Simon's spine, and he thought of his vision of the black ship. "Do you know anything more about the man in that story?"

Eppie gave him a look as if she could guess his thoughts. "He was a water witch who became a privateer, working for a patron in

Charleston. They said he stole cursed and haunted cargo and got rid of it where it couldn't hurt anyone again."

That triggered another memory, and Simon promised himself to make a phone call when their meeting was over.

"Would this have been back around the time of the Gallows Nine?" Simon pressed.

Miss Eppie nodded. "Probably. What are you thinking, Sebastian?"

"The rough water churned up the wreck of the *Annabelle*, the ship sailed by the Gallows Nine. People knew it went down off the coast, but no one had been able to find it before. I met one of the lead divers who's exploring the wreck. I'm just wondering whether that has anything to do with the rest of this mess."

"There's no such thing as coincidence," Gabriella said. "The question is, can you find the link?"

"We've got two sets of murders," Simon said and refilled his glass. "The men who are being driven to hang themselves, and Jacob Platz's killing out at the manor."

"Socastee Manor is a bad place," Miss Eppie said, and her fingers went to the mojo bag that was always in a pocket. "Been unlucky for a long, long time. I wish you'd have asked me before you promised that man you'd help un-haunt it. Some places are stained deep."

"What's so bad about it?" Simon asked. "I read up on the Dunwoods—at least, what I could find online."

Miss Eppie gave a snort. "Like you'd find the whole truth there. The man who settled that plantation, back before the Revolution, got the land from the king. Only it wasn't the king's to give—there were native people already living there. So the first Dunwood had to drive them off and steal their land, and people died."

She paused to sip her tea. "It didn't get better from there. Dunwood had slaves—of course he did. Working a rice plantation was a death sentence from malaria. At first, the Dunwoods didn't do well. Then all of a sudden, everything turned around, and they became rich. People I know whose ancestors worked that land say Jamie Dunwood made a deal with the devil. The slaves knew about the dark magic, but they didn't dare tell anyone. Then later there were rumors Dunwood had a hand in the smuggling trade. Wouldn't surprise me. His descendants weren't any better." She leaned forward. "That house should stay abandoned. That land is cursed, and the energy will just get worse with more people around."

"The developer isn't going to walk away from the project," Simon said, shaking his head. "Trevor—the general contractor—is afraid someone on his crews will get hurt badly. I can't just walk away if I could help. Maybe I can't un-curse the land, but if I can get rid of the vengeful ghost, at least nobody else will die."

"I agree with Eppie," Gabriella said, giving Simon a disapproving look. "But if you're not going to quit, take these." She pulled several charms made of shell and bone, feathers and seeds, from her purse and pushed them across the table to Simon. "They'll help protect you, but they won't hold off everything. Just remember —storms can make all kinds of bad things rise from where they've been buried."

Simon stopped at the store on the way back to the bungalow. He'd felt bad all day that he and Vic had argued, and he wanted to make up for it. A quick run through the Piggly Wiggly netted him two steaks, bagged salad, and fresh rolls. On impulse, he also grabbed a bouquet of red carnations, Vic's favorites.

When he got to the blue bungalow, Vic wasn't back yet. Simon hurried inside, heated the broiler, and set out candles and the flowers. He'd just finished fixing the salad when he heard Vic's key in the door.

"I'm in the kitchen," Simon called, giving the table a quick glance to make sure everything was as it should be.

He heard Vic toss his keys in the bowl near the front door and hang up his coat. His footsteps stopped in the doorway. "What's all this?"

"An apology," Simon said. "I shouldn't have gotten testy with you for trying to keep me safe."

Vic took him in his arms and kissed him, and Simon felt some of the day's tension melt. "Like you said, we're still figuring things out. We've got time."

"The steaks are ready," Simon said, reluctantly pulling away. "I thought we'd eat and then make an early night of it." His smile left no doubt that sleeping wasn't on his mind.

"I like the way you think."

The steaks turned out even better than Simon had hoped, since he preferred grilling to broiling, but the foul weather outside made that impossible. They kept the conversation light as they ate, and Simon promised himself he'd catch Vic up on everything he'd learned later, when they'd had time to decompress.

Just as they finished up the dishes and were heading toward the living room, Vic's phone chirped, with the tone Simon knew meant the MBPD. Vic met his gaze apologetically and took the call. His face fell as he listened, then nodded.

"Yeah. Okay. I'm on my way." He slipped his phone into his pocket and swore under his breath. "I'm sorry," he said, reaching for Simon and pulling him in by the hips until they were standing toe to toe. "That was Hargrove. There's been another hanging. I've got to go in."

Simon nodded and brushed Vic's cheek with the back of his hand. "That's okay. Go do what you need to do. I'll be here." Simon leaned in for a kiss, silently begging Vic to be careful, and promising what he could look forward to when he came home.

6

VIC

The dark, cold rainy night made Vic's mood more foul as he and Ross headed for the site of the latest death. He reminded himself that despite the interruption to his romantic evening, he was still having a much better time than the victim.

That thought didn't do much to lift his spirits.

"Hargrove said to handle this one with kid gloves," Ross warned. "Wealthy family, old money—the kind that can play havoc if they don't feel like they're being given special treatment."

"Fuck," Vic muttered. "Just what we need. You got any details?"

The windshield wipers slapped a beat as they drove down rain-soaked roads that reflected the Grand Strand's neon signage like a distorted rainbow.

"Corey Baucom, age forty-five, dentist. Married, no kids. I guess from what Hargrove said, the family used to be a big deal around here at one point, but everyone moved away or died off except Corey. Still, having the name come up in the system triggered Hargrove's 'special handling' warning, so I guess they used to have some pull."

"Who found him?"

"The wife," Ross replied. "That's pretty much all I know. Forensics is on the way, and so is the coroner. They'll probably beat us."

"How does Sheila take it, when you get called out?" Vic asked as they sat at one of the many stoplights on Kings Highway. He tried to sound off-handed, but he knew he hadn't imagined a trace of disappointment in Simon's eyes, despite the way he tried to make it seem like no big deal.

"It took some getting used to," Ross admitted. "I think that being married to a cop is a lot like being married to someone in the military—probably another reason we get so many ex-soldiers. You either get used to it, or you don't. The people who can't handle it don't stick around. The ones who do have made their peace with it."

"We're trying to use our words," Vic said. "It's hard."

Ross gave a snort. "Ya think? I don't know if I'll ever be comfortable with the touchy-feely stuff, but talking about it beats fighting about it."

"Simon is better at it than I am," Vic replied. "I know what I want to say, it just doesn't come out right."

"Simon is a word guy. I mean, he writes books and gives speeches. You shoot things and hit people. It's a different way of communicating."

"Thanks, I think."

"I'm gonna go out on a limb here. With me and Sheila, only one of us got brought up with all that macho bullshit. Girls get pushed to be the relationship fixers, be good listeners…talk it out. It's not fair that they get told they're responsible for the whole thing, but it's the culture, you know? I'm guessing that when it's two guys, and you both got brought up with the whole 'strong and silent, hide your feelings, never let 'em see you cry' BS, there's a little more unlearning to do, on both sides."

Vic raised an eyebrow. "That was actually rather profound. And…yes. Probably doesn't help that I'm in a macho job, from a family of cops. Being in academia might not have been quite as rough on Simon, at least in making him feel like he has to be a superhero."

"But we're not superheroes. This job breaks us, eventually," Ross replied. "And I think the guys who can't talk it out break faster and harder. At least that's what the counselor said."

"I don't know how to stop worrying," Vic admitted. "Simon doesn't like guns. And he's not trained to be a fighter. I can't be there all the time. And the kinds of things he goes up against—even that Kevlar vest won't protect him."

"He's a badass in his own way," Ross replied. "He took down the Slitter, remember? And that monster-thing at Christmas. He's got his own mad skills. Did you ever think that he might worry about you, because you don't have his magic woo-woo?"

No, he hadn't, Vic realized. "But like you said—I shoot things."

"Uh huh. But the stuff you two team up to fight now, you can't necessarily shoot, right?"

"No. At least, not with regular bullets." Vic really hadn't thought about it from Simon's viewpoint before. Vic might be learning to accept Simon's psychic abilities, but Simon had leaped into a relationship with someone who was essentially defenseless against supernatural threats.

"So cut him some slack," Ross replied. "He knows lots about the stuff that goes bump in the night—it makes sense that he worries because you don't. And you know just how bad human beings can be to each other, so you worry about him. I think that's kinda how it's supposed to work."

"Thank you, Dr. Phil." Vic's tone took the sting out of his words.

"Wait 'til you get my bill."

They pulled up to a closed iron gate and buzzed for admission. The metal grate swung back, allowing them onto a winding entrance road. Spotlights lit a clubhouse that looked like it belonged in the Greek Isles, and off to one side sprawled a pristine golf course. Tennis courts ranged on the other side, along with an outdoor pool. A sign at the cross street indicated the marina was to the right.

"Dr. Baucom must have been doing all right as a dentist," Vic observed. "Unless he inherited a boatload of money."

"I think he'd need more than just a boatload," Ross agreed. "A container ship-full? 'Cause in place like this, it's not just the house you gotta pay for—everything comes with extra fees. It's a racket."

"And you know this, how?"

"Sheila's sister, Shelly, married a cardiologist," Ross said. "Some nurses marry doctors, others marry cops. I lucked out with Sheila. Shelly traded up."

They pulled up in front of a house with Spanish-style architecture and a half dozen police cars in front. If the neighbors were gawking, the cold rainy night meant they rubbernecked from inside their houses. Hargrove was already on the scene as Ross and Vic flashed their badges at the patrolmen who were stationed at the end of the driveway.

"Glad you're here," Hargrove said. "Forensics is in there already, and so is the coroner. I asked them to preserve the scene until you got here so you could see for yourselves. And I'd like you to talk to the wife."

"Check the dead man's clothing for dried brine," Vic said quietly, in a voice only Hargrove could hear.

Hargrove gave him a look, then nodded. "Where's Simon?"

Vic cleared his throat. "He's had a rough couple of days with the ghosts from that old manor. I'm guessing the scene looks the same as the others, and Simon doesn't have to be on site to connect with the spirit, if it'll talk to him." He pitched his voice so that no one else would pick up on what he said.

Hargrove nodded. "Okay. I'd like his read on it—if he can make contact—as soon as you can."

The dead man had hanged himself from a light fixture in his study. The body now lay on the floor, clearly dead of strangulation, with evident petechial hemorrhaging. Once Vic and Ross had seen the corpse, the coroner maneuvered it into a body bag for transport.

"Matches the profile," Ross muttered. "Cap says the room was locked from inside, the guy stopped responding or answering his phone. Doesn't look like there was a struggle, and there's no note."

They walked to the living room, where Baucom's widow sat on the couch, crying quietly. Ross and Vic sat across from her.

"I'm Lieutenant Hamilton, this is Lieutenant D'Amato, and

we're very sorry about your loss," Ross said, taking the lead so Vic could observe. Christine Baucom's face was puffy and blotchy from crying. She wore an unremarkable sweater over jeans, what Vic would have expected for someone who thought she was going to have a quiet night at home. Either Christine was an excellent actress, or she was completely in shock.

"We need to ask a few questions," Ross said in his most sincere tone. "Was your husband depressed?"

Christine shook her head. "Not that I ever noticed. His practice is busy. We have—had—a big vacation coming up."

"Money problems?"

Again, a shake of the head. "I was just online paying bills this afternoon. The bank account was fine. We don't have much debt, other than a loan he took out for new equipment for his office. Nothing we couldn't handle."

"Drug or alcohol problems?"

"No. He was a good man, lieutenant," she said, pulling herself together enough to fix Ross with an accusing glare. "I don't know what happened, but this isn't like Corey. It just doesn't make sense."

"Yes, ma'am," Ross agreed. "That's why we're asking questions. Did he seem out of sorts, distracted, in an odd mood today?"

Christine frowned. "He had gone up to the bedroom for a nap after dinner, said he was very tired. That's not unusual; he'll often lie down while I clean up the kitchen, and then come back down to watch TV together. But he didn't tonight. He went right to his office. He didn't call out to let me know. I realized where he'd gone when I went to check on him, and he wasn't in the bedroom. By the time I really thought something was wrong…it was too late." Her voice caught, and she blinked back tears, then dabbed her eyes with a tissue. "If only I'd looked in on him earlier, talked to him. Maybe—"

They sat with her for a moment as she tried to collect herself. This was the part of the job Vic hated the most, because it made it impossible to avoid acknowledging the human toll.

"Thank you," Ross said quietly. "You've been very helpful. We'll be in touch."

Hargrove caught them on the way out. "Hey, there's another situation you might want to take a look at. A body just washed up north of the Second Avenue Pier. A guy in a dive suit—with one of the stolen historic knives sunk in his back."

"Shit." Vic exchanged a glance with Ross. "A knife. Just like out at Socastee Manor."

"We're on it," Ross said, and Hargrove clapped him on the shoulder.

"Thanks," Hargrove said. "Heads up—the Coast Guard has a man waiting to talk to you. He was the one who found the body."

Vic texted Simon while Ross called Sheila to let her know he'd be even later. "Yeah, not far from the pier," Vic said when Simon called him back. He gave the address. "Probably a good idea, but drive. See you there."

He buckled up as Ross pulled away from the curb. "Simon's going to meet us there."

"Sheila's binge-watching a baking show. She won't miss me for a couple more hours," Ross said.

"You get anything out of the conversation with Mrs. Baucom?" Vic asked.

"Only that something changed between taking a nap and locking himself in his office."

"Yeah, that's what I noticed, too. If Simon's right about this ghost possession thing, maybe it happened then. Maybe the poor guy really had no intention of offing himself when he came home from work, and it took him over while he was asleep."

"That's kinda terrifying," Ross replied. "Give me a random mugger any day. Crime makes sense."

Vic yawned. "Simon will tell you that supernatural shit also makes sense, if you know where to look for the motive. Which we still haven't figured out for the forced suicides."

"What are the chances that the gardener's murder out at the manor isn't related to the diver's killing?" Ross maneuvered through the rain around pokey drivers.

"Slim to nil," Vic replied, staring out the passenger window. "And while we try to figure it out, the bodies keep piling up."

Simon was waiting in his car when they arrived, parked right behind the first responders. He got out and joined them, hunching his shoulders against the rain despite his hooded jacket.

"Thanks for coming," Vic said, feeling better because Simon was with him, though that meant they both were miserable in the lousy weather.

"Sure. Why should you get all the fun?" Simon bumped his shoulder. The three walked together toward where headlights from patrol cars driven onto the beach lit the cordoned area. Vic saw the cops talking with Bret Timmons, a Coast Guard captain Vic had worked with before, and another man he didn't recognize.

"Simon!" The stranger called out when he spotted them. "How did you know to come?"

Simon shook the man's hand. "Josh, this is my boyfriend, Homicide Lieutenant Vic D'Amato and his partner, Ross Hamilton. Vic, Ross, this is Josh Williams—the guy in charge of the *Annabelle* dive."

That clicked as Vic remembered what Simon had told him. "Did you know the man who died?" Vic asked as the four of them headed toward where the wetsuit-clad corpse lay sprawled face-down on the sand. There was no missing the handle of the knife sticking out of the dead man's back.

"Unfortunately, yes. He wasn't one of mine. Sean Bradley. He's a dive poacher."

"A what?" Ross interrupted.

"There's a complicated process for getting permission to dive and reclaim objects from a historic wreck," Josh explained. "I've done that for the *Annabelle,* and I've got the licenses, permits, and sign-offs to prove it. We're supposed to be the only ones allowed near the ship. Bradley has a reputation for watching where other dive researchers post a find and then sneaking in and trying to loot the site."

"That's a pretty serious claim. Can you back it up?" Ross asked.

"Ask anyone reputable in the underwater recovery business," Josh replied. "Bradley's been brought up on multiple charges, but he always managed to skate free of the most serious ones."

"Had you noticed him near the wreck?" Vic tried to get a read on the explorer. He'd already admitted to having what might be a powerful motive. People had killed for lower stakes than a sunken treasure when professional jealousy was involved.

"No. But we can hardly post a guard," Josh said. "My team pulled out early today because the surf was too rough. If he went down after we left, he was insane."

"How much is the wreck worth?" Ross seemed to be sizing up the man as well. "Is there a treasure?"

To Vic's surprise, Josh barked out a laugh. "Are you kidding? You guys watch too much TV. There's no chest of doubloons on a wreck like this. Odds are, the *Annabelle* was smuggling rum, maybe cotton. Its cargo disintegrated long ago. The only treasure on this dive is knowledge."

Vic looked to Simon, needing him to translate from academic. "The *Annabelle* is famous because its crew included the Gallows Nine," Simon said. "There's always been some debate on whether that legend was based in fact. Being able to document the *Annabelle* and prove it was a real ship goes a long way toward verifying parts of the state's history. For some of us, that's a big freaking deal."

Vic couldn't say he totally understood, but then again, people had been killed over baseball cards. The crime scene photographers were battling the rain and darkness, and the coroner stood off to one side in a yellow rain slicker with reflective stripes, waiting his turn to take the corpse away and be done with it.

"Don't leave town," Ross warned Josh. "We'll have more questions for you."

"I figured," Josh replied. "I'm not going anywhere. I did my dissertation on the Gallows Nine. Protecting the wreck and the reputation of the survey means a lot to me."

Ross took down Josh's contact information, and then the diver walked back toward the street and, presumably, his car. Vic turned to Simon. "You getting anything?"

Simon frowned, concentrating. "From the dead guy? Surprise. Sadness. He didn't see his attacker. From Josh Williams? Less than usual. For some reason, I have difficulty reading much from him."

"Does that happen a lot?" Ross asked, turning his back to the wind.

"Occasionally," Simon admitted. "Some people have natural shielding. The other possibility is that he's got enough of a psychic gift that he's intentionally keeping me out. I don't know enough to guess right now." Simon went silent, and a strange expression crossed his face.

"Are you okay?" Vic asked.

A few seconds later, Simon shook off the distraction. "Yeah. I'm fine. Just thought I saw something."

Ross walked over to talk to the coroner and the patrol officers. With the wind, rain, and surf, the scene would deteriorate rapidly. Still, the autopsy might yield some information, Vic thought. He glanced at Simon, who looked thoroughly miserable.

"Sorry to drag you out on this."

Simon shrugged. "It goes with the deal. I think the wreck has something to do with all of this—I just don't know what, yet."

"Let's go home," Vic said as Ross headed back their way. Vic and Ross agreed to pick up again in the morning, and Vic headed to the Toyota with Simon. He was happy Simon was driving.

Inside the car, with the heat turned on and the knowledge that he was finally off-duty, Vic's exhaustion hit him hard, and despite being a short drive back, he started to nod off almost immediately.

Something evil watched him in the darkness. Vic found himself alone, in a place he didn't recognize. It felt like the inside of a huge, unlit warehouse, but no light broke the gloom to give him his bearings.

Primal instincts warned him that he was being stalked. He should run, but where? For all he knew, he might go straight toward the thing that hunted him or fall to his death if the floor suddenly opened to an abyss. Vic's hand fell to where his gun should be, only to find he was unarmed. Then his fingers went to where he usually kept the spelled kerchief, woven with protective magic, only to remember he'd left it in his other coat that morning. The bracelet on his wrist afforded some safety, but Vic wasn't sure that it was a match for the power that chased him.

He thought about crying out for help. Simon was nearby, wasn't he? Then he stayed silent, unwilling to give away his position. Vic had played a deadly game of hide-and-seek once with a suspect he had chased into a rail yard, but at least there, he'd been able to take cover behind boxcars and stacks of materials. Here, Vic was completely exposed, weaponless, and alone.

The creature attacked from behind, landing on Vic's back with enough force to drive them both to the floor. Vic fought, kicking and punching, but the thing on his back stayed out of reach, though it tightened a gnarled hand around his throat, slowly cutting off his air.

I'm going to die. Vic rammed his elbow back, taking satisfaction in the grunt earned as the sharp bone hit his attacker's ribs. Fingers dug into his neck, and Vic wheezed for breath. He bucked and twisted, managing to flip himself onto his back so he could land with all his weight on the thing that clawed at him from behind, stealing his breath. Bony legs locked around Vic's waist, making it impossible to throw the creature off, making it even harder to breathe.

In the distance, Vic thought he could hear shouting. Simon. Simon would come for him. But pinpricks of light danced in Vic's vision, and his lungs burned as he grew woozy from lack of oxygen. Simon was coming, but he was going to be too late.

No, Vic vowed. He'd only just found Simon, they'd barely begun a life together. This creature would not tear him away from Simon, not while Vic still had consciousness to fight back. Vic used all his waning strength for a final, defiant move, rising up and slamming down hard, using his weight and strength against the attacker, trying to buy time.

Simon's voice was louder now, along with another voice Vic didn't recognize, chanting in a foreign language. The monster from the darkness raked its claws across Vic's neck and chest, and he thought it might tear out his throat rather than just starve him for breath. It clamped down, squeezing his neck, cutting off his air, and Vic knew he had lost. He clung to the sound of Simon's far-away voice as everything faded to black.

7

SIMON

One minute, they were driving back from the murder scene at the beach, with Vic dozing in the passenger seat, and the next minute, Vic was gasping for breath and tearing at his throat.

"Vic! Vic, wake up!" Simon reached over and jostled Vic, but the awful wheezing sounds continued as Vic jerked and shook as if he were fighting for his life.

Should he pull over right now, although they were only a few blocks from home, or keep driving? Simon's Gift recoiled when he stretched out his senses toward Vic. He sensed a dark energy surrounding Vic, strong enough to overcome the basic wardings and protective charms Simon kept in the Toyota. This was a supernatural attack, not a physical problem, and Simon's gut told him to get home as fast as he could.

"Hang on, Vic," he said through gritted teeth, maneuvering the rain-soaked streets as quickly as he dared. Vic bucked and twisted, while his breathing became more labored, the long, rasping drags that made Simon think of a dying chain-smoker.

Whatever energy or entity attacked Vic had tried to get at Simon, back on the beach. He'd shut it down, holding it at bay with his abilities and his psychic shielding, driving it off with imagined white light infused with a banishing spell. Simon felt sick that in pushing the attacker away from himself, he might have put Vic in harm's way.

Simon chanted the banishing spell as he drove, his voice rising so that by the time he pulled up to the blue bungalow, he was shouting. For a few seconds, he thought the incantation might be working, but then Vic's whole body shuddered, and he went limp, making Simon panic.

"Vic!" Simon parked the car and ran around to Vic's side. He opened the door and struggled to get Vic out. Vic was solid muscle, taller and heavier than Simon, and while Vic had often supported Simon's weight when he wrapped his legs around Vic's waist, Simon had never even considered trying to pick his lover up. Now, Simon decided he needed to spend more time lifting weights.

He got under Vic's arm and half-carried, half-dragged him to the door, barely keeping both of them standing as he worked the key in the lock, and then he hauled Vic's limp body across the threshold and slammed the door behind them.

Simon dug for his phone and hit a number on speed dial. "Travis?"

"Simon?" The voice on the line sounded sleep-blurred, and Simon realized it was past midnight.

"I need help," Simon said, fighting down panic. He ran to the kitchen for a container of salt and pulled a bottle of holy water from his go-bag, then came back to where Vic lay, barely breathing, and sprinkled both over his prone form. "Something supernatural's attacking Vic. My banishing spell won't make it go away. Salt and holy water aren't working. He's got one of Teag Logan's woven bracelets, but it's not enough. He's breathing a little better since I got him inside the house with the wardings, but he won't wake up."

"What do you need?" Ex-priest Travis Dominick fought demons up in Pennsylvania. He was one of several hunters who relied on Simon for arcane lore. Now, Simon needed a favor in return.

"An exorcism," Simon replied breathlessly, as he continued to shake Vic and pat his face, but to no avail. Vic's pallor and his shallow, labored breathing scared Simon, especially since every intake sounded like a death rattle. "You're on speakerphone. Now!"

Thankfully, Travis didn't argue. *"Exorcizamos te, omnus immundus spiritus…"* The Latin exorcism flowed easily from Travis, and even across the distance, Simon felt the power in the words.

Simon sensed the dark energy fluctuate, and added his own banishment spell to the effort, pushing with all his might against the entity that trapped Vic, unashamed of the tears running down his face. When Vic drew in a deep breath without struggling, Simon felt a wave of relief.

"It's working!" he shouted at the phone. "Keep going!"

Travis's voice continued, steady and sure, and Simon felt the hostile energy fight to keep its hold. He took Vic's hand, twining their fingers, making sure his own protective silver bracelet came in contact with Vic's skin. Simon dug his jack ball and gris-gris bag out of his pocket and pressed them between the flat of his palm and Vic's chest, sending all of his protective magic into his touch.

Simon knew the instant the dark entity released Vic. He felt it tear free, like a cloth carried away on a storm wind, and Vic came to with a start, jerking upright and heaving for breath like he'd been trapped underwater.

"It's gone!" Simon called out to Travis. "Thank you so much!"

Travis finished the last of the exorcism litany, then cleared his throat. "Any time. Glad it worked. Call me at a decent hour and fill me in on what's going on. I'm going back to bed."

Vic had a wide-eyed deer-in-the-headlights look as he sat, trembling and breathing hard. Simon couldn't blame him for freaking out.

"It's okay. You're safe. We're home. I'm here." Simon reached out to lay a hand on Vic's shoulder. Vic jerked away, pale and shocky, as if he still wasn't sure that the nightmare was over. Simon remembered his own dark visions and how Vic had patiently talked him down.

"Whatever attacked you, it's gone." Simon didn't try to touch again, but he stayed close, hoping that his presence and the calming energy he sent Vic's way would help clear away the fog of terror.

"Simon?" Vic croaked as if noticing him for the first time. His voice rasped, and Simon saw red marks where unseen hands had choked him.

"I'm here. I love you. You're safe." Simon met Vic's gaze.

Vic took a long, shuddering breath, and covered his face with his hands. "God. What was that thing?"

"I'll tell you, but first I want to reset the warding on the front door to make sure nothing can come in." Simon jumped up, taking the salt container with him, and laid down a fresh line inside and outside the door. He added a blessing Gabriella had taught him, and a splash of Four Thieves vinegar as well as a sprinkle of brick dust.

That will do for now, he thought, feeling the protective energy strengthen. In the morning, he'd do a proper, full warding. He felt certain that whatever he and Travis had cast out would not be coming back soon.

Simon poured a Coke for Vic and returned to the living room. He handed off the glass, and Vic drank it down.

"Was that a demon?" Vic's voice still wasn't completely steady.

Simon shook his head. "I'm thinking boo hag. Demons are harder to summon and manage. Lesser spirits can be conscripted more easily."

Vic stared at him. "You sound like this was a hit."

Simon met his gaze. "I think it was. I had the feeling that something was watching us down on the beach, but I couldn't get a read on it. Whatever's behind the knife murders and the hangings, it's not afraid of the police—but I think it does see me as a threat." He looked away, awash in guilt. "I think it went after you because it couldn't get to me."

Vic took Simon's hand, squeezing hard. "If it had gotten to you, I wouldn't have known what to do," he said quietly. "And it's my fault—I have the bracelet but not the pocket square you gave me. It's in my other coat."

Simon got up and ran to fetch the kerchief, and returned in a moment, pressing it into Vic's hand. "This will help you feel better," he assured, "but it probably wouldn't have held off the spirit. It was very strong."

Vic slumped, and Simon gathered him into his arms. So many times, Vic had been the one comforting Simon after a disturbing vision or nightmare. Now, Simon was grateful to be able to return the favor. Vic leaned against him, and Simon pulled him close.

"Come on," Simon urged. "Let's get some sleep. I promise you'll feel better in the morning."

When Simon woke at his usual time, he called Pete and told him he would be a few hours late. Then he slipped out of bed, letting Vic sleep, and padded to the kitchen to make breakfast.

Later, he'd finish up strengthening the wardings and call Travis to explain. But first, Simon wanted to make sure Vic was all right, and help him make sense of the attack from the night before.

"Morning." Vic stood in the doorway, sleep rumpled and half awake. Simon had managed to strip Vic's clothes off except for his briefs before they fell asleep, and Vic hadn't bothered to grab anything on his way to the kitchen. The tension in Vic's jaw told Simon that Vic's first instinct when he woke alone was to find him and assure himself that Simon was all right and nearby.

"Morning," Simon returned, giving Vic a once-over. In daylight, he could see the bruising where the boo hag had tried to strangle Vic and the red welts where her sharp nails had scored across his chest.

Vic still looked spooked, understandably so. "I saw the marks when I went in the bathroom. It really happened, didn't it?"

Simon nodded. He poured Vic a cup of coffee and brought it over to the table, waiting for Vic to have a seat. Then he grabbed a cup for himself and joined him. "Yeah. It was real. It would have sucked for it to be a nightmare, but it sucks even worse that it wasn't."

Vic wrapped both hands around his mug, closing his eyes and breathing in the aroma as if he were trying to steady himself. If the attack had been purely physical, a Mob hitman or a jacked-up addict, Simon knew that Vic would have had a frame of reference to process it. Sure, he would have been thrown for the proverbial loop, but that would have fallen within the range of "normal." But Vic was relatively new to the idea that supernatural creatures were real, magic worked, and ghosts existed. Getting jumped by an invisible monster was clearly shaking his concept of reality.

"How do you do it?" Vic asked, opening his eyes and staring at Simon intensely.

"Do what?"

"Deal with all…this." He made a gesture that Simon took to mean everything supernatural.

Simon stretched across to take Vic's hand. "It takes some getting used to," he admitted. "But I've had all my life to figure it out. It's a little overwhelming to dive in head first."

Vic's laugh sounded brittle. "You could say that." He took a deep breath and seemed to collect his thoughts. "I can fight what I can see. But I don't have your mojo. I can't punch or shoot or kick things like that boo hag. It almost got me."

Simon repressed a shiver. "You scared me," he said in a voice just above a whisper. "All of a sudden, you couldn't breathe, and I didn't know what was happening. Then I reached out with my Gift, and I knew it was a supernatural attack. The car's wardings aren't as strong, but I knew if I got you in here, the hag would have to fight the wardings to keep her grip on you. And I gambled that an exorcism would work."

Vic nodded. "Thank you."

"I love you, Vic D'Amato. I'll do anything to protect you. I'm not much good in your kind of fight, but on my territory, I can usually hold my own."

Vic raised their clasped hands to his lips and kissed Simon's knuckles. "Love you, too." He sighed. "I have no idea how I'm going to explain the bruises and marks. I mean, I can tell Cap and Ross the truth, but everyone else?"

"Just make sure no one thinks I did it," Simon cautioned. "I don't need a bunch of pissed-off cops with misplaced protective instincts coming after me."

"I think I'll chalk it up to a mugging, but the perp got away," Vic said. "As long as Hargrove and Ross know what really happened, that should cover it."

Vic declared himself fine to go to work. Simon knew that Vic would deal better with what happened if he stayed busy, and trusted Ross to keep an eye on him. Hargrove and Ross had Simon's number if they needed him.

Once Vic left, Simon strengthened the wardings on the house, including dusting the front stoop with red brick dust and washing it down with water mixed with Four Thieves vinegar, one of Miss Eppie's hoodoo protections. He refreshed salt lines at all the windows and sprinkled fresh salt on the carpet around the bed. That wouldn't hold off any of his visions—they came from his Gift—but it was a second line of defense should any hostile spirit make it inside the bungalow. Once that was done, Simon lit a bundle of dried sage and let its smoke fill the house. Sage was a protective plant, and burning it drove out negative energy.

When the smudging was complete, Simon poured a fresh cup of coffee and called Travis.

"I wondered when you'd get back to me," Travis said when he picked up. "Everything go okay last night?"

Simon let out a long breath. He'd tried to stay calm for Vic's sake, but with Travis he could admit to his own fears. "I almost lost him, Travis. And I don't think the attack was random."

"Start at the beginning," Travis said. "Tell me what's going on."

Travis listened patiently as Simon told him about the hanging "suicides" and the vengeful ghosts at Socastee Manor, as well as the knife murders. He trusted Travis's discretion, although neither he nor his hunting partner, Brent Lawson, worked for law enforcement.

"I agree that the wreck is the key," Travis said after he'd mulled over Simon's story. "But I don't know how or why. There are pieces missing to the puzzle. It takes a powerful spirit to possess someone and ride them hard enough that they'd kill themselves. And if the boo hag really was sent, then whoever had the power to do that is certainly out to get you. That means they think you've got the ability to hurt them or stop them, even if you don't quite know what's going on."

"You sound like I should be flattered."

Travis laughed. "Encouraged is more like it, because if the killer fears you, then it isn't invincible."

"Vic's working the knife angle," Simon replied. "That's solidly cop stuff, although I think the killer has a supernatural influence."

"I'd agree, from what you told me. My suggestion is to try to connect with the ghosts who've reached out to you. They might not have the juice to come to you unless you seek them out. Maybe they can help you fill in the gaps." Since Travis was also a psychic medium and had at one time worked for a secret Vatican group of demon-hunting vigilantes, Simon appreciated his input.

"Will do. Thanks. And if you get any brilliant ideas, let me know, okay?" Simon ended the call and decided he needed to make a side trip before he went into the shop.

He hadn't visited the Horry Area Museum in a while, which meant seeing new-to-him exhibits—a distraction Simon couldn't resist. He found himself in an art display titled "Wrecks and Rogues," staring at paintings of pirate ships and sea battles from the South Carolina coast. In one of the paintings, a black-hulled corsair dogged a larger ship with a strangely familiar red-haired figurehead.

"Beautiful, isn't it?" Edith Lindsay, the curator of the museum, spoke from just behind him. She wore a trim pantsuit, and reading glasses dangled from a crystal-beaded lanyard around her neck. Her gray hair was tucked into a smooth chignon. Simon had done several ghost lore presentations for the museum and counted Edith among his friends.

"I love the exhibit," Simon replied. "Are the paintings on loan?"

She shrugged. "Some were in our collection but not on display, and others were loaned by private collectors. With all the interest in the *Annabelle*, it's turned out to be very timely."

"Is that ship the *Annabelle*?" Simon asked, pointing to the one with the figurehead. He was almost sure it was the one from his vision.

Edith nodded. "Probably an artist's fancy, but yes. And that's the *Vengeance* in pursuit, one of the most infamous privateer ships of that period. Its record against pirates is positively spooky."

She might not have meant that literally, but Simon felt a chill down his spine as he recalled his vision of the two young men aboard the dark ship and the way the dark-haired man had seemed to stare right at him, through space and time.

"What do you know about the *Vengeance*?" Simon wondered if there could be any connection to the men and ship in his vision.

"Not as much as I'd like," Edith admitted. "Although privateers were legal because they carried a Letter of Marque authorizing them to pirate the pirates, they often kept their identities secret since they straddled the line on legality. From what we've been able to find out, the captain and first mate were from a fishing village that was wiped out by pirates, and they swore to take vengeance—hence the name. I think they were based somewhere near Charleston, which was quite the hotbed back in the day. Rumor has it one of the privateers was a witch," she added with a confidential tone. "They say the men had ties to an old Charleston family."

"And the *Annabelle*?" Simon asked.

"Everyone talks about pirates like Bluebeard and Blackbeard, but ships like the *Annabelle* terrorized the shipping lanes for years without the fame. The *Vengeance* is said to have helped scuttle the *Annabelle*, and led to the capture of the Gallows Nine." She smiled. "Nowadays, there's an 'outlaw chic' attached to the Nine, but they were unrepentant killers who didn't just steal cargo, they slaughtered the crews of ships they boarded to leave no witnesses."

"They were hanged here in what's now Myrtle Beach, weren't they?"

She frowned. "Closer to Georgetown, which was the bigger city back then. But the judge and jury were all local. I think most of the families are still around this area."

That caught Simon's attention. "Do you know the names of the men involved in passing judgment on the Gallows Nine?"

"I should be able to find it. Is that what brought you to the museum today?"

"Actually, I wanted to know more about the three knives that were stolen. Did they, by any chance, have a connection to the *Annabelle* or to Socastee Manor?"

Edith gave him a look as if she were trying to figure out his reason for asking. Simon managed his most innocent smile. "I'm working up some new ghost stories, and I want to get the background history right."

"The knives were said to belong to Jamie Dunwood, the man who built Socastee Manor," Edith replied. "You know it's being renovated?"

"I'd heard," Simon answered, unwilling to disclose his role. "I'm guessing that at some point, all the personal effects were removed?"

She nodded. "Yes. Such a shame, but the mansion sat empty for a long while. The family left the area after a series of scandals, and whatever they didn't take was auctioned off for tax purposes. Scandal or not, the Dunwoods left an imprint on this area, and collectors wanted to own a piece of their history. Those knives were purchased by a collector who just recently donated them."

Edith put her hand to her heart. "You can imagine how we feel, not just that the knives were stolen, but that two of them have been used in crimes." She shook her head. "It's awful."

"Any leads on the thieves?"

"Not yet. The truth is, we're not a big museum with a big budget. Our security systems are adequate, but nothing like the big museums have. The police said it wouldn't have required a genius to get in—just someone who knew what they were doing."

"I'm sorry to hear that. I know the police are working to find whoever is responsible."

Edith patted Simon's arm. "I'm sure they are. But even if they catch the thieves, those knives will be tied up as evidence in the murders for a long time. Who knows when—or if—the museum will get them back?" She sighed. "Ah well. That's out of my hands. Give me a few minutes, and I'll look up those names for you. Have a walk around the rest of the exhibit—it's really quite nice."

With that, Edith bustled off, leaving Simon alone in the exhibit. He moved from painting to painting, hoping to find more clues about the *Annabelle* or the *Vengeance*. Instead, he found himself in front of a large canvas showing what had to be Socastee Manor overlooking a stormy sea. Frigates armed with canons fought in the distance, illuminated by exploding gunpowder. In the foreground, a small ship made its way across the dark water.

He was still staring at the painting when Edith returned. "Oh, you found the controversial one!"

"What makes it controversial?"

"It's during the Civil War, and those are Union and Confederate frigates fighting," Edith said, pointing to the sea battle in the background. "Of course, the Union blockaded the South, but there were plenty of blockade runners, like the small ship off the coast. There have always been rumors—unproven, but persistent—that the Dunwoods had a hand in first smuggling, then blockade running, and during prohibition, in rum-running."

She patted her hair, a nervous gesture. "While the Dunwoods were still a force locally, they denounced any attempt to link them to those activities, maybe a little too forcefully," Edith replied. Simon thought she was probably old enough to remember when Patrick Dunwood still lived at Socastee Manor. "They were used to getting their way, and quick to defend their honor. With duels back in the day, and later with lawsuits."

"When was this painted?" Simon asked.

"In the early seventies. The family was still living at the manor, and when a local gallery displayed the work, Mr. Dunwood went ballistic. He threatened both the artist and the gallery with a lawsuit and created quite a stir. Of course, that just made the painting more notable to collectors and drove the price up. This is the first time it's been publicly exhibited since then."

She passed a thick envelope to Simon. "Here's what my system printed out as far as people who were involved with the Gallows Nine trial. It was a long time ago, so some of the families may have died out or moved from the area, or even changed the spelling of their name. But it should give you a good start." She winked at him. "And any time you want to come back and do another Night at the Haunted Museum tour, we'd love to have you! That was our biggest event last year."

Simon left, after assuring Edith that he would call her with dates to do another tour. He stopped to pick up sandwiches and coffee for himself and Pete, then went in to finish out the afternoon at Grand Strand Ghost Tours. The storm forecast hadn't changed, and gray skies supported the predictions that the bad weather would continue to worsen.

"I've already gotten the inventory done and priced everything in the back room," Pete said as they ate. "We had one actual customer this morning, one browser who I think really just came inside to get warm, and a man selling books of discount coupons."

"I'm glad you weren't run ragged," Simon said through a mouthful of sandwich.

"I also lost fourteen games of solitaire on my phone, dusted everything in the shop, put the t-shirts in size order, and made a list of what we need to restock," Pete added. "Just a thrill a minute."

Since the afternoon didn't look likely to suddenly attract crowds of customers, Simon worked on invoices and orders in his office, while Pete cleaned, straightened, and puttered in the front of the shop. After Simon had soothed his conscience by getting some work done, he leaned back and pulled out his phone.

"Cassidy? It's Simon. Did I catch you at a bad time?" Simon's cousin, Cassidy Kincaide, ran Trifles and Folly, an antique and curio shop in Charleston, SC. Cassidy was a psychometric, able to read the history of objects by touching them. Simon had never quite made up his mind whether that Gift was a benefit or a liability in her line of work. Teag Logan, the witch who had made Vic's protective bracelet and pocket square, worked with Cassidy and was her best friend.

"No, it's quiet here," she told him. "Off-season and people are spooked by the storm warnings."

"It's been dead here," he said, then winced at the choice of words. "Actually, that's what I need to talk to you about. Did we have any ancestors who might have been privateers?"

Cassidy was quiet for a moment. "What makes you ask?"

Simon caught her up on what had happened, and how everything seemed to circle back to what he saw in his vision, the *Annabelle*, and the Gallows Nine.

"One of our ancestors, Dante Morris, was the captain of the

Vengeance," Cassidy said when Simon finished. "Coltt, the first mate, was Dante's best friend."

"So I'm related—distantly—to the *Vengeance's* captain?" Simon repeated, thinking of the dark-haired man who had given him such an intense look in his vision. "Do you think it's possible that what I saw in my vision might have been real? Could that have been Dante and the *Vengeance*?"

"My visions work a little differently from yours," Cassidy replied. "Since I'm working off stored memories in actual objects. Most of what I see is like getting snippets of a movie. I don't have your ability with ghosts. If Dante's spirit hasn't moved on, then maybe he sent you a warning."

"I heard that the *Vengeance* was the ship that captured the Gallows Nine. If they're back, could their ghosts possibly know that I'm a descendant of Dante's? And is it true that Dante was a witch?"

He held his breath while Cassidy mulled that over. "I need to look into that and get back to you," she said after a moment. "I'll ask the family historian," she added, in a tone that left Simon thinking there was another, hidden meaning to her words. But before he could ask, she went on. "You know, if the storm's coming your way, you and Vic are welcome to come here. We're not supposed to get hit as badly as Myrtle Beach."

"Thanks," Simon told her. "But Vic's going to have to work emergency shifts, and I promised to help out at the shelter if it really gets bad."

"Just…be careful, Simon," Cassidy warned. "I have a bad feeling about that wreck and the pirate ghosts. And I'll check with my history sources about Socastee Manor and the Dunwoods. You know that down here, everyone's related to everyone else one way or another. If there's a story, I'm connected to the people who are going to know."

"Thanks, Cassidy. And thank you for offering to take us in. We really do want to come down and visit, but it would be more fun when we aren't storm refugees."

"Stay safe, and I'll call you back as soon as I know more,"

Cassidy promised. Simon said goodbye and ended the call, musing about the conversation. He always had a feeling that Cassidy knew more about some of the supernatural stuff than she let on, and he vowed to get to the bottom of that someday.

He headed to the front, taking the packet from Edith with him. Pete had done all the daily chores and most of the weekly chores, so he now sat at the register, losing another game of solitaire. Simon fetched them both fresh coffee, then spread out the papers and began to take notes.

8

VIC

Jacob Platz's apartment was several blocks back from the ocean in Surfside Beach. The building looked like it might have been a hotel at one time. Each unit opened to an outside hallway that doubled as a balcony. Vic and Ross looked around before they let the forensics folks loose.

The one bedroom rental didn't have the extras common in new, more expensive places. The galley kitchen was tidy, but looked well-used, suggesting that Platz cooked many meals himself. A worn but serviceable couch and recliner plus a coffee table filled the living room, and a small table doubled as a desk. Most of the furnishings were older, but the flatscreen TV was recent, although Vic recognized it as a less expensive brand.

A few car magazines lay on the coffee table, along with an empty cup. A set of bookshelves held some action movie DVDs, quite a few mystery and adventure paperbacks, and a framed photograph of a younger Platz standing arm-in-arm with a woman Vic guessed was his wife.

"Sixty years old, widowed, no children," Ross read off the report. "Clean record, no arrests, no trouble of any kind. Been a landscaper all his life."

Vic glanced into Platz's bedroom, only to find a neatly made bed and a set of furniture that looked as old as the couch. "Guy kept things tidy for being on his own."

"Not everyone's a slob, Vic," Ross replied without looking up, but Vic saw a hint of a smile.

"You get anything from the landlady about him?" Nothing in the apartment triggered Vic's cop senses. Platz seemed like a decent guy who was in the wrong place at the wrong time.

"Said he was friends with Gus Thompson, down in 4B. I guess they played poker together, watched a lot of football."

The forensics team started to swarm, making the small apartment feel even more cramped. "Let's let them do what they do." Vic said with a nod toward the technicians, "and see if Gus is at home."

A rangy man with salt and pepper hair sat in a retro metal lawn chair outside apartment 4B, watching the cops arrive. He looked like he might have played college football in his younger days, and had the leathery tan of someone who spent a lifetime outdoors.

"Are you Gus?" Vic asked.

The man nodded. "You come to find out what sorry son of a bitch killed Jacob?" His blue eyes held fire.

"That's as good a description as any," Ross replied and introduced them. "The landlady said you and Jacob were friends."

Gus shrugged. "We got along good. He didn't cheat much at poker, and we rooted for the same football teams. He was a decent guy. And he didn't deserve what happened to him. So I hope you catch the bastard and send him away."

Vic leaned against the railing. "Did Jacob have any enemies? Anyone who might have wanted to hurt him?"

Gus raised an eyebrow. "Is that a way of asking if he played the horses or owed a bookie? Far as I ever knew, no to all that shit. Never saw him gamble. Liked a cold beer after work—who doesn't? But never saw him get drunk. Seemed to have enough money to do what he wanted to do."

He gave a wave toward the parking lot, filled with older-model cars. "In case you didn't notice, this ain't the Ritz. Rent's afford-able, bugs aren't too bad, and the neighbors—for the most part—

keep the noise down and don't bust up the place. Folks here do too much work for too little money and don't cause problems. Jacob liked to go out for breakfast on Sunday to the waffle place, and now and again we saw a movie. He was widowed; I'm divorced. It was nicer to do some things together than by ourselves."

Vic nodded. "Did Jacob say anything that might have made you think he was worried about his safety?"

Gus thought for a moment, then sighed and shook his head. "He'd gotten hired on to work at some old mansion that was getting redone. Jacob liked that, because his dad had done the landscaping there back in the seventies, and Jacob said he spent time helping his dad when he was young. He liked the work, but the boss man was an asshole. No surprise."

"Jonah Camden or Trevor Nichols?" Ross asked.

"Camden," Gus replied. "Nichols was okay. Jacob liked him. Camden was a stuck-up prick, but those kinds usually are." Vic wondered whether "those kinds" meant bosses, executives, or people with money—maybe all three.

"Did you notice any changes in Jacob's routines right before he died?" Ross asked. "Sudden plans to go out of town, acting like he might be afraid someone was following him? That sort of thing?"

"Jacob was just Jacob," Gus replied. "We were going to go to the bar and watch the big game together this weekend. He was talking about taking a couple days off so we could go fishing when the storm blew over. So I don't think he was worried about getting killed." He lit a cigarette and took a long drag.

"The only thing Jacob talked about that worried him were the ghosts."

Vic and Ross exchanged a look. "Ghosts?" Vic asked, wondering if Gus was pulling his leg.

"You can believe or not, that's up to you," Gus replied. "Jacob said that the mansion and the grounds were haunted. It didn't bother him much—said that the ghosts left him alone. Thought maybe they remembered him being around as a kid. Like he belonged there. But lately, they seemed to be riled up more than usual. Not the ghosts outside, the ones in the mansion. He wasn't afraid for himself, but he worried that the workmen might get hurt."

"Thank you," Vic said and handed Gus his business card. "If you think of anything else, give us a call. We want to find the person who did this just as much as you do."

Vic and Ross walked back out to their unmarked department sedan. "You get any vibes from Gus?" he asked.

Ross shrugged. "Seemed to be telling the truth. I'm not surprised—were you expecting Platz to be running a drug ring or something?"

Vic shook his head. "Nah. And the last time I checked, drug lords don't steal antique knives to use in their hits. I think it's all tied together somehow—Platz's murder and the suicides—but fuck if I know where the connection is."

Ross drove them to the next stop, which was the by-the-week hotel room where Sean Bradley, the dive poacher, had been staying. Vic recognized the area from the police blotter, a rundown neighborhood with more than its share of drug busts and domestic disputes.

"Nice digs," he said sarcastically as they pulled up in front of the motel. It looked like a 1950s one-story mom-and-pop sort of place, but the years had not been kind. Leaking rain gutters had stained the white stucco. A vending machine at the corner of the building appeared to have been broken into. Vic was glad he and Ross were both carrying.

The forensics team had finished with Bradley's room. The small space held a cheap bed, dresser, nightstand, and table, along with a coffee maker, microwave and a hot plate Bradley had probably snuck in against the rules. A small refrigerator and a plastic cooler sat in one corner. The room smelled of old cigarette smoke and cheap beer. An ashtray and a wastebasket full of empty cans provided proof.

"Looks like he was living out of his suitcase." Ross nodded toward where the bag had been rummaged through. "I guess he didn't intend to stay long."

"If he really did make a living claim jumping other divers, he probably needed to keep moving." Vic made a slow walk around the perimeter, not sure what he expected to see.

"Bradley was thirty-six, former Navy diver. You saw his priors—he had a rap sheet as long as my arm," Ross said. "Most of the charges didn't stick, but where there's that much smoke, there's got to be fire."

Vic nodded. "Yeah. And plenty of enemies who are probably toasting his death. But how many of them could take on a Navy guy underwater—with a stolen knife?"

"Maybe more than you think," Ross replied. "I wouldn't be surprised if a lot of pro divers are ex-military. But why bother with an antique knife? And if they were going to jump him, it'd be a lot easier in the parking lot here, just sayin'."

"Was there anything you saw about him having a dive team? Because I wouldn't think he'd salvage wrecks all by himself," Vic asked.

"Not that there's a record of," Ross confirmed. "But if he was looting other people's projects, maybe he didn't want a regular crew. Maybe he hired guys by the job who didn't ask too many questions."

In a place like Myrtle Beach, finding divers wasn't difficult. And it was never hard to find people who needed cash badly enough to look the other way on the details.

"The hotel manager says Bradley mostly kept to himself, but he saw him walking over to that bar across the street several times," Ross said, indicating a rough looking place with a sign *"Buccaneer."* The motorcycles and the beat-up trucks in the parking lot made it clear the bar was a locals' joint.

"Let's see what the bartender knows," Vic said. "We can leave the car here and walk. Just as likely to get boosted either place."

Buccaneer was the kind of joint where Vic couldn't make up his mind whether it was safer or more dangerous to be made as a cop. Mid-afternoon, barflies were already lined up on their stools, half-watching the sporting matches on a row of TVs. Most of the tables were empty, but a few guys in biker leathers were playing pool. Everyone looked up when Vic and Ross walked in, gave them the once-over, and went back to what they were doing.

Vic led the way to the bar. He'd been in tougher places back in Pittsburgh, and he knew both he and Ross could hold their own in a fight if it came to that. But Vic hoped they could get their questions answered without causing any trouble.

"What can I getcha?" the bartender asked. He was probably in his fifties, with a full head of dark hair and a bit of a belly. Vic guessed he was the owner.

"Just a little information," Vic replied and flashed his badge. Conversation stopped, and he felt the barflies stare.

"I've paid all my taxes, and the license is good," the bartender said. "And we card anyone who looks under thirty."

"We're from homicide, not ATF." Ross held up a photo of Bradley. "You know this guy?"

"Seen him in here a few times," the bartender said. "Just in the last couple of weeks. What do you want him for?"

"Caught a knife in the back," Vic replied, watching for a reaction. The barkeeper's wince seemed genuine. "Wondered if he'd met up with anyone here."

The barflies had gone back to watching TV or staring at their drinks.

"He told me he was looking for guys who could dive in rough weather and who wanted to earn some good money. I gave him a couple of names. Don't know whether he hired them or not. After that, he came over in the evening for a beer and a burger, but he didn't say much, and he didn't hang around."

"Who did you recommend to him?" At the barkeeper's hesitation, Ross added, "They might be in danger if the person who killed Bradley thinks they have what he didn't."

"Shit." The barkeeper pushed a hand through his hair like he was debating two bad choices. "Okay. Yeah." He wrote down three names on the back of an order slip. "Here. Look—these guys, they're a little down on their luck, but they're not bad people so go easy. Work's hard to come by. They're just tryin' to get by."

Ross pocketed the slip. "We'll keep that in mind. Thanks for your help."

When they stepped back outside and no one tried to follow

them, Vic fished out his phone. "I'm going to call Simon, see if he can pick up anything of Bradley's ghost from his room." After a brief conversation, he pocketed his phone as they walked through the bar parking lot and breathed a sigh of relief. "Well, that went better than it might have."

Across the street, their unmarked car exploded in a ball of flames.

9

SIMON

All morning Simon's gut warned him of danger. He checked his phone frequently, but Vic hadn't texted, and there were no messages from any of his friends. Staying busy didn't lessen the sense of impending doom. He stepped away from the few customers and took a couple moments in the kitchen to settle his thoughts, reaching out to the spirits to see if they were the source of his concern. None of the ghosts answered his call.

"Everything okay, boss?" Pete asked, coming to the doorway.

Simon nodded, trying not to be sick. "Yeah. Just getting a reading I can't quite make out."

"I brought a six-pack of Coke. It's in the fridge. Might help."

Simon drank a soda, and it kept him from throwing up. Still, he knew that his nausea was a portent, not the result of iffy lunchmeat. Something was going on—or about to happen—that was going to be very bad. Not for the first time he wished his psychic abilities worked like they did in the TV shows. He couldn't pick up anything except the certainty of disaster. Just in case, he texted "be extra careful" to Vic mid-morning, willing to put up with some ribbing from his partner if Vic would just come home safely.

Vic's call caught Simon in the middle of selling a t-shirt to a customer, but he promised to drive over as soon as he was done. Pete sent him on his way, and Simon walked to where he had parked the Camry, trying to figure out the best route to the address Vic had given him. In the distance, he heard the wail of fire trucks and the honking of horns, sounds that just magnified the distress he'd been trying to ignore.

As he wound his way through the streets, Simon wondered what he would find in Sean Bradley's room. So far, his attempts to contact the diver's ghost had been unsuccessful. Maybe Bradley had moved on, or perhaps he hadn't figured out how to make himself heard, even to a medium of Simon's ability. *Or perhaps he's still afraid of whoever killed him.*

Simon didn't have much cause to come to this part of town. It had a reputation for crime, and there was nothing here Simon couldn't find elsewhere. But for a guy like Bradley, looking for somewhere to live on the cheap while he pirated dive projects, the neighborhood was probably perfect.

The sound of sirens grew louder as he drove toward the motel, and an uneasy knot settled in his stomach. A block from the address Vic had given him, two squad cars and several wooden barriers blocked the road. Simon pulled into a parking lot and locked the car, then took his police ID from his pocket before approaching the uniformed officers at the roadblock.

"I'm sorry sir, you'll have to—"

"Police business," Simon said. "I'm looking for Homicide Lieutenant Vic D'Amato. He asked me to meet him here."

The officer looked to his partner then shrugged. "Go on, but stay out of the way. It's a shitstorm over there."

Simon broke into a jog once he was past the roadblock, driven by a sudden, gut-deep fear. Black smoke billowed from near the motel, and several fire trucks and ambulances took up all the space in the small parking lot. Simon came to a sudden halt when he saw the charred wreckage of a car. And near the car, under a sheet, lay a body.

Firefighters still battled the blaze, trying to put out a fire that Simon knew couldn't have been spontaneous.

A bomb. Someone bombed their car. Oh, God—

Everything went still in Simon's head, except for the pounding of his heart. He stood, frozen in place, needing to know where Vic was and afraid to find out. His breath came in sharp, shallow pants.

Vic. I need to find Vic. Sweet Jesus, let him be okay.

One of the uniformed cops noticed Simon and started toward him. "This is a restricted area. You need to leave."

"Simon!" Captain Hargrove's voice stopped the cop in his tracks and broke through the haze of fear that had Simon paralyzed.

Simon looked up as Hargrove approached, unable to find his voice. The look on his face must have been sufficient.

"Vic and Ross are okay. They're safe."

"Then who—" Simon managed, staring at the body under the sheet. Hargrove grabbed his bicep and steered him through the chaos, maneuvering around officers, EMTs, and firefighters, making sure Simon didn't trip over the hoses.

"We don't know for sure. But the winning theory at the moment is that he's a would-be thief with the world's worst luck," Hargrove replied. "From the surveillance video, we know a guy in a hoodie broke the car window and tossed something inside. The other guy came out a few seconds later, saw the smashed window and must have decided to look for spare change or valuables. He caught the full blast."

Later, Simon would feel bad for the dead man. Now, all he could process was that Vic and Ross were alive. The words "they're safe" echoed in his mind, but he knew he wouldn't really believe it until he saw them.

"Found him!" Hargrove announced as he led Simon into the apartment complex office where a small crowd of first responders was gathered.

Vic plowed through the group, with Ross right behind. Simon laid a hand on Vic's shoulder, unsure how much Vic felt comfortable showing in front of the crowd. Vic pulled him into an embrace, and Simon hugged him hard in return before stepping back.

"What happened?" Simon asked.

Vic shook his head. "We're not sure yet. Ross and I went across the street to ask about Bradley at the bar. When we came out, ka-boom."

Simon shivered. The twisted, melted metal suggested a true inferno. "Did anyone see—"

Vic jerked his head toward where two cops were hunched over the shoulder of the hotel manager in front of a computer. "They're going over the security tapes now. All I've seen so far is a guy in a hoodie running away after breaking into the car. Tape's black and white, so we can't even get a color on the damn sweatshirt."

Simon could see the tension in the line of Vic's jaw, and in the way he held his shoulders. The attack terrified Simon, but it clearly made Vic mad as fuck.

"Come on," Vic said, guiding Simon back outside with Ross right behind them. "Since you're here, let's have a look at Bradley's room—if you're up for it." He met Simon's gaze as if he could guess the emotional roller coaster of the past few minutes.

Simon swallowed hard and then nodded. *Vic's safe. He's alive. He's here. It's okay.* "That's why I'm here."

"I'm sorry you came in on it like this, but I'm glad you weren't around for the show," Vic continued as they sidestepped pools of whatever the firefighters had used to extinguish the blaze and contain spilled fluids.

Now that he was closer, Simon could see where the fire had scorched part of the roof overhang and melted the asphalt around the car. The plume of black smoke had lessened, but not the noxious odor of burning plastic, rubber and gasoline. An oily residue in the air meant Simon could taste the fumes, and he knew he would still smell the fire for hours afterward.

"Whoever did it knew you weren't in the car, and set it to blow anyhow," Simon reasoned out loud. "So they weren't trying to kill."

Ross nodded, a tight-lipped expression on his face. "A warning is our guess. Helluva way to send a message."

"But was it about the wreck of the *Annabelle*, Bradley's murder, or the stolen knives?" Simon mused.

"Your guess is as good as ours," Vic replied.

Simon stopped just before they got to Bradley's door, which was directly behind the burned car. The paint had bubbled and charred from the explosion, and the outside walls were streaked with soot. After the way the fire had turned his emotions inside-out, Simon wanted to be prepared in case Bradley's ghost was waiting to whammy him. But as he sent out his psychic "feelers," Simon didn't sense a ghostly ambush waiting to happen.

"What?" Ross asked.

Simon blinked and came back to himself. "Sorry. Just…the psychic equivalent of peering around corners. Wanted to know what I'm walking into."

Ross unlocked the door, and the three stepped inside. Ross closed the door behind them to shut out the chaos of the parking lot. Light-blocking curtains pulled partway across the windows had protected the room somewhat from the blast, but the glass had shattered, and shards sprayed out from the explosion.

Simon stopped in the middle of the room and closed his eyes, taking several deep breaths to ground himself. Bradley's ghost didn't respond to his call; no surprise, since Simon had been attempting to connect with the spirit since the murder. All he picked up were echoes of strong emotions. Anticipation, nervousness, worry, resentment, and bitter loneliness.

"Anything?" Vic asked when Simon shook himself out of his trance.

"Bradley either can't hear me or doesn't want to make an appearance," Simon replied. "And I've been trying." He glanced at Ross. "Not all souls become ghosts. Some go right on to…wherever. As for the others, it's a little different for each one. It takes some people a while before they figure out how to show themselves as a spirit, while others get the knack pretty quickly."

"Were you able to read anything?" Ross asked.

Simon nodded. "More like picking up on his mood. He was excited about something good in the future—maybe the payday he thought he'd get from whatever he found in the dive. But he was also uneasy—probably about how rough the water was. If Bradley was a serious diver, he had to know that the conditions made it treacherous."

He paused, parsing through his impressions. "Josh Williams said that Bradley had a reputation as a dive poacher, so he definitely made enemies. I think he resented not having his ability as a wreck diver appreciated, that he didn't get the professional recognition he thought he deserved. Not like Josh, who's made quite a name for himself."

Simon hesitated, thinking through the jumble of feelings he picked up from the room's resonance. "If I had to guess—and I'm filling in a lot of blanks here—I'd say that somewhere along the line, Bradley lost out to Josh or someone like him, and Bradley didn't think it was fair. So there's a lot of anger, and a dangerous need to prove himself, show he was good enough—or better."

He frowned. "I'm also betting that his poaching isolated him from the exploration community—understandably. So he was alone—and blamed other people for it."

"That's one hell of a ghostly shrink session," Ross replied. "You got all that from an empty room?"

Simon managed a wan smile. "It's not really empty if you know where to look. And a lot of what I told you is interpretation. We already knew Bradley was a greedy asshole who didn't care about the history of the wrecks or whose research he hurt by poaching."

"So the question is, was the explosion meant to warn us off investigating Bradley's murder, or did the bomber think the car belonged to Bradley and was telling him to fuck off?" Vic mused.

"Possible," Ross replied. "We'll have to see if there's enough left of the bomb for forensics to come up with details."

Vic gave Simon an apologetic look. "I'm sorry for dragging you into the middle of this when I'm going to have to stay—probably late. Are you okay to drive back?"

Simon nodded. "Yeah. And believe me, I'm glad I didn't see the explosion on TV."

He left Vic and Ross with the swarm of cops at the apartment and headed back to the shop. A glance at his watch told him that it was nearly closing time. Simon called Pete to close, figuring that with the storm threat the shop wouldn't be busy. Then he headed back to the blue bungalow, needing to clear his mind and let go of the tension from the events of the afternoon.

Simon had set the slow cooker before he left that morning, so the house smelled of pot roast. He checked to make sure there was enough liquid on the meat, and then gathered the items he needed to soothe his nerves.

He lit a bundle of dried sage and smudged, letting the smell relax him. Simon put on water for tea, choosing a mix of matcha, chamomile, and citrus to help him unwind and get a second wind. Then he lit candles on the kitchen table, focusing on his thankfulness that Vic and Ross were all right, and his desire to stop more people from getting hurt.

Simon sat at the table and narrowed his concentration to the dancing flames in front of him. He took deep breaths to center himself and ran through a guided meditation he had memorized. Before long, he felt much less jangled. When his tea finished steeping, Simon brought the cup with him, inhaling the soothing vapors.

All of his preparations helped, but deep down they couldn't erase the bone-deep fear he'd felt when he saw the burned-out car and the body. Logically, he knew that being a cop was a dangerous job and that Vic knew how to handle it. But deep inside, he struggled.

Bad things can happen to people in office jobs, he reminded himself, thinking of the Twin Towers and workplace violence. He understood that nowhere was one hundred percent safe. And he knew when he fell in love with Vic that the badge came with the deal, in the same way Simon's psychic abilities were part of who he was. But most days, the dangers were theoretical. Today, they were frighteningly real.

His phone rang, and he recognized the number. "Hi, Travis. What's up?"

"I wondered whether you'd had any more trouble with the boo hag," Travis replied. "And, to be honest, I got a really strong psychic image of you and fire. Is everything okay?"

Simon couldn't help smiling, touched that his fellow psychic was worried. He told Travis what had happened at Bradley's apartment, and the new twists with the ghosts since their previous conversation.

"That's quite a lot going on," Travis said. "Watch your back on the man's ghost in the house. He sounds like the kind who could be big trouble."

"Yeah, I'm bringing backup to the séance," Simon replied. "But if I'm right about the ghost possession for the hangings, then there has to be a way to figure out whose ghost is causing the problem and what's giving it power. The deaths only started a couple of weeks ago."

"I guess there's no way you can get a closer look at that wreck?"

"Diving isn't my thing, even in good weather. And even the professional and military divers admit that going down in the weather we've been having is insane. Do you think it could be the wreck itself?"

Travis considered for a moment. "Maybe. Men get attached to a favorite car. I've seen more than one haunted automobile—not to mention that Stephen King movie. So if the captain felt that way about his ship, I guess it's possible. But I think the anchor would be more likely to be a personal possession, maybe something that's still trapped in the wreckage? And I don't know how you'll find some-thing like that and destroy it without going down there."

"I'll talk to Josh Williams," Simon conceded. "With the storm coming up, I don't know if he's planning to dive again, but if so, I'll ask him to take a look."

"Sounds like a plan." Travis hesitated. "Look, I know you didn't ask for my advice…but here's my two cents on the cop thing, for what it's worth. I wasn't a cop or in the military, but the organiza-tion I was part of was very much a militant priesthood," he said, referring to the role he'd played with Vatican black ops. "We were trained to be warriors against the supernatural. Often that included bad people, too. And I can tell you that it takes a special kind of person to do the job."

Travis paused. "I see the same thing in Brent," he added, mentioning his work partner, a demon-hunting former FBI agent. "And he *was* military, and a cop, and a Fed. It's not that we don't care about our own safety. We just don't worry about it the way normal people do. It's not about thinking we're invincible—because we're not—but the fear doesn't carry the same weight as it does for most folks. The same way that you and I aren't scared of ghosts and supernatural things like regular people."

Simon nodded. That made sense. "Here's the thing," Travis went on. "When a soldier—or a cop—gets spooked by something that happened on the job and starts to worry, that's the beginning of the end. It's not a job you can do looking over your shoulder. You've got to have the arrogance to think you can go into a firefight and come back out again, because while it's okay to be careful, you can't afford to be fearful. Does that make sense?"

"Yeah. Kinda the way I ask Vic to trust me when I let a spirit take me over so I can do a séance," Simon replied.

"Having done both, I'd say it's exactly the same. No room to doubt yourself."

"Thank you," Simon said. "There aren't many people I can talk to about this kind of thing."

"Any time," Travis replied. "And while I don't really expect one of your Southern ghosts to show up here in Pittsburgh, I'll keep an ear out, just in case."

When the call ended, Simon found that much of the weight had been lifted. He glanced at the time and remembered that Vic expected to be late. The slow cooker meal would hold for a while. Since he found himself with extra time, Simon settled in and made another attempt to reach any of the ghosts involved with suicides, the *Annabelle,* or Platz's death.

The vision hit him quickly.

He was aboard a sailing ship, in the middle of a bloody battle. Sailors with muskets and sabers defended their ship against pirates who would stop at nothing to steal precious cargo. The deck ran red with blood, as dark clouds filled the horizon and choppy seas made the deck pitch.

Time skipped, and Simon saw the inside of what must have been the captain's quarters. For a cabin aboard a ship, the room was well-appointed with mahogany furnishings and brass fittings. Simon saw through the captain's eyes as he took a box down from a shelf and glanced inside. A blue stone lay inside, and whether the captain could see it, Simon's Gift picked up on the stone's power and its strange glow.

The captain snapped the lid shut, then moved books to one side on a shelf and pressed a hidden button that made a panel slide, revealing a secret compartment. He pushed the box inside and had barely finished resetting the shelves when the door to his cabin burst open, and three ruffians forced their way inside.

"We'll take your special delivery now," a tall man said, crowding closer, his musket aimed at the captain's chest. Simon recognized the three men from the prior vision. They were part of the Gallows Nine.

"I don't keep cargo in my quarters," the captain snapped. "Anything you want is in the hold."

The other two pirates began a rough search, tossing bedding and clothing out of their way as they rummaged through the captain's belongings. The tall pirate kept his musket trained at the captain's heart. Up on deck, the sounds of battle had slowed, and Simon knew the captain feared his crew had lost.

"It's not here," one of the men said, straightening from where he'd gone through the captain's clothing. The other pirate pulled all the books from the shelves and began shooting holes in the woodwork. On the third blast, the secret door opened, revealing the prize.

"Well, well," the tall man said. "Look what we found."

"You can't—" A musket shot silenced the captain's objections, and he slumped to the floor.

Simon wobbled in his chair and nearly fell as the vision ended as abruptly as it began.

Minutes later Simon stretched out on the couch for a nap, too restless to read or research, and almost afraid of what he might see if he turned on the TV. He woke to the sound of Vic's key in the door and figured by how groggy he felt, that he must have slept for a while.

"It smells great, but you didn't need to hold dinner for me," Vic said, hanging up his coat and toeing out of his boots. "I'm starving. You should have eaten already."

Simon shrugged. "I'd rather wait for you." He grinned as his stomach rumbled. "Although I might have gone ahead if you'd been much later."

He went to greet Vic with a kiss, but Vic pulled him close,

holding on to Simon's hips, drawing their bodies together. The kiss deepened and grew more desperate. Simon felt all the emotions he'd struggled to suppress rise to the surface, a mixture of fear for Vic's safety and abiding love.

It felt to Simon that here in the privacy of the bungalow, Vic was showing him everything he hadn't been able to share at the bomb scene. He hung on to Simon like he'd drown if he let go, as if their kisses reassured him that he was alive and safe, and home.

"God, Vic," Simon panted. He shifted to rut against Vic's leg, making his erection impossible to ignore. Vic ground against him, equally hard, backing Simon against the kitchen counter.

"Quick and dirty now; slow and good later," Vic promised.

"It's always good." Simon took back the initiative, cupping Vic's face with one hand for another long, deep kiss. Simon's other hand lazily traced the ink on Vic's forearm. He worshipped the art with his hands and tongue at every opportunity, tracing the swirls and symbols and turning his tats into one big erogenous zone.

Vic moaned and bucked against Simon, rutting like teenagers behind the bleachers. He reached between them, eager to get their jeans and briefs out of the way. Vic worked Simon's belt open, then his jeans as Simon kept kissing his jaw and neck, stroking the patterns on his skin. It took two tries for Vic to get his own belt unbuckled, and he pushed down his button fly jeans rather than take the time to pop them open.

Simon's cut cock stood proud and leaking against his pale skin. Vic's dusky member left a sticky trail of pre-come when he pulled it free from his briefs. He wrapped his hand around both of them, and they both began to thrust against the friction.

"So good," Simon murmured, letting his fingers brush across Vic's short hair as their lips met, as his other hand joined Vic's around their stiff cocks. Vic pulled Simon closer with a grip on his ass that might leave fingerprints, even through the material. Vic returned the fervor in Simon's kiss, and Simon understood that Vic said with his body the things words often failed to convey.

Later, there'd be all the time in the world to edge each other to madness and take their time with satisfaction. This was "I was scared for you" and "I love you" and so much more, as their bodies found a rhythm that drove them both higher. Simon gave a choked groan and spilled his release over their hands. Vic followed seconds later, adding his spend.

They collapsed against each other, held up by the counter, wrapped in each other's arms. Simon ducked his head to rest his forehead on Vic's shoulder, and Vic buried his face in Simon's hair, breathing in the smell of sweat, shampoo, and sex. Simon tightened his grip, too overcome to bear meeting Vic's gaze for a moment. *I love you…don't ever leave me…please always be here.*

Before Vic, sex with other partners had always just been about getting off, making the other person feel good, having a good time. There hadn't been intimacy, the way even a hand job with Vic stripped away Simon's walls and left him vulnerable. He'd longed for that to happen with previous partners, but he craved it with Vic. He hungered for those moments when it felt like they were joined body and soul. Vic's harsh panting told Simon that maybe he wasn't the only one who felt shaken.

"I've been thinking about doing that ever since you left the apartment building," Vic confessed, resting his cheek against Simon's hair. "I've always heard about 'fighting and fucking,' like they go together. I guess they do."

"When I got there, and I saw the fire and the body, I was so afraid," Simon confessed, safe in the circle of Vic's arms, tucked against his chest. "I should have trusted my Gift to know you were all right, but for a moment—"

"Yeah. Ross and I weren't even close—across the street. But when it went up in a fireball, and the pieces came raining down, all I could think about was making it home to you," Vic said, his voice no more than a whisper.

"I'm glad you're here," Simon replied. Vic stepped back, and they moved apart to tuck themselves back in and clean up. By the time Vic finished in the bathroom, Simon had dinner on the table, along with glasses of Australian Shiraz.

"So far, tracing the bomber is a dead end," Vic admitted after Simon had told him about the call with Travis and his newest vision.

"But my gut says it's connected to the mess here, not Bradley's past."

"So now what?" Simon savored the roast and washed it down with a mouthful of wine.

"Now, we go back to pounding the pavement, old school," Vic replied. "Somebody somewhere has to know something, and we're going to find out what they're hiding. Today, this shit got real personal."

10

VIC

"I've read so much about these guys, I feel like I know them." Ross tossed a folder onto the table and leaned back in his chair. He drained the now-cold coffee in his cup and grimaced.

"Yeah. Same here," Vic agreed and glanced up at the whiteboard scribbled full of notes.

"All the forced suicides are from the area, from families that have been around here for a long time," he recapped. "We know there was brine residue on the clothing of all of the latest victims, but no one was looking for that on the first bodies."

"The families weren't all wealthy, but they often had members who were prominent in some way—mayors, judges, military officers," Ross added. Vic and Ross often found that reviewing aloud made familiar material new again, helping them gain insight.

"And the Socastee Manor folks—the Dunwoods—were a real piece of work," Vic said with a sigh. "Crooked as all get out, but no one ever made it stick. Smuggling, blockade running, rum-running. They were wealthy enough that people had to put up with them, but no one seemed to actually like the family. Can't blame folks—the Dunwoods were big into duels and lawsuits."

"Don't forget the charges of art and relic misappropriation in later years," Ross reminded him. "Sounds like when you come from a family of high-class thieves, some habits die hard."

"It's like something out of one of Simon's ghost stories, but I don't know how all that connects to Jacob Platz's murder or the dead diver, unless they stumbled onto contraband that someone else didn't want found."

"Nice theory, but we don't have said contraband to prove it," Ross pointed out. "And if it was just a matter of running across a hidden stash, then why the gardener and the diver? The two men wouldn't have had reason to be in the same places. I really doubt Platz was diving the wreck in his spare time."

"Speaking of which," Vic said, "Josh Williams has had a few run-ins with salvage law." He handed a printout to Ross. "Just came through this morning. But from what I see, the disputes all got settled in his favor. So he's probably legit."

"Or he has a patron with enough pull to get charges dismissed," Ross added cynically.

"That, too."

"Hargrove said he heard from Jonah Camden, the developer behind the Socastee Manor renovation. Apparently the guy is hyper to have us close the investigation 'before it hurts resale value.'" Ross's voice took on a mocking note on the last few words. "I imagine to a guy like him, that's what matters. After all, it was 'only' the gardener who got killed—no one important." He'd gotten downright bitter on that last observation.

Before Vic could respond, his phone buzzed with Simon's ringtone. He took the call, surprised because Simon usually only texted during work hours unless it was important.

"They're all connected to the Gallows Nine," Simon said, sounding a little breathless.

Vic frowned, completely lost. "Who? What?"

Simon paused, and Vic could imagine him taking a deep breath to quell his excitement. "The hanging suicides. All the families of the dead men were somehow involved in condemning the Gallows Nine pirates from the *Annabelle* to hang, back in the day."

"You think the suicide hangings have something to do with an execution over two hundred years ago?"

Ross's head came up, as he followed Vic's side of the conversation. "Hold up—I'm putting you on speaker, so I don't have to repeat it all to Ross."

"I got a list of the people who played a prominent role in the Gallows Nine execution," Simon went on. "From the Horry Area Museum. And I've spent all afternoon matching names and looking up genealogies. Some of the families involved died out, and others moved out of the area. But of the families that are still here—yeah. The dead men were related."

Vic and Ross exchanged a glance. "Do you know which families that are still here haven't had a death yet?" Vic asked.

"Emailing you the list," Simon said.

"How the fucking hell do we warn people not to let themselves get possessed by a pirate ghost that wants to make them hang themselves?" Ross wondered aloud.

"Er…I hadn't figured that out, either," Simon admitted. "But if we can stop the ghost, we can stop the killings, and then we don't have to explain it to anyone else."

Vic sighed. "That part's up to you. Good lead on the families—I'm just not sure what to do. We can't exactly put them in protective custody against ghosts."

"Working on it," Simon promised. He hesitated as if he might have something more to add, then said, "I'll let you know if I find out anything else," and ended the call.

Vic stared at his phone. "He knows something he's not telling."

Ross gave him a warning look. "Do not apply cop intuition to your significant other. That way lies madness…and sleeping on the couch."

"But— "

"He'll tell you when he's got it worked out," Ross said. "You've got to trust him."

Vic slumped in his chair. "I do trust him. But if both cases really center on something ghostly, then it all rests on Simon, and I don't know how to help."

"Take a look at the email he sent you," Ross advised. "We'll come up with the names of possible next victims."

"Because that won't look suspicious as fuck."

"I didn't say we had to show it to anyone. But we work the angles we've got, and see where it goes."

Vic was silent for a moment. "What year was the Gallows Nine incident?"

Ross ran a search, then looked up. "Would it be a big surprise that in two days, it'll be the two hundred and fiftieth anniversary?"

Vic thumped his fist on the table. "Fuck. So what if the suicides date from when the hurricane unearthed the *Annabelle?* Betcha they do. It's probably building toward a big ugly climax. And there's a storm coming in."

"Situation normal—all fucked up," Ross agreed.

Vic's phone rang again, another familiar ring tone. "Mom?" Vic answered, exchanging a confused look with Ross.

"We've been hearing about the big storm," Bernadette D'Amato said. "I've been worried."

Vic managed a smile. "Nothing yet except rain," he replied. "Not supposed to get bad for a couple more days. And you know how the forecasts are near the ocean—everything could change in an hour. I'm not going to worry about it until we know for sure."

"Mrs. Johnson and her husband canceled their trip because of the storm, and the Schmidts are going inland to Savannah."

"That's probably a good idea," Vic told her. "But I'll be on duty here if it does get bad, and Simon helps out at the shelter. We'll be okay."

"I worry," she replied, and he rolled his eyes, although he couldn't help appreciating her concern. "I also wanted to tell you that Uncle Stu is back in the hospital for his gallbladder, Aunt Maggie is doing rehab for her hip, and Mrs. Caudle from across the street said to tell you 'thanks' for the recommendation you wrote for her son. He got into the police academy."

"Glad to hear it."

"Oh. And one more thing. The Internal Affairs investigation did not go well for Nate. The decision just came down last week. He's been fired, and he's out on bail pending trial. Your father thinks Nate'll do time."

"Shit." Vic ran a hand back through his short hair. Nate might have been a crappy boyfriend, but there had been a time when Vic trusted him to be a good cop. When he and Simon had gone to visit Vic's family over Christmas, he'd seen another side of his old partner. Nate had attacked Simon, and they'd uncovered hard evidence that he had thrown investigations to satisfy powerful friends. Nate deserved to go to jail, but Vic couldn't help feeling a pang of misplaced guilt for playing a role in sending him there.

"I didn't want to tell you, but your father said you should know." Vic's dad—and his brothers and uncles—were cops.

"No, that's okay. I needed to know. It's just—"

"I understand."

Vic rubbed his eyes. "Okay. I've got to go. I'm working a case. Don't worry about the storm. We've been through worse. Just take care of everyone up there, and give them my best."

"Give Simon a hug for me, and think about coming up for Easter," Bernadette replied. "Talk to you soon." She ended the call, and Vic let his head fall back, eyes closed, as his hand with the phone dropped to his side.

"Something wrong?" Ross asked.

"Nate's being charged. She didn't say, but I'd bet obstruction of justice, falsifying and destroying evidence, lying under oath…it's not going to go well." Vic sighed. "How did I not know he was a dirty cop?"

"Because he was a good liar," Ross replied. "Those kinds always are. If he'd been easy to spot, he'd have had his ass handed to him long ago." He leaned forward. "This is not your fault."

"I turned him in."

"Because you're a good cop. Nate made his choices. Ever think that might have been the real reason he wouldn't leave town with you? Or kept you at arm's length? He knew you wouldn't go along with what he was doing."

"Maybe. Yeah. It's just…fuck." Vic didn't understand the tangle of feelings in his chest, so it wasn't surprising he didn't have the words to explain. He'd left Pittsburgh under a cloud because something supernatural had put him in a difficult position during a hostage situation. Vic had been cleared of wrongdoing, but that wasn't the same as having people fully believe his side of the story. He'd jumped at the chance when an old friend put in his name for a job with the Myrtle Beach PD, but it wasn't until he met Simon that everything finally clicked. Now, he was happier than he'd ever been, and he knew that Nate could have never given him what he needed. But he'd never wished for Nate to come to harm.

It seemed Nate hadn't needed any help with that.

Ross got up and stretched. "Go ahead and pull up that email from Simon. I'm going to get us more coffee, and then we can go over Simon's list. You know what Cap says."

"Work what you've got, and you'll find what you need," Vic answered, knowing Hargrove's catchphrases by heart. "I'm on it."

11

SIMON

After he called Vic with news about the link between the Gallows Nine and the suicides, Simon felt restless. Cassidy hadn't called him back, and Simon's instincts told him that he didn't have time to waste. The shop was empty, and he and Pete had finished all their regular chores as well as all the monthly to-do list. They had even filled and stacked sandbags at the shop's front and back doors, and got the storm shutters ready in the storage room so they could be put up quickly when the weather turned.

"I'm going to see if I can connect with a ghost who might know something about this whole mess," Simon announced, setting aside the book he'd been trying to read. His concentration was crap since he couldn't get his mind off the case.

"I'll watch the door," Pete replied, looking up from his phone. "It might do tricks."

Simon headed to the back corner, where a table and chairs awaited customers who wanted a private psychic reading. He pulled the thin curtain to screen off the area from the main shop and settled in on his side of the table. Simon took several deep breaths, trying to relax. Spirits tended to approach more readily if he wasn't tense.

He slowed his breathing and ran through a memorized meditation that always helped put him into a light trance. With the heightened impressions of the trance state, Simon could feel the protective wardings on the shop and see them in his mind's eye like ribbons of white light. When he felt receptive, he reached out into the ether, hoping to connect with Dante's spirit.

Even here, within warded walls, Simon remained cautious. He wore protective charms in addition to the many ways he had used magic to safeguard the shop, and he stayed alert, knowing that all kinds of entities were attracted to any show of mediumship. Usually, spirits came looking for Simon, not the other way around. They were easy to find, eager to be heard. Now, he was trying to contact a spirit from more than two hundred years ago. It would have felt like a needle in a haystack, except for Simon's certainty that Dante's ghost had recognized him in the visions.

"Dante Morris, if you can hear me…I'm kin. The crew of the *Annabelle* is still causing problems. I need your help."

He waited, remaining open to the spirits, listening for a particular voice among the garbled background noise of thousands of restless ghosts. Simon didn't pretend to know how ghosts "got the message," he just knew that sometimes a general summons attracted the spirit he needed, and other times, the call went unanswered.

Simon shook out his shoulders and arms, rotated his neck, cracked his knuckles, and tried to relax. "Dante Morris. I need your help."

He felt a stirring in the gray cloud of souls, his imagination's way of providing a representation for the unknowable. Simon caught a flash of dark eyes, windswept black hair, and the stubborn set of a jaw he remembered from his vision. The years had faded the spirit's substance, and Simon had the feeling that the ability to reach across time rested in Dante's willful refusal to be denied.

The Wilton Stone, a voice carried across the void. *Should have been destroyed.*

Simon felt certain Dante's spirit intended to say more. But before he could continue, another entity burst into Simon's mind. The dark energy threw itself against the shop's wardings, growing increasingly angry when it could not breach the protections to get to Simon.

Simon drew back, although the threat wasn't actually physical. He trusted the magic that secured the store, but he had rarely tested it against such a powerful foe. Simon redirected his concentration, grounding himself and drawing on his Gifts to reinforce the wards and help drive back the entity.

Unlike Dante's ghost, this intruder didn't use words. The impressions were primal. Rage. Fear. Frustration. And a hunger for revenge that chilled Simon to his core.

Simon clasped his gris-gris bag with one hand and pressed the blessed silver of his bracelet tight against his skin. He spoke the words of the banishment spell, then cycled through an invocation against evil. The litanies might not have the power of the Rite of Exorcism, but they still seemed to weaken the spirit's energy, or perhaps it had spent itself in its futile assault against the protective white light encircling the store.

"You are not welcome. You have no power here. By all that is good and holy, all the power of creation and the enemies of darkness, be gone, and do not trouble us again!"

The entity made one final salvo, shrieking its fury when it did not succeed, and then vanished. The enemy was gone, but so was Dante's fragile connection. Simon remained alert, tense, and watchful, until he felt certain that the attacker would not return. Then exhaustion caught up to him, and he slumped forward, feeling like he'd just run a gauntlet.

"Simon?" Pete's voice cut through Simon's mental fog. "Is everything okay? You were kinda yelling."

Simon winced. When he was in a trance, it was hard to know what was spoken aloud, and what was just in his mind. "It's all right," he replied. "You can pull the curtain."

Pete obliged and placed a cold bottle of soda in front of Simon. "Thought you might need this. Whatever happened sounded intense."

Simon massaged his temples, fighting the headache that often accompanied a difficult session. "Thanks. Just…don't go outside for a while. You have those charms I gave you?"

"Yeah. In my pockets." Pete moved to look out the front window, past the books and t-shirts on display. "Is there something out there?"

There's always something out there, Simon thought, but it served no purpose to freak out his assistant. "Not anymore. Grab a couple more of the onyx stones out of the cabinet. Did you ward your apartment the way I told you?"

Pete's eyes went wide. "Okay, I'm a little weirded out now. I mean, yeah, I did the salt thing, and I hung the dried herbs at all the windows. But…do you think something is going to follow me?"

Simon didn't want to overly worry Pete, but at the same time, he wasn't sure just what they were up against. "I don't know. Whatever it is, we think it has killed several times—and probably will again. But so far it's also stuck to a very clear pattern. If you're really worried, you're welcome to stay in my old apartment upstairs until we get this worked out."

"I'd be fine with that," Pete said, jumping on the offer so fast that Simon knew he was truly scared. "That way, I can keep an eye on the store, too."

"If anything happens, call the police. Don't try to be a hero," Simon warned.

Pete grinned. "Me? I'm more like the comedic sidekick who runs away to live to fight another day."

"Wait a couple of hours, then go back to your place to grab whatever you need to stay for a few days."

"Even better," Pete proposed, "I'll just ask my roommate to chuck some clothes and my toothbrush and a few things in a bag and drop it off. He'll be thrilled—his brother is visiting, and this way, they can have the place to themselves."

Simon mentally promised to give Pete a bonus for watching over the store. Pete went back up front, just as Simon's phone buzzed with a call from Cassidy.

"Hi, Simon. I've got some info for you about that wreck and Dante," Cassidy said. "The *Annabelle* smuggled a lot of different things, but it often carried occult or magical items from the Caribbean to witches and practitioners on the mainland. Dante and Coltt and the *Vengeance* skirmished with the *Annabelle* frequently, trying to reclaim dangerous stuff."

"Okay," Simon replied. "So do you know anything about what the *Annabelle* was carrying when it went down?"

Cassidy hesitated as if debating how much to say. "According to the family stories, the *Annabelle* was supposed to be carrying a load of illegal bourbon. Dante believed they also had an amulet stolen from a wealthy family in Barbados that was a powerful focus stone. It—and the bourbon—went down with the ship."

"If the current brought the wreckage up closer to shore, and the focus stone was with it, could it juice up a vengeful ghost?"

"Maybe," Cassidy allowed.

"Could the depth of the water, or the sand, or the current have possibly kept the ghosts from being able to draw on the focus stone before this?"

"It's possible," she mused. "Water can interfere with magic, sort of dampen the signal. I'd guess that ghosts can also take a while to learn how to manifest. Maybe the combination of time and being brought back into shallow water made the difference."

"What about Dante? Was he a water witch?"

Cassidy hesitated a bit longer this time. "According to the stories, yes. Our store, Trifles and Folly, is always passed down from one psychometric to another. But apparently some other talents run in the family—like Dante's magic and your psychic abilities."

"I tried to reach Dante's ghost today. He gave me a warning, about something called the Wilton Stone."

Cassidy caught her breath. "That's it. The focus stone that the *Annabelle* was supposed to be carrying."

"He said it should have been destroyed. Then something tried to attack from outside the wardings, and I lost the connection to Dante."

"Be careful, Simon. This doesn't sound like your usual haunting, and there were rumors that the crew of the *Annabelle* made pacts with the darkness for their success."

Simon chuckled. "Funny, but I've heard the same kind of stories about the *Vengeance*."

"I know enough about Dante and Coltt to tell you that whatever agreements they made, it wasn't with anything evil," Cassidy assured him.

"Good to know," Simon replied. "Any suggestions on what to do if the Wilton Stone washes up on shore?"

"Put it in a lead box and bring it to me. I've got someone who can make sure it doesn't bother anyone ever again."

"I'm hoping I don't have to get that close to it, but it's nice to have a Plan B. Thanks a lot, Cassidy."

"Please be careful," Cassidy warned. "I've got a friend who's a witch—"

"Thanks, but I'm going to bring Miss Eppie and Gabriella in on this. If it's more than the three of us can handle, I'll definitely be calling you back."

He ended the call and sat back, thinking about his options. The storm was supposed to hit late tomorrow, although the forecasts varied. Simon couldn't shake the feeling that all the different threads were converging, and the storm would be the least of their worries if he didn't stay ahead of the game.

That meant taking charge of the agenda, Simon decided. Until now, he and Vic had been reacting. But if Simon could flip the script and put the vengeful spirits on the defensive, he might be able to push them into making a mistake. Or goad the entity behind the suicide hangings into revealing itself and giving the investigation a crucial lead. And he felt certain he knew what to do to make that happen.

"You want me to come to a what?" Tracey replied, hitting a shrill note that made Simon move his phone away from his ear.

"A séance. Tonight, at Socastee Manor. Bring Shayna. I need people who believe, and who have positive energy."

"Uh huh. What's your boy think about this?" Tracey demanded. Simon could practically see her tapping her toe.

"Vic's going to be there. And so are Miss Eppie and Gabriella, although Gabriella is really riding shotgun. She's not going to be part of the circle."

"Ooooo-kay," Tracey said, drawing out her syllables. "And is this on the sly, or is the owner in on it?"

"Not exactly the owner. Trevor, the General Contractor, invited us. He'll be there in the circle, too."

"How about the real estate guy? I thought you said he was cranky."

Simon snorted. "Cranky" was as good a word as any. He figured Tracey must be in a public area because her assessments were usually more frank—and profane.

"You know we'll be there to watch your back," Tracey assured him. "Has Vic ever seen you do a séance before? Hell—has he ever been to one? Does he know how they work?"

Simon knew what she was really asking—had Vic ever seen him allow a ghost to possess him? "I've explained what goes on, but he hasn't been to a séance or seen me hold one before."

"You think he can handle it?" Tracey sounded skeptical. Simon knew that she liked Vic, but questioned his tolerance for what he had once termed "woo-woo."

"I think he'll do his damnedest to," Simon replied. "He knows this is part of who I am, the way I know being a cop is part of him. So we're both working on it. And I know he'd be pissed if I didn't include him."

"Yeah, I imagine so. Okay. Count us in. We'll see you there at seven."

Vic insisted on driving, which Simon appreciated because a séance could leave him badly drained, depending on how difficult the spirits chose to be. They arrived at Socastee Manor as soon as Vic got off work and Simon closed the shop. Trevor's car was in the lot, but they were still ahead of the others.

"You really think this is a good idea?" Vic asked as he walked beside Simon toward the old house.

"I'm running short on options. And we need answers or more people are going to die." Simon understood the risk involved, but with Miss Eppie and Gabriella here to help, Simon felt safer. Having Vic and the others as part of the circle would strengthen him. That was the good news. He looked out across the dark ocean, toward the lights of the Grand Strand. For just a second, he thought he saw the silhouette of a man in an old-fashioned frock coat, the kind associated with buccaneers.

Blackcoat Benny, Simon thought. He froze, and Vic jostled his arm.

"You're seeing them." Vic didn't even make it a question.

"Yeah," Simon replied, unwilling to commit to a Blackcoat Benny sighting. They had enough to worry about, without adding the storm to the list. "Let's get inside."

Trevor greeted them when they entered. He had a few electric lanterns set up to light the main parlor, along with a round folding table and enough chairs for all the guests.

"I didn't know if you needed an Ouija board or a crystal ball or anything," Trevor said apologetically. "So I hope you brought them if you do. I didn't think to ask."

Simon smiled. "Contrary to everything you see in the movies, they're not required. This is perfect. Thank you."

"I really appreciate you doing this," Trevor added, shaking hands with Simon and then Vic.

"How about Camden?" Vic asked.

Trevor glanced at Simon, unsure. "He's not asking as a cop," Simon replied. "Just wondering whether he'll be here."

"I might have forgotten to mention it to him," Trevor said, clearing his throat. "He has so much on his mind."

Simon felt relieved to know Jonah Camden wouldn't be present. If the man was hostile to the idea, he might shut them down without a chance to contact the spirits. If not, his negative energy could put a damper on Simon's efforts.

The crunch of tires on gravel had Vic going to the window. "Tracey and Shayna," he reported. "And I think the other car is Miss Eppie and Gabriella." Out of habit, Vic's hand fell to his holster. He was off duty, but he'd insisted on wearing one of his own personal handguns, a sleek Sig, just in case.

The old house was quiet enough that Simon could hear rain hitting the windows. Socastee Manor felt restless, an uneasiness that went down to its foundation. He'd heard that the first house built on Dunwood land had washed out to sea in a hurricane, taking family members and servants with it. This newer house was no stranger to tragedy and bloodshed, and Simon could feel where darkness had stained the home like blood sunk into the floorboards.

He had done his research and determined that the ghosts haunting the manor were not buried in the family graveyard on the hill that he had contained with a salt ring. Jamie Dunwood was buried in Charleston, since he'd died of a fever and bringing the body home posed a risk. The body of his first wife had been sent back to her family after her untimely death. Any servants whose ghosts remained would have been buried in a separate graveyard, away from the family. That meant their ghosts were free to haunt the house, and communicate with Simon.

"You picked a helluva night to do this, Sebastian," Miss Eppie scolded as she and Gabriella came through the door, shaking off their umbrellas on the porch. "I wouldn't consider this auspicious."

"I hadn't counted on the rain," he replied. "Come in and get settled. I want to get us all home before the roads get bad."

"We'll be okay for a while," Trevor told them. "It takes a long, hard rain to flood the access drive."

While the others took their places around the table, Gabriella assessed the room, then picked a corner and laid down a circle of salt and aconite to protect her as she stood sentry over the séance. Simon would be open to the spirits, and the others who were linked to him could be equally vulnerable. Gabriella would make sure that nothing human or supernatural tried to take advantage.

Simon sat with Vic to his right and Miss Eppie on his left. Tracey sat next to her. Shayna was next to Tracey, and Trevor sat on the other side of Vic. Simon glanced at the friends assembled around the table.

"Ready to begin?" Nods and murmurs let him know everyone was set. Simon reached out and clasped hands with Vic and Miss Eppie as the others followed his lead. Then he closed his eyes, took a deep breath, and opened his Gift to the friendly, supportive energy at the table. He sensed Gabriella's protective magic, and beneath everything, the house's restlessness.

"Spirits of Socastee Manor. We mean you no harm," Simon began. "We wish to understand why some of the workers here have been hurt, and ask you to let them work in peace. Please, show yourselves."

They waited in silence for several heartbeats. Simon felt Vic fidget, despite his warnings that a real séance took far more time than the re-enactments on TV ghost-hunter shows. Miss Eppie's energy felt solid and steady, reassuring. Tracey and Shayna were excited and curious, while Trevor's wariness came through the link. Gradually, the room grew colder, until Simon was certain he would see his breath mist if he opened his eyes.

"Who has come to us?" he asked as he sensed a spirit in the room. "You are welcome to speak to the others through me, if you like."

Vic's hand clenched his, worried. Simon smoothed the pad of his thumb over the back of Vic's hand to reassure him. Then he opened himself and felt the ghost wink into his consciousness.

"My name was Marilee, and I was a kitchen girl. I died in the year of our Lord, seventeen fifty-two." Simon hadn't known how to explain this fully to Vic, how he could speak for Marilee, and still retain his sense of self. Her voice sounded higher pitched than his own, with an accent that was not quite British, but definitely not modern.

"What do you want us to know, Marilee?" Simon asked in his own voice.

"I saw what I wasn't supposed to and died for it," the ghost replied. Under her influence, Simon's voice turned thin and reedy. "I went out late to use the privy and saw men carrying boxes up from the shore. They caught me, though I cared nothing about their business, and beat me for it. I died before I woke again."

"We hear you, Marilee. What happened to you was wrong. Does something hold you here?" Simon asked.

"I wanted the truth of it known. They told the others it was a cutpurse who killed me."

"We know now, and we will honor you. It's all right to move on and rest."

Simon felt the ghost hesitate and understood. Socastee Manor had not been a good place for her but leaving meant uncertainty. Then the ghost gathered its energy and left Simon, feeling lighter and less burdened. Simon felt it rise, then vanish from his Sight.

One down. Let's see what shows up next.

"I know you're out there," Simon said, with his eyes still closed. Vic's hand was warm in his, reassuring. Miss Eppie's grip was a conduit for her energy, sustaining Simon and sharing her energy.

Simon sensed a cloud of spirits hovering just beyond reach, drawn to his power. Some were too faded to manifest, even with his help—mere shadows of their former selves. Others hung back, afraid still in death of the family that ruled the manor with brutal authority. Finally, a woman's ghost appeared to Simon, wearing a fine, high-necked dress that might have been Colonial-era and carrying herself like an aristocrat. He shivered as her spirit filled him, anchoring himself to Vic and Miss Eppie as the unfamiliar presence took hold.

"Dear Lady, who are you? And how can we ease your way?"

Marilee's ghost wanted to be heard. This spirit wanted justice.

"My name is Katarina, and I was married to Jamie Dunwood. For a time, I was the mistress of this house." Her voice was lower in pitch from Marilee's, with a Deep South accent, and very different from Simon's own. Simon recognized the name from his research.

"What brings you to us?" Simon asked.

"My faithless husband pushed me down the steps, because he

wished to wed another." Katarina's voice grew hard and bitter. "A more profitable bride."

"I grieve for your death," Simon told her. "And Jamie Dunwood is long dead, as are his descendants. The family came to ruin. What will help you to pass on?"

Simon felt the ghost consider. "I am pleased that the family did not prosper," Katarina said after a pause. "I had learned that my husband was a criminal, smuggling guns. He meant to profit from the war, and I told him that was wrong. I would have everyone know that he was a cad."

Simon thought of all the stories he had read about the Dunwoods and how hated they were by the other plantation aristocrats, even though no one had been able to prove all the allegations of lawbreaking. Ghostly testimony wouldn't count, although it affirmed what those around the table suspected. Katarina had her justice many times over.

"It's time to let go," Simon coaxed. "You can rest now. We've heard your testimony."

"It's not over yet," Katarina replied through Simon. "They're still here. Still keeping secrets and hurting people."

Simon sensed everyone's attention focus. "What do you mean?" Simon asked.

Before Katarina could answer, a frigid wind blasted through the closed room. Simon held on tightly to Vic and Miss Eppie and felt a powerful dark force rip Katarina's ghost away from him. Simon sensed her terror as she sped toward the light.

The new ghost battered at Simon's shielding. It felt like his head was going to split open. The spirit pushed relentlessly, strong enough to tear at Simon's protections.

"Get out!" A gravelly voice shouted against Simon's will. "Get out of my house! You're not welcome here. I will kill you all!"

Simon rallied his strength even as he felt Gabriella turn her magic toward the unwelcome newcomer. Vic kept a bone-crushing grip on Simon's hand. Miss Eppie shifted her arm, and a mojo bag slid down into their joined palms.

The counterattack from Gabriella and Miss Eppie startled the ghost, and Simon saw his chance. He imagined someone attempting to force their way through a partially closed door, an intruder trying to break in. In his mind's eye, Simon saw himself hurtle toward the door, slamming against it with his consciousness and his magic.

The psychic door almost closed, but the vindictive ghost pushed back, wedging the opening wider. Simon fought, knowing that he dared not lose. The ghost was old and strong, stinking of hate and fury. Simon knew that this was the revenant behind the "accidents" here at the manor, and he felt certain it had a hand in the death of the groundsman. He could feel the spirit's glee in the turmoil he caused among the séance attendees, although to their credit, no one broke the circle.

The ghost shoved hard, but Simon held his ground. He could not imagine the damage a spirit like this could do if it gained control of him and his abilities.

I don't belong to you, Simon growled in his mind. He felt Vic's grip on his hand, steady and sure. Simon drew in the energy his worried friends sent to him through their link and threw everything he had against the intruder, as he felt another wave of Gabriella's magic wash over him.

Again, the mental door inched toward closing, with the vengeful ghost fighting mightily. Simon strained to shut the door, surprised the spirit could hold out with so much psychic power arrayed against it. The ghost's rage and fury flared like a forest fire, bent on forcing the opening wide enough to seize control.

Who are you? Simon shouted in his mind.

I am the master of this house! The voice roared back, and Simon no longer could tell whether he had screamed the words himself, or they just echoed in his brain. He saw an image of a man in an old-fashioned frock coat and guessed it might be Jamie Dunwood. In that moment of shared knowledge, other images flashed in Simon's mind, almost too fast to process. *I will not be denied.*

Simon was determined to keep on denying the entitled asshole of a ghost. He drew on his love for Vic, his friendship with Tracey, and the affection he felt for Miss Eppie and Gabriella, Trevor's trust that Simon could make a difference. Reaching down to the core of his being, Simon mustered his power and pushed.

The mental door slammed shut. Simon threw himself against it, digging in his heels, as the ghost on the other side raged and threatened.

Dimly, Simon became aware of the rain outside, driving hard against the walls, making the windows rattle. And in the storm, he felt another spirit, old and familiar. Dante's ghost swept toward them, but instead of focusing on Simon, Dante brought his power against Dunwood.

Dunwood was fury and fire. Dante's ghost felt like storm surge and lightning. Simon rallied for another salvo, channeling his own Gift, the energy of the séance circle, Vic's love, Gabriella's magic, and Miss Eppie's hoodoo to support Dante.

With a scream of sheer rage, Dunwood's spirit wrenched away from Simon and vanished.

When you need me, call to me. I will come. Dante promised, then disappeared into the storm.

Finally free of the spirits, barely conscious, Simon slumped in his chair. "The séance is over. Go in peace."

1 2

VIC

Vic had no idea what to expect from a real séance beyond what he'd seen in cheesy horror movies. Simon tried to assure him that wasn't the way things worked in real life, but Vic had been skeptical. He couldn't remember a single film when a séance had gone well.

And yet, Simon knew much more about ghosts and the spirit world, and Vic wanted to trust his boyfriend's judgment. Even if doing the séance was dangerous, it couldn't be worse than Vic's job, which all-too-often required dodging bullets. Whatever it took, Vic intended to show Simon that he was all in. So he came along, seeing it as a milestone in their relationship that he hadn't learned about the séance after the fact, determined to prove that he deserved Simon's trust.

Damn, Vic hadn't counted on how hard it was to see Simon taken over by something else, to hear him speak and know it wasn't really him. To trust that Simon's Gift was strong enough to protect him if the ghost's intentions were bad.

When the first ghost settled into Simon's skin, Vic felt the shift on a gut level. He knew, bone-deep, that the entity speaking through those familiar lips was not Simon. Everything felt wrong on a hind-brain level, sending his intuition screaming. But Vic held on.

When Marilee's spirit left quietly, Vic breathed a sigh of relief. Then Katarina came, angry about her murder but respecting Simon's boundaries until the end, when she was about to tell them something vital, and another presence forced its way to the front.

Vic thought he had been terrified the night he'd spent pacing in the hospital waiting room, not knowing if Simon would survive a gunshot. Now he knew a different kind of fear. The gun at his side couldn't fight this threat. Vic knew how to tackle an armed assailant, could hold his own with his fists. But this attacker was beyond his reach. Simon needed help, and all Vic could do was hang on and pray.

After the third ghost's terrifying threats, Simon went silent, but Vic felt his struggle. Every line of Simon's body tensed with the invisible fight. The cords in his neck strained, his jaw clenched, and his eyes rolled back in his head like he might have a seizure. Simon's rigid form and his death grip on Vic's hand proved that Simon was fighting, but Vic was locked out.

This is how he feels when I'm on duty. The truth of that insight cut through Vic's terror. When Vic went to work, he trusted his partner, his gun, his own skills, and the system. He had backup, training, experience. He believed in those things to protect him, even though his job was hunting down killers, men and women who had nothing to lose. And except for the cases they worked together, when the culprit was supernatural, Simon was on the outside, powerless to protect Vic.

I get it. Sweet Holy Mother of God, save us both.

Vic wasn't very religious, but he'd been brought up Catholic in an old-school parish, and old habits died hard. He'd prayed that night at the hospital, and now the words came to memory again, the only kind of incantation he knew, one he had been promised carried power.

Hail Mary, full of grace. The Lord is with thee. Vic chanted silently and held on to Simon's hand as if the storm outside might tear Simon from his grip.

Suddenly Simon jerked and trembled. The expressions that played across Simon's face hinted at a silent, internal battle. Gabriella's voice sounded from her corner of the room, low and commanding. Vic could see the fear on the faces of the other participants. Tracey's gaze never left Simon's face, as if she could will him to be all right. Shayna looked like she might bolt. Trevor had a thunderstruck expression as if he got far more than he bargained for. Vic couldn't see Miss Eppie's face, but she had a white-knuckled grip on Simon's hand and had managed to slip a mojo bag between their palms, drawing on her spirit guardians.

Vic didn't have a mojo bag, but he had the woven bracelet and pocket square that Simon swore had protective magic incorporated into their warp and woof. He kept on repeating the Hail Mary, and focused on the bracelet and kerchief, willing himself to be a conduit for whatever white light they might share with Simon. His own fear didn't matter. All that counted was helping Simon win his battle.

Vic noticed that the rain had turned to a storm, with wind that howled around the manor's chimneys and a downpour that lashed the windows. Lightning flashed far out to sea. The hairs on the back of Vic's neck stood up, and he knew another presence had joined them.

Simon jerked back and forth, twitching in the throes of a nightmare battle. A stranger's voice roared threats, controlling Simon's body to speak through him. Simon gasped for breath and tensed hard enough that his back arched. Then suddenly his eyes flew open. Thunder crashed outside. The energy in the room shifted, and the cold, oppressive feeling vanished. Simon let out a long breath with a whoosh, and slumped in his chair, eyes closed.

"The séance is over. Go in peace," he mumbled, barely coherent.

"Simon!" Vic released his grip, and his hand ached from being clenched tight for so long. He reached for Simon, but Miss Eppie batted his hand away, leaning in from the other side.

"Give him room to breathe. He's gonna be okay," she said, folding both of her hands around the mojo bag in his fist. Vic didn't understand the words in Gabriella's chant, but it felt more protective than defensive, a benediction perhaps, instead of a battle cry.

"What. The. Fuck." Trevor looked completely shell-shocked. Shayna let out a sob, and Tracey wrapped her arms around her girlfriend, rocking slowly and murmuring reassurances.

Simon groaned, and Vic's attention shifted immediately. This time, Miss Eppie moved back, allowing Vic to lean forward to see Simon's face.

"Simon?" Vic's heart pounded, waiting for a response. Simon opened his eyes, groggy and disoriented. "Hey," Vic said gently, reaching to touch Simon's cheek. "Are you okay?"

Simon nodded. "Yeah. Just…give me a minute."

Gabriella stopped chanting, but she didn't leave her warded circle, still on guard should the angry spirit return. Trevor walked to the windows, and from his stance, Vic figured that the contractor was trying to compose himself.

"Is he okay?" Tracey asked. She had an arm around Shayna, who sniffled against Tracey's shoulder, looking shaken.

"He will be, child. Just give him a chance to collect himself," Miss Eppie said. "He did real good. Just needs to catch his breath."

Vic realized that the storm outside had ended. He hoped that the roads were passable, because he wanted to get the hell away from Socastee Manor and never come back.

Simon shifted, straightening in his chair. He shook his head like he was tossing off a bad dream. His long hair had pulled loose from the tie that held it, and strands fell into his face. Vic reached out to smooth them back.

"Hey," he said, offering a smile that he hoped said "I love you" and "You scared me" and "Are you okay?"

"Hey." Simon sounded exhausted, but completely himself once more.

"What happened?" Trevor turned from where he stood at the window. "One minute you were talking about a woman, and in the next—"

"I was attacked," Simon said quietly. Vic scooted closer and put his arm around Simon, who leaned into him for support. "One of the Dunwoods—Jamie, I think. He didn't want Katarina to finish telling us whatever it was she meant to say. I think there's something here that ties him to the manor, something he doesn't want found."

"Did he have anything to do with the groundskeeper's murder?" Vic asked.

Simon nodded. Tracey dug a bottle of water out of her backpack and pressed it into Simon's hand. He drank it down and it seemed to revive him.

"I'm certain he did. But…I don't think he's the one behind the hangings," Simon replied, turning to look at Vic.

Shit. There were a million questions Vic wanted to ask, but he could see that Simon was barely staying awake.

"I need to get him home," Vic announced. He looked to Trevor. "Do you think we can get out?"

Trevor nodded, still shaken by what he'd witnessed. "Yeah. It sounded like we had a hurricane out there, but when I looked there's nothing. No branches or leaves down, and it's wet but not flooded. Go figure."

Vic exchanged a look with Miss Eppie that confirmed much more had transpired than met the eye. Vic could bide his time to get the answers. His priority was taking care of Simon.

"Come on," he said, helping Simon to his feet. "I've got sports drinks in the car. I need to take you home."

Simon leaned heavily on Vic, proof that the séance had badly drained him. Gabriella and Miss Eppie flanked them as they left the house, like supernatural bodyguards. Shayna wiped her face with the back of her hand and took a few breaths, regaining her composure. Tracey looked torn between worry for Simon and her concern for Shayna. Trevor followed, still poleaxed.

Gabriella turned to Trevor as they reached the cars. "Darkness clings to this house. Much evil has been done here. It would be smart to burn it to the ground."

"I can't do that," Trevor replied. "It's not my call to make."

Gabriella nodded. "I understand. I don't agree, but I understand. We will help, but you must realize the bad energy is very old, very strong. When he is rested," she added with a nod toward Simon, "we will see what can be done."

"Take him home, put him to bed, feed him. Let him draw energy from you if he needs to," Miss Eppie cautioned Vic as he helped Simon to the car. "He'll be all right, but he's had a day of it." She and Gabriella headed for their car.

"Call me if you need me," Tracey told Vic, with a worried glance toward Simon. "If you get called out or something. Don't leave him alone."

Vic promised and watched as she and Shayna drove off. Simon was already asleep as Vic started the car. The rain had slowed to a light drizzle, just enough to require wipers and to make the road dark and reflective.

Vic struggled to keep his mind on his driving, but his thoughts and feelings were a jumble. A year ago he would have doubted his sanity after what he'd seen tonight or concluded that somehow, the entire performance had been rigged. He'd accused Simon of being a fraud the first time Simon had done a reading for him. Now Vic knew better, both about the supernatural and about Simon's abilities. That knowledge did not help him sleep at night.

Simon woke when they pulled in beside the blue bungalow. Vic came around to help him out, but Simon managed on his own, although he did accept Vic's arm around him as they climbed the steps. As soon as they were inside Simon relaxed, and Vic wondered if the protective wardings on the house made him feel more at ease.

"Come on," Vic said, tugging Simon toward the couch. "You get comfortable, and I'll get dinner." Simon didn't object, and he had gone from sitting to lying down before Vic had even left the room.

Vic pulled a container of leftover homemade lasagna from the fridge and split it into two portions. It would take several minutes to microwave, so he checked his phone, which had been on silent. He realized he'd missed several calls from Ross.

Vic glanced at Simon, asleep on the couch. Rather than listen to his messages, he just hit speed dial.

"What's up?" Vic asked when Ross answered.

"You didn't listen to the messages, did you?"

Vic couldn't resist a smile. "Of course not. That's why I called you back."

Ross gave an exaggerated sigh in response. "Hargrove called me since he couldn't reach you. Turned up some more details on Josh Williams, the guy who's heading up the dive on the *Annabelle*. Seems like Jonah Camden has filed a cease and desist against him that is pretty much of a gag order on saying anything that links the Gallows Nine to the Dunwood family or Socastee Manor. Apparently, Camden tried to get the whole dive project shut down, even called in favors with a couple of his rich buddies to throw their weight around, but he couldn't swing it."

"Interesting," Vic said, splitting his attention between the call and the timer on the microwave.

"Oh, and it turns out that Williams not only crossed paths with Sean Bradley, his fist also crossed Bradley's face a time or two. They were graduate students together, and diving partners, until Bradley double-crossed Williams and got caught selling relics to private collectors on the black market. The scandal almost ruined Williams's career and cost him a high-profile reclamation project."

"Some details Williams managed not to mention."

"Yeah. I want to bring him back in for questioning, but right now we're not having much luck finding the guy."

Vic frowned. "You think he's going to turn up dead? And if he does—are you betting on 'suicide' or the third missing knife?"

Ross swore under his breath. "Your guess is as good as mine." He paused. "You sound a little off. Simon okay?"

Vic grimaced, even though Ross couldn't see his expression. "He did a séance out at Socastee Manor and it got fucked up."

"A séance. What happened? Accidentally summon a demon or something?"

Vic winced. He'd been around Simon enough to know some things shouldn't be joked about. "Not quite. I don't have all the details yet. It went hard on him. I'm trying to get him to eat. Kinda afraid he's going to have a hangover headache tomorrow."

Ross believed in Simon's abilities, but he hadn't seen as much close up as Vic had, and the whole supernatural aspect was new to him. "You gonna be in tomorrow?"

"Planning on it," Vic replied. He bent to take the lasagna out of the microwave and nearly burned his fingers on the plate. "I'm hoping that a good meal and some TLC will set things right."

"TMI on the TLC," Ross answered with a laugh. "Just let me know if anything changes, and I'll keep you posted if I hear from Cap."

Vic ended the call and slipped his phone in his pocket. He thought about setting dinner out on the table, then set up a couple of retro TV trays that had come with the bungalow. He and Simon could eat on the couch. He found a movie they'd both seen a dozen times, figuring that neither of them were up to paying full attention.

"Hey," he said, gently jostling Simon to wake him. "Dinner."

Simon looked rumpled and vulnerable, making Vic's heart squeeze. God, he loved this man. He'd fallen for Simon harder than he ever thought he could.

"I'm not—"

"Tracey's going to whip my ass if I don't get you to eat," Vic said, hands on hips. "You know it's true. She's gonna call me and be all 'did Simon eat dinner'? And I'll have to say, 'no, I let him sleep,' and then she's gonna come over here and we're gonna have a come-to-Jesus moment, and I'll get my ass whupped."

Despite everything, Simon had to chuckle. Vic hid a smile. Tracey was unquestionably fierce, and she had no problem telling Vic when she thought he was off base when it came to Simon. She was also Simon's second-biggest supporter, after Vic, and Simon's oldest friend in Myrtle Beach. That counted for a lot in Vic's book.

"We wouldn't want that." Simon looked utterly exhausted but dug into the lasagna with determination. The dish was one of Simon's favorites, made from Vic's mother's recipe, so Vic trusted the tasty pasta would win out, even over an adrenaline crash.

"How are you feeling?" Vic asked after they had finished their food.

Simon drank the last of his sweet tea and leaned back. "Like someone played tug of war with my brain—and I lost."

"We weren't really sure what was going on." Vic tried to keep his voice level. "One minute you were talking with Katarina, and then you went stiff and started shouting about killing us."

Simon winced. "Yeah. About that. I need to check my notes, but the glimpse I got of the spirit made me think it was Jamie Dunwood, the guy who built the place. He'd be the right time period for Marilee and Katarina."

"Why did he come after you? You said he wasn't the same spirit who's been killing the descendants of the Gallows Nine officials."

"Think about it," Simon replied. "Dunwood sided against the Gallows Nine. So he backed the side that hanged them. But there've always been rumors that Dunwood actually hired the *Annabelle* to do some of his smuggling." He shut his eyes, and Vic could tell the day's activities were catching up to Simon.

"Dunwood wanted us out of the house. I think there's something hidden that he doesn't want anyone to find—something that might prove the smuggling accusations."

"Why would he care? He's been dead for two hundred years."

Simon shrugged. "Jamie Dunwood was obsessed with gaining respectability with the plantation class. He earned the money, but never got the respect."

"Maybe that explains Platz, the groundskeeper, but what about the diver? And who held the knife?"

"I'm working on it," Simon mumbled in a sleepy voice. "Also… how likely are criminals to change the way they do things?"

Vic raised an eyebrow. "Not very. That's what makes most of them easy to catch."

Simon nodded. "So we've got criminal ghosts. Why would the same ghost stab some people and possess others to make them hang themselves?"

"He wouldn't—at least a live perp wouldn't."

"Two ghosts, different sides, they want different things. Now we just have to figure out who and what."

Simon's voice faded as he fell asleep. Vic eased him onto his side so he could lie down, and carried the dishes out to the kitchen. He thought about what Simon had told him as he loaded the dishwasher and cleaned up. Vic had overlooked something basic, because he forgot that the ghosts involved were just dead criminals. He replayed that in his mind and shook his head, deciding that was an insight he might not share with Ross—at least, not worded quite that way.

Still, Simon was right. The methods were too different to be the same perp. And since he didn't share Simon's ability to talk to ghosts, Vic was sidelined on that track until Simon recovered. But when it came to living suspects, Vic felt certain that Jonah Camden and Josh Williams were tangled up in this somehow. And tomorrow, he intended to figure out how.

But tonight, he had a hurt partner to take care of. Simon might not have taken visible damage from the séance, but he'd been wounded nonetheless.

Vic checked the wardings the way Simon had taught him and made sure all the doors were locked. He turned off the television and put the trays away. Simon didn't really wake up when Vic got him to his feet, but he sleepwalked to the bedroom, and collapsed bonelessly onto their bed, making it easy for Vic to strip him down to his underwear.

Vic thought about trying to get Simon to brush his teeth, then decided he'd probably end up falling and hurting himself even more. Vic got ready for bed, put his phone on the nightstand and turned out the lights, managing to get both of them under the covers.

"I love you," Vic whispered, snuggling up against Simon's back with an arm over his chest. "I'm here. You were badass. But you can rest now. I'll keep watch. Gonna protect you. I promise." But as he drifted into restless sleep, Vic wasn't sure how he was going to be able to make good on that vow.

13

SIMON

Simon dragged himself out of bed the next morning, more from sheer stubbornness and the need for coffee than because he felt up for dealing with the world. He'd never been much of a party animal, and the splitting headache reminded him of his worst freshman hangover. Vic made sure he could manage by himself, made coffee, and fixed him breakfast, then headed to the precinct—after Simon promised to call if he needed help.

With the storm rolling in, Grand Strand Ghost Tours and most of the rest of Myrtle Beach was closed for business, except for hotels and a few gas stations and grocery stores. Pete was happy to stay at the store, assuring Simon that not only was the shop better warded against supernatural threats but also better made than his apartment to withstand the weather.

The weather forecast droned on as Simon finished his coffee, calling for heavy rain and very high winds. Not a hurricane, but bad enough that there would likely be plenty of downed trees, damaged roofs, and power outages once it hit. He was glad that Vic had helped him sandbag the bungalow, just in case.

Simon checked in once more with his Skeleton Crew contacts, making sure they had somewhere safe to hunker down, and asking them to call if they found out anything about a ghost coaxing people to kill themselves. Text messages began to flow in, assuring Simon that the senders had a place to stay, but no one had a lead on either the ghost or the next victim.

He poured himself another cup and settled down at the table with the list of names he'd sent to Vic, the potential victims he'd identified from the information on the Gallows Nine trial from the museum. He agreed with Vic—there was no good way to warn any of these people, not without being reported as a suspect. He sipped his coffee and thought about what he'd learned from the museum, from Cassidy, and from the séance.

The Gallows Nine were the crew of the *Annabelle*, ruthless smugglers and pirates, hardened criminals who very likely might have been sometimes employed by the Dunwoods for secret projects. And who, in their time of need, were abandoned by their patron. The Dunwoods viciously protected their family's reputation with duels and lawyers. So what were the odds that the proceedings were rigged against the Gallows Nine, despite their guilt?

The *Annabelle's* crew weren't angels, but they deserved a fair trial —and fairness would have also damned their patron with them. Instead, they'd been rushed to justice at the end of a noose, so that they couldn't implicate the Dunwoods. And now, two hundred years later, with the storm disturbing the ship's wreckage and the renovations disturbing Socastee Manor, ghosts on both sides had risen, one for revenge and the other to protect a legacy.

What a mess. Simon combed his fingers back through his hair and tried to figure out a way to come at the rat's nest of clues. He'd barely made it through the list when his phone rang.

"Sebastian. I need you to come to my house. Right away." Miss Eppie didn't mince words.

"What's going on?"

"I have someone here you need to meet. And Gabriella and I think you should try to talk to the ghost who helped you last night. There isn't much time left."

Simon knew better than to argue. "Okay," he said, since he was at a standstill following his own leads. "I'll head right over." He'd promised to help at the shelter, so he wouldn't stay at Eppie's long.

He finished his coffee, then texted Vic to let him know where he was heading. Miss Eppie's house was down toward Socastee Manor, in Murrells Inlet. Simon glanced at the forecast again. With the storm's predicted route, he had time to get down to Miss Eppie's and spend a few hours, before the worst of the weather hit. Just in case, Simon grabbed a pair of Wellington boots and his best rain slicker, then headed out.

Miss Eppie's home was a tidy ranch house down a sandy lane, away from the bustle of tourist traffic. While she had her shop in town, many of her hoodoo customers in dire need found their way to her home in the off hours, and she obliged them, taking her responsibility as a root worker very seriously. Simon wasn't surprised to see Gabriella's car parked in front, although he did not recognize the late-model Honda sedan next to it.

He sprinted through the rain to the front door and felt a frisson of magic as he passed through the protective wardings. Simon and Vic had visited here before, and he knew that if he wasn't welcome, the wards would have deterred him from entering.

"Leave those boots in the mudroom and come inside before you catch your death," Miss Eppie called as Simon let himself in. He left his wet boots on the mat and hung his dripping coat from a peg, then headed into the cozy living room. Comfortably worn furnishings combined with a color scheme of muted oranges, reds, and yellows made the room feel warm, cozy, and safe. Simon knew that some of that had to do with the protection spells Miss Eppie laid over everything, nurtured and reinforced over time. He caught the scent of gumbo, perhaps left over from last night's dinner, and the tang of sage.

"Sit down, Sebastian. We need to talk about a few things." Miss Eppie already had a pitcher of sweet tea and four glasses ready on her coffee table. Gabriella gave Simon a welcoming nod. A man Simon didn't know sat stiffly in an armchair near the fireplace with a slightly glazed look in his eyes.

"I'd like you to meet Reggie Henderson," Miss Eppie said, and

Simon stepped toward the chair and shook the stranger's hand. "He's come here for protection. I think you'll want to hear what he has to say." She turned her attention to Reggie. "Go on."

Reggie looked to be in his early forties, with dishwater blond hair and a receding hairline. He had a doughy build that suggested a desk job and wore a pair of glasses that looked more functional than hipster accessory. The poor fellow also looked like he would rather be anywhere else.

"I came to ask Miss Eppie for help because something is trying to kill me," Reggie said, so quietly that Simon had to strain to hear him. But he clearly caught the key word—"something," not "someone." And the name registered immediately. Reggie Henderson was on Simon's list of descendants from the Gallows Nine incident—and a potential victim of the vengeful ghost.

"What kind of thing?" Simon asked, giving Reggie an encouraging smile. "I'm a psychic medium. Maybe I can help."

Reggie looked only partly reassured. "I'm not sure. Twice now it's come at me, just in the last couple of days. There's a dark shadow, but it's not normal darkness. Something's in the shadow, but I can't see it. It knows where I am, and it wants me. I realized what was happening when I was outside, and this awful sadness came over me."

He wiped his mouth with the back of his hand, a nervous gesture. "All of a sudden, it's like I didn't want to live anymore. I thought about every mistake I've made, everything I've done wrong, and I just couldn't bear it. So I got thinking, maybe the world would be better off without me, and I went in my house, not sure yet how I meant to do it." He swallowed. "And as soon as I went across the threshold, the sadness went away, like flicking a switch. That's when I knew, something had tried to get to me."

Simon exchanged a look with Miss Eppie, who wore a triumphant little smile. "What was special about going into your house?" Simon asked, as his thoughts raced.

"I've been a good customer of Miss Eppie's," Reggie said. "Grew up in these parts, and so did all my family. My mama swore by Miss Eppie's charms, and when I got my place, first thing I did was wash down the entrances with red brick dust and Four Thieves vinegar, just like mama told me."

Simon opened his Gift, trying to get a read on Reggie. He suspected that, like his Skeleton Crew misfits, Reggie had an untrained psychic gift. That made him more susceptible to supernatural attacks, but it also meant that he might sense danger that those without a gift would not.

"You said the…entity…attacked you more than once?"

Reggie nodded. He seemed to loosen up once he realized that Simon believed him. "The first time, I was walking home from the grocery store, and all of a sudden this bleak mood just came over me, like nothing would ever go right and no one would ever want me…it was awful." His voice caught, and Simon guessed the vengeful ghost knew how to exploit its targets' weaknesses.

"How did you get away that time?" Simon asked.

"I felt so upset that I ducked into the first church I came to," Reggie confessed. "I don't even know what kind of church it was. I'm not real religious, but I just felt the need to be there. And like at home, as soon as I stepped inside, whatever came over me let me go."

Sacred spaces often deterred dark entities, Simon thought. Either Reggie had very good instincts, or he'd been exceptionally lucky. "And it wasn't waiting for you when you went back out?"

Reggie shrugged. "I stayed inside for about half an hour, said a prayer, and sort of soaked up the atmosphere. You know what I mean? Then when I went out, nothing."

"When did all this happen?" Simon didn't know whether Miss Eppie and Gabriella had already questioned Reggie, or if they were just letting him take the lead.

"The first time, with the church, was two days ago. The second time, earlier today. Only when it happened the second time, it was a lot worse. So when I could go back outside and it wasn't waiting for me, I got myself here to beg Miss Eppie for help."

Two days, Simon thought. It's been three since the last suicide hanging. Which meant Reggie was intended to be the ghost's next victim.

"You did the right thing, coming here," Miss Eppie told Reggie. "We can help."

Simon sat back and turned to Miss Eppie and Gabriella. "What did you have in mind?"

"The spirit who came to you at the end of the séance last night, the one who helped drive off the bad ghost. I think we need to talk more to him," Gabriella replied. "He might be able to give us some answers."

"His name is Dante. He was a privateer back around the time of the Revolution, and his ship scuttled the *Annabelle* and led to the capture of its crew—the Gallows Nine," Simon told them. "He's a distant relative of mine. I've seen visions of him before. There's an occult object that went down with the *Annabelle*, the Wilton Stone. Having the wreck wash closer to shore woke up the stone—and the vengeful ghost that was attached to it."

"You're related?" Gabriella asked. "That's very interesting. It makes your bond with Dante stronger, and might make you a target for the *Annabelle's* ghost."

Simon had spent some time reading up on the *Annabelle* and its doomed pirates. Little was known about seven of the men, but the ship's captain and first mate were infamous in their time. William "Red Hands" Beecher, the captain, earned his nickname from his fondness for slitting throats. Hastings "Dog" Anders, the first mate, was said to be as loyal and ferocious as an attack dog. From what Simon could find in newspaper accounts from the period, Anders was a follower, though no less guilty for his crimes. Beecher, on the other hand, sounded like a sociopath, someone who enjoyed killing, even when it could have been avoided. Simon's money was on Beecher as their vengeful ghost. The others listened intently as Simon filled them in on what he had discovered.

"Why me?" Reggie asked, looking from one of them to the others. "Why did this thing pick me?"

Simon explained his theory about Reggie's connection to the townsfolk involved in the hanging of the Gallows Nine. When Simon finished, Reggie nodded.

"I'd heard something about that from my grandfather, only a

little different," Reggie said. "He said that his grandfather claimed that our ancestor, Ronald Henderson, was a judge. He sentenced the Gallows Nine to hang. But on his deathbed, he supposedly told his son a secret that he needed to get off his chest."

Simon had a good idea of what that secret might be. "Do you know what he said?"

Reggie shook his head. "It was a warning, but the message has been lost over time. My grandfather thought there was a curse to go with the Gallows Nine because it seemed like there'd been bad luck in the family ever since."

Simon told them his theory about the connection between the *Annabelle* and the Dunwoods of Socastee Manor. "I think your ancestor may have confessed to presiding over an unjust trial," Simon added. "Not that Beecher and his crew didn't deserve to hang, but Dunwood should have been on the gallows with them, and the town protected him because they were afraid of what he could do with his wealth and power. And now, I think the storm and the renovation brought both ghosts back for a showdown."

"Is it after me because my ancestor was the judge?" Reggie looked worried.

"It's come after people whose families were involved in the trial," Simon told him. "The ghost takes over the person and forces him to kill himself."

Reggie's eyes grew wide. "Oh my God. That's what it tried to do to me, what I was thinking of doing before I went into the house and broke the connection."

"I know what happened last night went hard on you," Gabriella said to Simon. "But I think the only way we're going to get to the bottom of this is by contacting Dante's ghost. And when I read the omens, they pointed to tonight's storm as the critical event."

Simon refilled his glass of sweet tea and drank it, gathering his courage. "All right," he said. "You want to do it here?"

"Reggie is safe here. I don't think we dare take him elsewhere," Miss Eppie replied. "He can help make the circle." That confirmed to Simon that Miss Eppie suspected the man had a bit of a Gift, which would strengthen the séance circle, and the connection to Dante, if the ghost answered their summons.

Gabriella and Eppie set up the table and chairs, while Simon ran through a few breathing exercises to calm himself and let go of his nervousness and exhaustion in order to open his Gift more fully to Dante's presence. When he opened his eyes, he saw that they had prepared the space with a candle and a batik tablecloth whose block print design hid protective runes.

"Ready when you are, Sebastian," Miss Eppie said, holding out her hand.

"I'm not going to let him talk through me," Simon said, worried that would require too much after the strain of the previous night. "But I'll tell you everything he says to me."

Simon pushed off the couch and fell into step beside Reggie. Their guest still looked unnerved, but Simon wasn't worried the man would freak out on him. When this was all over, assuming they survived, Simon intended to talk to Reggie and see if he needed to be one of the Skeleton Crew to help protect him and hone his abilities.

Settling in at Miss Eppie's table felt nothing like the séance at Socastee Manor. Then, Simon had been acutely aware of all the darkness and misery etched into the mansion by the troubled lives of its former occupants. He'd needed to expend energy to hold off those negative vibes, which left him with less power to connect with the spirits.

Here, the house exuded calm and safety within strong wardings. Simon already knew that neither Beecher's ghost nor Dunwood's could attack him inside these walls, thanks to Miss Eppie's layers of protective magic. With both Gabriella and Miss Eppie as part of the circle—as well as Reggie with his latent, untested abilities—Simon felt a surge of power that wiped away his exhaustion.

They joined hands, forming the circle. Simon took in a deep breath and let it center him. He tuned in to the energy the others sent his way. "Dante Morris. Please come back and finish our conversation. Your old enemy has returned, and I need your help to stop him before more people die."

Simon sent a wave of psychic power behind his summons, trusting it to carry into the ether. They waited, and Simon watched the flickering candle in the middle of the table. He tried to relax and stop the chatter of his thoughts so that he could be open for Dante's response. After a few minutes, the temperature dropped, and the flame flickered wildly.

Simon. I am glad you came back.

Thank you for helping me fight off Dunwood's ghost.

Of course. You are kin. What help can I provide now?

We think Dunwood's ghost is killing to keep people from finding out a secret —maybe something hidden in the manor.

Dante was silent for a moment. *There would have been ledgers, somewhere, of his dealings. He was too active not to have his shipments recorded.*

Can you see where they are?

Dante's laugh sounded like a gust of wind. *I'm just a ghost. Not all-knowing.*

Simon wasn't surprised, but he thought it had been worth asking. *Your energy feels stronger tonight.*

I was a water witch. The storm feeds me. I can't usually show myself this strongly.

Simon knew the connection between them could falter at any moment, so he pushed on, setting aside the many questions he would have loved to ask about his ancestor and the time period. *William Beecher's ghost is killing the descendants of the men who hanged him. How can I stop him? The Wilton Stone is underwater, and it's treacherous to dive there.*

This is new?

Yes. Just since the storms washed the wreck to shallower water.

If he has been quiet for so long, with the stone deep in the ocean, then lend me your power at the peak of the storm tonight, and together we will push it back to the abyss.

That just might work, Simon thought. *When and where?*

You'll feel the storm crest and know it's time, Dante promised. *Just have a line of sight to where the wreck lies. We'll send that son of a cur back to Davy Jones.*

Dante's ghost slipped from Simon's consciousness, but this time the parting was gentle, not the wrenching violence of the night at the manor. For a few seconds, Simon drifted peacefully. Then an image appeared full-blown in his mind, of the diver, Josh Williams, slipping up the front steps of a darkened Socastee Manor.

Simon jolted awake, eyes wide, heart thudding. "Josh Williams. He broke into the manor. He must be looking for the ledger." Simon looked around the table. "He was on the dive to the *Annabelle*. If he was near the Wilton Stone, maybe Beecher's ghost has been possessing him all this time. We've got to stop him."

Simon told them what Dante had revealed. "We need to destroy the ledger to break Dunwood's hold on the manor and stop him from hurting the workers. And we have to stop Josh Williams so Beecher's ghost won't kill more people."

"Socastee Manor is only a mile from here," Miss Eppie said. "Let's go."

Simon shook his head. "You shouldn't come with me. It's bad out there—the storm is going to get worse."

Miss Eppie tilted her head and gave him a look. "Child, do you know how many hurricanes I've seen in my lifetime? I respect the ocean, but I don't fear the storm. Where you go tonight, Gabriella and I are coming, too. Right?"

Gabriella cussed under her breath in Spanish, then nodded. "Of course." She glared at Reggie. "You, stay here. That way Beecher won't make you his hostage. Stay inside, and don't touch anything unless you want to be turned into a frog."

Simon knew that wasn't possible, but Reggie's eyes widened and he paled. Miss Eppie clucked her tongue at Gabriella and laid a hand on Reggie's arm. "No frogs. But there are items best not handled if you don't know what you're doing. So stay inside, and stay out of trouble."

Gabriella went to the window. "If we're going out to the Manor, we should go now. The rain's coming down hard, and the water's rising. That access road could get cut off."

Simon fished his phone out of his pocket and hit Vic's number on speed dial. He had no idea what Vic might be doing at the moment, since he'd been called in for emergency storm duty—

directing traffic around accidents, helping get stranded motorists out of flooded cars, setting up barricades, and any other police duties that needed extra manpower. He didn't really expect Vic to pick up, but he knew he needed to let him know that they might be closing in on two killers.

"Vic—I know what to look for at the Manor to break Dunwood's link, and Dante's ghost told me how to stop the Gallows Nine killer. But we've got to go out to the mansion to do it, and we've got to go now. Miss Eppie and Gabriella are coming with me. And I had a vision of Josh Williams breaking in—I think he's the one who's been possessed by the ghost of the *Annabelle's* captain to cause the hangings. If you get this message, we could use some backup. Stay safe. I love you." He disconnected, swallowed hard, called the shelter to say he might not be coming to help, and then pocketed his phone.

"Come on. We've got some ghosts to wrangle."

14

VIC

On nice days in Myrtle Beach, even a boring stakeout wasn't all bad. This definitely wasn't a nice day. At least it wasn't snowing, like back in Pittsburgh. But nights like this, in the driving rain and pitch black, with power outages taking down traffic lights at major intersections and alarm systems going wacko, Vic sometimes thought a little snow wasn't as bad as he remembered it.

"We should be shadowing those guys on the list Simon gave us," Vic grumbled to Ross as they struggled through water that nearly went over their hip waders, in the glare of the blue and red strobing lights from the parked cruiser at the flooded intersection.

"Probably. But until you figure out how we can show up and warn them that they're going to get ganked by a ghost, we're going to follow orders and push cars out of flooded streets because drivers are too stupid to know their Honda isn't a Jet Ski," Ross replied.

They were cold and soaked, despite the heavy-duty police rain gear. Vic's short hair was plastered to his skull, sending drips of icy rain down his back. Sure, it wasn't snow, but being wet clear through in a gale force wind in late January was still fucking cold. His feet might not be wet, but Vic swore he hadn't felt his toes for at least the last hour.

"There was a reason I applied to be a detective," Vic said as he and Ross pushed yet another stranded car out of water that had stalled it.

"Look at the bright side. It's too cold for the gators to be out, and the snakes are hibernating."

Vic glared at his partner, not feeling the humor. "And it's not mosquito season. I'm thankful for small fucking favors."

He looked out over the main stretch of the Grand Strand. Usually, Ocean Boulevard and Kings Highway were lit up like the Vegas Strip, awash in neon and tail lights. From the never-ending carnival of Family Kingdom amusement park to the huge glowing signs of the big beach shops, the party never ended. Except now, whole blocks were dark. Stoplights blinked without changing colors or were out completely. Sirens wailed from every direction, and the crashing of the ocean that was normally just background noise sounded unnervingly loud and rough.

A car came through on the opposite side of the road, going too fast for conditions, and sent up a chest-high spray of water, dousing them. Vic sputtered and wiped his eyes, muttering at the driver.

"You know, you're usually not this surly. Did Simon make you sleep on the couch or something?"

Vic bit back a retort that Ross didn't deserve because his partner was right; Vic's mood was out of line. They had done this job in dozens of storms, under worse conditions, with more danger, and Vic had taken it all in stride.

Tonight, Vic's intuition—what Simon jokingly called his Spidey sense—was jangling, putting him on edge. Not for himself, but for Simon. Something wasn't right, and Vic had no way to do anything about it.

He'd gotten a message earlier in the day from Simon, before the storm got bad, saying that he was going to see Miss Eppie. Vic knew that Simon had intended to spend the evening helping out at the shelter where people went when their homes flooded, so his change of plans told Vic that Simon was chasing a lead on the case. At least if Simon was with Eppie and Gabriella, he wasn't alone, and he'd be safe. Vic hoped.

They were supposed to get a break every hour, a chance to guzzle hot coffee, take a leak, and dry off. In reality, they were lucky if they got the chance every couple of hours. At their previous break, Vic had checked his messages. Nothing new from Simon— Vic wasn't sure whether that made him feel better or worse.

He did have a new email from the crime lab. "Hey," Vic said, getting Ross's attention. "Take a look at this. They ran the prints on one of the knives and got a match."

They read through the message once, then again, and stared at each other. "Shit," Ross said, breaking the stunned silence. "I was sure it was going to be Josh Williams. I would have bet money."

"Jonah Camden," Vic said, feeling sucker-punched. "If Simon's right, Dunwood was worried about his reputation. Camden would have been in the right place to kill the groundskeeper, if the guy found something incriminating."

"But what about the dead diver?" Ross argued. "Williams had the means."

"Do you remember that day at the manor, when we met Camden? His Beemer? The license plate had a dive flag."

"Half the cars in Myrtle Beach have a dive flag on them some-where," Ross countered.

"I need to let Simon know." Vic started to dial, just as a streak of lightning raced across the sky and a deafening peal of thunder followed. More lights went out, and Vic's signal faded.

"Fuck. I can't get any bars."

"You can try again later. We need to get out and help with traffic. Simon'll be safe. That root woman won't let him do anything stupid," Ross assured him.

Vic glared at his phone, shaking it as if that would improve his signal. Maybe he'd get moved to a part of town that still had reception, and he could get the call to go through. Vic shivered, but this time it had nothing to do with the rain. His intuition told him that Simon was in trouble.

They spent the next hour going from one disaster to another— wrecked cars, stalled vehicles, flooding that required evacuations for people who couldn't manage on their own. Whenever Vic had the chance, he checked to see if he had signal, desperate to let Simon know about Camden and make sure he was okay.

Just when Vic had resigned himself to having a phone that was just a fancy paperweight, he and Ross responded to a dispatch that took them into a different area of downtown.

"I've got a signal!" Vic crowed. A text message popped up from Simon—over an hour old.

"No, no, no," he muttered as he read the message.

"What's wrong?" Ross asked, daring a side glance as he navigated through the obstacle course of standing water and stranded cars.

"Simon got a vision about Josh Williams going to the Manor, and he thinks he's the killer. Shit. If Camden's there, both Simon and Josh are in a lot of danger."

"Tell Hargrove. This could be the big break in the case."

Vic didn't bother with his cell phone; he used the dispatch radio. "Cap, Simon got a lead on the killer, so he's headed to Socastee Manor. Josh Williams might be there, too. But forensics just confirmed Camden's fingerprints on one of the murder knives. Simon and Josh are in danger. Permission to head for the Manor?"

"Go," Hargrove said. "You and Ross. Just watch yourselves. The way the storm surge is rising, you might need a boat. If the road out that way floods, you won't get a car through there."

"Got it," Vic said. "We're heading out."

"How are we going to get to Socastee Manor if the road is swamped?" Ross asked.

Vic smiled. "I'm going to call in a few favors." He toggled the handset on his police radio. "Dispatch? I need you to patch me through to the Coast Guard. Captain Bret Timmons."

15

———

SIMON

Simon's Toyota had good tires, but traction wasn't the problem. As he skirted standing water and went around stalled cars, he found himself wishing for a Humvee, or at least a big SUV with high clearance and enough power to not get stuck in soft sand. The rain fell in sheets. Dante's ghost whispered that the storm had begun in earnest, the big one that had the forecasters in a tizzy.

Socastee Manor was just a mile away, but with the torrential rain, Simon had no choice except to crawl with his four-ways flashing, hoping none of the other idiots who were out in the awful weather were going to hit him. Miss Eppie rode shotgun, while Gabriella was in the back. Reggie had been all too glad to stay at Miss Eppie's house, and Simon agreed that he would be safer there. But if they got stuck, he wouldn't have objected to having another man to help push the car.

Puddles covered the road, deceptively deep. The side roads weren't quite as well maintained, leaving them with dips and potholes, but Simon didn't dare try to go around on the wet sand. All the while he chafed at the delay while simultaneously dreading the confrontation to come. He couldn't use Dante's weather magic while driving, and he didn't want to squander his energy when he knew the fight to come would be brutal. But Simon definitely wanted the ability to pause the rain and stop the wind, just until he got to his destination.

You know it doesn't exactly work like that, Dante's ghost confided.

We're going to lose the battle by default if we can't get there. Simon gripped the wheel white-knuckled, hunched forward and jaw set as he tried to see through the downpour.

He worried about Vic, something Simon was coming to accept as just a given. On normal days, if he thought too hard about it, Simon worried about bullets, knives, and ambushes. But pulling emergency duty meant going up against the worst Mother Nature had to throw at them, wading into dangerous situations to protect people, animals, and property. High water could be deceptively swift, and many people had drowned in storm water ditches. Fallen electric wires and snapped trees could be lethal, and the high winds were notorious for flinging debris with the speed of a pro baseball player hitting a line drive. Simon could conjure up far too many scenarios that were just as deadly as a shoot-out, and harder to protect against.

But worry came with loving a cop, just like it did for military families, and Simon was resolved to learn how to balance reasonable concerns with dark imaginings. After all, Vic had a much harder adjustment to make, accepting all the "woo-woo" that went with loving Simon. He vowed to be worth the trouble.

The closer they got to Socastee Manor, the more Simon's sense of foreboding grew. He asked and got no response from Dante, probably meaning that the ghost knew no more than he did about what to expect.

"Are you picking up on anything?" Simon asked Miss Eppie and Gabriella. Before they could answer, a deep puddle dragged one of his wheels, making him adjust sharply to keep them on the road.

"A storm like this stores a lot of energy for magic that can tap into it," Gabriella replied. "I'm not a weather witch, but I'll do my best to pull what I can when you need it."

"I have what I need to cross the person responsible for those poor men's deaths, but I have to know I'm putting a root on the right person," Miss Eppie said. "It's strong magic, and I want to have it right."

Simon knew just how powerful Miss Eppie's hoodoo was, having seen the result of one of her curses firsthand in his battle against a serial killer. He'd been in the Lowcountry long enough to understand that having a hoodoo practitioner cross someone or put a root on them was nothing to be trifled with.

By comparison, Simon had his psychic Gifts—his visions and the ability to talk to ghosts—and a few minor spells he learned by rote. Patience and persistence more than native magic honed the ability to burn with a touch, open a lock with a word, send a stream of fire a few feet, hurl a small object farther and harder than usual, and summon a small protective barrier. They were, at best, a distraction against the kind of power Simon feared they faced from both Dunwood's ghost and Beecher's vengeful spirit. He wasn't sure they'd be worth the drain to his power, given the bigger goal in mind, but Simon felt better knowing he had at least a little magic of his own.

Heavy storm clouds blocked the moon, and the rain dimmed the reach of the Toyota's headlights so that Simon could barely see a few yards in front of them. He had traveled this road enough lately to know they were nearly to the manor. He wondered if Vic had gotten his text, and assumed that since he'd had no response, that Vic was either too busy to read his messages, or unable to get a call through. As much as Simon wished for reinforcements, he feared that the battle fell to them.

"Josh Williams is definitely here. That's his car," Simon said, as they pulled up near the manor. "And so is Jonah Camden, the developer. That's his BMW."

"If Josh came looking for the ledger, would Camden be able to stop him?" Miss Eppie asked.

Simon remembered Josh's muscular build and Camden's slender frame. "I wouldn't bet on Camden in a fist fight. Josh is a bigger guy."

"If Dunwood is riding Josh, then Camden doesn't have much of a chance without magic to counter him," Gabriella warned.

Simon pulled in, threw the car in park, and they ran for the manor. The wild wind made umbrellas useless and drove the rain nearly sideways, soaking them before they got to the door. He had to lean against the gusts, keeping a tight grip on a shotgun he'd brought, while Gabriella and Miss Eppie linked arms.

Dante loved the storm; Simon could feel the ghost's contentment with the wind and rain, the primal energy he commanded from the tempest. Simon could only hope that Dante could marshal those forces on their behalf, or things were going to go very badly.

The door swung on its hinges, banging open and shut. Simon and the others hesitated before entering, trying to get a read on where Josh and Camden might be. Then he felt the approach of dark power and sensed Dante's sudden departure as the ghost went to hold off Beecher's spirit so they could take on Dunwood.

Dante's absence made Simon feel vulnerable, though he knew Miss Eppie and Gabriella were fierce and powerful in their own right. Simon refused to carry a gun with lethal ammunition, but he had come prepared with a shotgun with rounds filled with rock salt. He also had an iron dagger in a sheath on his belt and plenty of salt in his backpack, as well as a container of holy water. As they entered, Simon lifted a hand to touch the silver medallions he wore, drawing strength from them.

"Go," Gabriella whispered after a moment to sense the entranceway.

Simon swung inside with the shotgun leveled and found an empty front room. Crashes and banging came from farther inside, and Simon fought the urge to run forward, fearing that Camden was in danger from Josh and the ghost of Jamie Dunwood.

The unfinished parlor looked much as it had the last time Simon visited, with an electric lantern set on a board between two saw horses providing a pool of light that did not extend farther into the house.

"Where are they?" Simon murmured. "They've got to be here."

A crash in the next room and a man's shout made them jump. Seconds later, Jonah Camden appeared in the doorway to the parlor, shirt untucked and hair askew. "He's right behind me!" He panted, wide-eyed and fearful.

"We can protect you," Simon offered. "Come with us."

"Simon! No! He's the one who killed Platz!" Josh's voice carried over the storm from the parlor Camden had just left.

"He's lying," Camden said, heading toward Simon and the others. "I got here, and found him tearing the place apart."

"Liar!" Josh hurtled from the parlor and flung himself at Camden's back. Simon glimpsed just enough to see that Josh's left shoulder was bloodied and his right eye was nearly swollen shut. Just before Josh should have tackled Camden to the floor, the developer wheeled and grabbed Josh by his wounded shoulder. Josh cried out in pain, and Camden pulled Josh in front of him like a shield, drawing the third missing knife from his belt.

"You shouldn't be here," Camden said, eyeing Simon and the others. "Josh made a mistake coming here. He thought he'd steal what's rightfully mine, expose what doesn't need to be shared. I caught him in my house, and I'm going to deal with him like a thief deserves."

"He's out of his mind!" Josh shouted, then bit back a cry as Camden dug his fingers into Josh's bloody shoulder.

"You came to find the ledger. Do you deny it?"

"I had permission! Trevor told me I could come."

"I will deal with his betrayal when we are through."

Simon took in Camden's features, which were his own and yet, altered. Gone was Camden's citified hipster arrogance, replaced by a much colder aristocratic entitlement used to holding men's lives and fortunes in the balance. Simon was willing to bet that Jonah Camden couldn't hold his own in a fight, but the spirit possessing his trim body carried himself like someone with military experience who had been no stranger to brawls.

"How'd you figure out about the ledgers, Josh?" Simon asked, buying time to figure out what to do.

"An old journal, from one of the jurors," Josh replied through gritted teeth, panting from the pain as Camden kept a cruel grip on his shoulder. "Said something about Dunwood keeping track of what was owed him in his ledger. It didn't sound like a business transaction."

"Doesn't matter how you found out about it; the ledger stays at Socastee Manor," Camden said, keeping the blade at Josh's throat.

The front door slammed again in the wind. Camden jumped, and Josh tried to twist out of his grip. Camden growled and dug the blade into Josh's neck just enough to raise a thin line of blood.

"Don't!" Simon shouted, desperate to keep Josh alive and Camden talking. He wondered how much of Camden was aware of the possession, or whether the developer had been a willing participant. After all, anything that damaged the Dunwood reputation might bring down property values, Camden's one true priority.

Josh's gaze darted toward the door. Simon didn't dare take his focus off Camden, but a glance out of the corner of his eye told him Miss Eppie was no longer behind him. He thought about hoodoo, and what it took to cross someone and hex their luck. She needed something personal from the target, like a hair or a possession.

The cars, Simon thought. *She's gone to find something she can use in Camden's car. At the least, he'll find himself very unlucky.*

Just turning Camden's luck wouldn't be enough. Simon knew that between the two of them and their abilities, he and Gabriella could probably best Camden and drive out Dunwood's ghost. But they hadn't counted on a hostage, and right now, with the blade digging into Josh's throat, Camden held all the cards.

"Why'd you kill the gardener?" Simon asked, figuring that if he could keep Camden monologuing, he'd give Eppie room to work her hoodoo, and maybe he and Gabriella could seize an opportunity.

"Too damn nosy," Camden said with a sneer. Now that he paid close attention, Simon could hear the difference in the possessed man's voice. Camden's normal tone was higher pitched, and he usually spoke like he was giving a presentation to investors, stilted and full of jargon. Dunwood's voice had the same odd hint of a British accent Simon had heard when Beecher the pirate spoke in his mind, a reminder that Colonial America wasn't far removed yet from its English roots.

"Why would Platz have cared about an old ledger?" Simon asked, needing to know and desperate to keep the conversation going.

"He might have sold it, or someone else could have gotten a hold of it, figured things out. I couldn't risk that." Dunwood's inflection made it clear that protecting his interests justified whatever action was required—including murder.

"If you hid it in the house, why would Platz be anywhere near the ledger?"

"He heard stories and told them to the contractor, Nichols," Camden snapped. "I couldn't get rid of Nichols without the investors noticing, but if an old man got jumped…well, that's just too bad, isn't it?" A cold smile touched Camden's thin lips.

"How'd you kill the diver?"

Camden's smile broadened, and Simon got the feeling that Dunwood was enjoying a private joke. "I'm dive certified," Camden replied. "Never did much with it except some vacation scuba, but it was enough to stop the looter from bringing up that accursed stone." His answer was an odd mix of Camden and Dunwood, juxtaposing a difference of centuries.

"You knew about the Wilton Stone." Simon figured Camden kept talking because he wanted someone among the living to know of his exploits…even if he intended to kill that "someone" later.

"Of course I knew. I purchased the damned thing!" Camden's eyes were glazed, and the fury that glinted in them belonged to the spirit who possessed him. "Would have made me an even bigger fortune, if they'd delivered it like we planned. But when the privateers scuttled the ship, the stone went with it. And I guess Beecher's had time enough to make it his. Couldn't take the risk he'd get even stronger if it came to the surface."

Simon felt sick with the confirmation of Dunwood's malice. "Did you know Beecher's ghost was killing off the descendants of those you bribed to throw the trial?"

Camden tittered, a chilling, mirthless sound. "Figured that out, did you? I owned this town in my day. Those pirates had a good thing going until they didn't deliver. I couldn't let them damage the Dunwood name."

"Because murder doesn't count?" Simon challenged.

"Fortunes aren't built by playing nice," Camden scoffed, and Simon wondered if the developer and the long-dead plantation owner had found common cause in kindred souls. He couldn't say he'd put it past Camden to ignore the law if it suited his needs, just like Camden hadn't cared whether the workers on the job site got hurt, so long as the deadlines were met.

Time was running out. Simon felt the struggle between Dante and Beecher's ghost in the background and knew that Dante couldn't hold off the angry spirit much longer. Before they left Miss Eppie's house, Simon had already figured out that he'd be able to see the site of the *Annabelle's* wreck from Socastee Manor, to help Dante push it and the Wilton Stone out to sea forever. But first, they had to find a way to stop Dunwood's ghost without costing Josh his life.

Outside, the wind howled and thunder rattled the windows.

"That ledger isn't just a way to protect your reputation, is it? It's what holds your spirit to this world."

Simon sensed the malice in Dunwood's ghost and its need for control. They'd guessed the secret of Dunwood's long stranglehold on his property, and Simon felt certain that the ghost did not intend to let any of them leave alive.

"This ledger?" Trevor's voice sounded from the next room, and he emerged holding a leather-bound book—and a cigarette lighter with its flame dancing perilously close to the tinder-dry pages.

"Give me that book!" Camden tried to turn on Trevor and still keep hold of Josh. The knife slipped away, just for a second, but it was enough for Josh to elbow his attacker and evade his grip. Simon pulled the trigger as soon as Josh was out of the way, and the round of rock salt hit Camden squarely in the torso.

The salt blast weakened the ghost's power, and Simon pulled on his ability as a medium and sent the psychic equivalent of a body block, using his Gift to try to knock Dunwood free of his vessel. In the same instant, Trevor's lighter set pages of the ledger aflame.

Camden screamed.

Josh scrambled out of the line of fire, holding his injured shoulder. Simon was too tangled up with fighting off Dunwood's ghost to get in another shot, locked in a life-or-death battle to wrest Dunwood out of Camden's body.

Josh scooped up the shotgun and sent another round of rock salt into Camden, hitting him in the back this time. Trevor dropped the burning ledger into an empty metal paint bucket as the flames danced high in the darkened room.

Simon lunged for Camden, struggling both physically and psychically to force Dunwood to release his hold. Camden growled and swung the knife at Simon, who brought his arm up to deflect. The blade arced downward, stabbing into Simon's thigh. Simon cried out in pain, but he hung on, resolute, and spoke the words of power that made his hands burning hot to the touch, trying anything to drive Dunwood's ghost out.

Camden fought him, trying to get away from the burning touch, and Gabriella called out an incantation of her own, ending with a shout. Camden suddenly went limp in Simon's grip, and Dunwood's ghost tore free. Simon didn't know whether that was because of Gabriella's spell, or because Dunwood's possession had drained Camden to unconsciousness. Simon rolled off Camden's limp form, still locked in an unseen battle with Dunwood's ghost.

Dunwood had no intention of letting go of this world, and he battered at Simon's mental shields, trying to take him over as he had Camden. Simon felt the spirit's age and its cold fury. Jamie Dunwood did not abide being denied, not in life and not in death. But as the flames leapt and the old book crackled and burned, Simon sensed the spirit's connection to its anchor wane.

This house is mine! Dunwood shrieked.

Not anymore.

Simon called on all his power and training and pushed with his mind and Gift, hurling the ghost away, toward the fire. For an instant, he saw Jamie Dunwood silhouetted against the flames in his frock coat and tricorn hat, the imperious master of Socastee Manor. Then the edges of the images began to burn and crackle like old celluloid film, and the image curled and distorted until Dunwood vanished with one last, piercing shriek of defiance.

Simon dropped onto his back, breathing hard, knowing the battle was only half won.

"We'll secure Camden," Trevor assured him. "Go do what you need to do."

Simon climbed to his feet, triaging the effects of his fight. He'd spent some of his energy, but thanks to the help of his friends, not nearly as much as if he had needed to wrest the victory from Dunwood all by himself. His leg throbbed, and the knife still protruded from his thigh, as blood ran down, soaking his jeans and sock. Pushing away fatigue, Simon hobbled to the windows in the front room that overlooked the ocean. He opened the French doors and stepped outside onto the balcony, into the lashing rain and howling wind.

Dante, are you ready?

"We're here, Sebastian." Miss Eppie came to stand next to him, soaking wet, but undeterred. She took his left hand, as Gabriella took his right. He heard Trevor and Josh take their places to make the circle, lending him their energy. He hoped it would be enough. Simon centered himself, gathering his courage, and thought of Vic, hoping that both of them would make it home alive this night. Then he reached out with his abilities and connected to Dante's spirit.

"Dante," Simon murmured. "Come in."

Dante's ghost rushed into Simon's consciousness, filling his mind, possessing him fully. Usually, Simon fought to hold back, but he knew that they would not win against Beecher's ghost without total commitment on both their parts. It was an all-or-nothing bet. If Simon and Dante succeeded, Beecher and the Wilton Stone would be lost to the depths of the Atlantic Ocean forever. And if Beecher won, his vengeful ghost would continue its killing spree, unfettered, and both Simon and Dante might cease to exist.

Dante's magic roiled through Simon like fire in his blood. He'd had a taste of the ghost's water magic before, but nothing like this. The full measure of Dante's power filled Simon, attuned to the storm that raged outside, giving and receiving energy until Simon wasn't sure where he ended, and Dante and the storm began.

Beecher's ghost dove and swooped at them like a hawk, furiously intent on its prey. The energy of the circle forced Beecher back, and Simon was vaguely aware of protective magic rising from both Miss Eppie and Gabriella, passing through Josh like an amplifier. He didn't have time to question, promising himself that if he survived, he'd get to the bottom of that mystery. Now, Simon emptied his thoughts, sharpened his focus, and joined his energy with Dante and the storm.

He knew from the dive charts where the *Annabelle* lay beneath the water, although he couldn't see the wreck itself. Simon fixed his concentration on what remained of the old pirate ship. Dante's magic showed him the old timbers and the skeletal hull, a far cry from its heyday as the terror of the seas. The wreck looked more like the bones of a dinosaur, half-hidden in the sand. Time and the waves had not been kind. Only part of the ship was still intact.

Somehow the Wilton Stone had been dragged along with the bones of the *Annabelle,* or its pernicious magic had attached it like a barnacle to the rotting keel, keeping it with the vessel that had been its last home. Even at a distance, Simon could feel the stone's power. It drew Dante's magic like a beacon. Two hundred and fifty years of connection with the stone had fueled Beecher's ghost, along with cold rage and an iron will. But now, with Simon's mediumship lending the energy of his Gift and the séance circle to Dante, the Wilton Stone was about to pass into oblivion

Give me all you've got, Dante urged, as his energy twined with Simon's to dislodge the wreck from its resting place. The violent waves worked with them, and when they found the riptide, Dante's magic only had to keep the hull from scraping bottom until the water carried it to the end of the relatively shallow ledge, and it could drop off into the depths far below.

Beecher didn't give up easily, slamming against Simon's mental shields and the wardings Gabriella and Miss Eppie raised around them. But the farther the waves carried the *Annabelle* from shore, the weaker Beecher's ghost became, still raging and furious, but no longer able to wreak its vengeance on anyone ever again.

When the rotting timbers and the Wilton Stone plunged to the abyss, Beecher's ghost fell silent.

The nightmare was over.

Thank you, cousin. Dante's voice sounded weary in Simon's mind, but proud of what they had accomplished.

Will you go away, too? There was so much Simon wanted to ask Dante, and there'd been no time for conversation.

I'm strongest in the storm, Dante replied. *Call me when you need me, and if it's in my power to do so, I will come. Fare thee well.*

Dante's presence vanished, leaving Simon himself once more. He felt like he'd been turned inside out and bled dry from the power Dante had channeled through him and the energy he had expended. Bone weary, soaked to the skin and freezing cold, Simon couldn't stay upright. He thought he heard Vic's voice in the distance, and that was the final thing he needed to let go and surrender to the exhaustion.

Vic will make sure everything's all right. He's here. I'm safe.

16

VIC

Vic and Ross burst into the parlor at Socastee Manor with Coast Guard Captain Bret Timmons on their heels and came to a screeching halt. Vic wasn't sure what he had expected, but the scene in front of him wasn't it.

Jonah Camden lay bound with duct tape, apparently unconscious. Everyone else stood near the French doors, which had been thrown open like this was a balmy summer night. Vic spotted Trevor Nichols and Josh Williams, bloody and battered, standing in the wind and rain, hands clasped in a circle with Miss Eppie and Gabriella—and Simon.

Good God, is that a knife sticking out of his leg?

Vic took a step toward them, but Ross grabbed his arm. "Don't. Whatever's happening, let it be." Everything inside Vic wanted to go to Simon and protect him. It took all of his self-control to stay back.

"What the hell is going on?" Timmons knelt next to Camden, taking his pulse to assure that the developer was still alive.

"I don't honestly know," Vic replied, torn between awe and terror. Lightning lit up the sky, streaking from the clouds to the sea. Simon was soaked, face raised to the wind, head back, long hair sodden and dripping. And just like last time, Vic knew on a primal level that the man who channeled the storm wasn't *only* Simon, He was something else, *someone* else, too.

Damned if Vic knew if he could ever quite get used to that, seeing his lover's body taken for a joyride by a visiting ghost. But he would, he'd manage, because this was Simon and Vic's love for him was as fierce as the storm.

A bolt of lightning illuminated the balcony, and the thunder boomed so loudly that Vic felt certain it struck somewhere between the manor and the beach. The tang of ozone hung in the air. Simon's whole body stiffened, and the same tension seemed to run through the circle of those who'd joined hands. Vic could practically feel the hum of the energy, and he knew in his gut that this was a showdown between Simon and the *Annabelle's* ghostly murderer, a battle that Vic had to sit out on the sidelines.

"Fuck that," he muttered, striding up to the circle with Ross close on his heels. Vic put one hand on Trevor's shoulder and the other on Josh's. Ross followed his example even if he didn't fully understand, doing the same with Josh and Gabriella. If Vic could lend anything to the fight without breaking the circle, he promised Simon silently that he would give it his all.

Vic thought about the woven bracelet and the pocket square with their magic, and the silver St. George medallion around his neck, willing all their protections toward Simon. Maybe it was his imagination, but Vic could have sworn that he felt a tug on his energy, and he didn't resist. He'd give Simon his blood if he needed it; maybe this was not so different. So Vic hung on, chanting the Hail Mary in his mind, hoping the cost of victory would not be more than he was willing to pay.

Simon gave a guttural cry. The wind battered the porch and snapped a tree with a crack like gunfire. All of a sudden the tension vanished, and the wind died. Simon dropped like a rock.

"Simon!" Vic plowed past everyone to reach Simon's side. The third stolen knife from the museum was buried deep in Simon's leg, which made Vic's stomach twist. Simon wasn't responding, and his skin was ice cold. Vic grabbed him under the arms and dragged him inside. Ross and Trevor shut the doors, although the rain had soaked the floor several feet into the room.

"We need to get him warm and stabilize the knife until we can get him to the hospital," Vic snapped. He looked to Trevor. "Supplies?"

Trevor disappeared and returned in a few moments carrying an armful of canvas painter's drop cloths. "We can wrap him in these. They're the closest thing to blankets I've got." He also held out a field med-kit. "There's gauze and an Ace bandage, plus tape."

Bret was on his portable radio, calling the Coast Guard for help. Josh Williams sat on an upturned utility bucket while Miss Eppie dabbed at a gash on his shoulder. A bloody line on Williams's throat gave Vic an idea that whatever had happened here had been intense. The whole house stank of fresh smoke, and Vic saw tendrils still rising from a metal bucket.

Gabriella knelt on Simon's other side and laid a hand on his forehead.

"Is he going to be okay?" Vic felt his heart in his throat.

"Dunwood's ghost is gone, and so is Beecher's spirit," she told him. "I can't heal his wound like it never happened, but I can use my magic to staunch the bleeding and keep him stable until help arrives."

"Thank you," Vic said in a ragged voice.

Josh joined them next, and Gabriella moved out of the way. He looked like he'd gone a couple of rounds with a boxer. "Let me have a look at that blade," he said. "I was a medic in the Navy."

Vic sat back on his haunches as Josh examined the wound without disturbing the knife. "He's lost blood, and we don't want to remove the knife until he gets to the hospital because it's sealing the wound. As best as I can tell, the blade didn't hit anything vital. It's going to need a hell of a lot of stitches, but it's fixable. Hitting an artery would have been a whole 'nother story."

Vic and Gabriella wrapped Simon in the drop cloths, careful not to jostle the knife. Vic had gotten stabbed more than once in the line of duty, and he knew it would hurt like hell when Simon woke up.

He held Simon's hand, trying to share his body heat, willing Simon to know, somehow, that he was close by.

"How did you get here?" Trevor asked. "The road is a mess. I came out because I'd told Josh I'd let him in to look for some old book. I was also worried that we'd both get stranded if the road flooded—which it did. My truck barely made it in."

"Thank the Coast Guard. We came by boat."

"In the middle of the storm?"

Vic nodded. "Yeah. Not a fun ride."

Bret wandered over. "The storm's dying down. They should be able to have an extra boat out to pick us all up in about an hour, since we can't all fit in the skiff. And I don't want to chance a return trip in that little boat with Simon injured if we don't have to. They'll have an ambulance standing by at the dock. We'll make sure Simon's in good hands."

Ross had been pacing near the French doors, trying to get a signal. He finally gave up with a disgusted expression. "I promised Cap I'd let him know that we got here, but I can't get any bars."

"I asked my commander to radio Captain Hargrove and relay my report," Bret said. "He and Hargrove go way back."

The next hour passed slowly. Ross and Vic took statements from Miss Eppie, Gabriella, Trevor, and Josh. Camden remained unconscious, and—more to Vic's concern—so did Simon.

"Why isn't he waking up?" Vic fretted. Simon's pulse was steady, but he was pale and colder than usual.

"He's been through a lot," Gabriella replied. "Shock, exhaustion, and blood loss. He put on one hell of a show."

Simon and his friends had managed to shut down two murderous ghosts. Vic was proud of Simon's bravery and cleverness, but right now all he cared about was that Simon was too cold, too quiet, too still.

Please be okay. I can't lose you.

Vic felt certain that the statements the others provided were edited somewhat, especially since none of them were sure where Bret stood on the supernatural issue. Vic promised himself he'd eventually get the full story. When Bret came over to check on them, Vic figured he might as well find out.

"So…about what happened here," Vic began.

Bret raised an eyebrow. "I don't need to know," he replied. "Although, since you partner up with a psychic medium on cases, I'd wager there was more going on that meets the eye." He shrugged. "We've got Camden on the hook for two killings and witnesses for his confession. Since one of those is the diver's murder, my boss will be happy. As for the rest? What I don't know, I don't have to do paperwork on." He slapped Vic on the shoulder and headed over to talk to Josh.

Over in the other corner, Vic could hear Trevor talking with Miss Eppie and Gabriella about how to cleanse Socastee Manor of the psychic stain from Jamie Dunwood's ghost and the general unpleasantness of the Dunwood descendants. Miss Eppie and Gabriella appeared to agree to something, then moved farther into the house carrying flashlights. Trevor noticed Vic watching, and came over.

"There isn't time for a full cleansing now, but they said they'd do what they could, and I promised to pay them if they'd come back and finish it after the storm." Trevor pushed his wet hair off his face. "Damn, it'll be a wonderful thing not to have that ghost fucking with us, after all that lost time and worry."

"What about Camden? He's going to have a date with the police. Will that hurt the project?" Vic didn't care much about the house itself, but he respected Trevor's efforts to keep his crew safe.

"Not really. The investment company will assign someone else to the account. Camden never really did as much as he thought he did. I won't miss him. And I'm glad he didn't kill Simon or Josh."

Vic knew he'd never get the real story of what happened until Simon woke up, or Miss Eppie and Gabriella had a chance to fill him in without the chance of being overheard. Obviously, Simon had figured out that his initial mistrust of Josh was wrong, since Camden lay trussed up like a Thanksgiving turkey. But what had happened out on the porch, and why was Simon so badly drained?

Vic tightened his grip on Simon's hand and hoped he'd be able to get the answers from Simon himself before long.

When the boat finally arrived, Vic carried Simon down to the dock and refused to let go until they landed and an ambulance crew stood ready to take Simon to the hospital.

"Go with him," Ross said. "I'll talk to Hargrove. Keep me posted."

Vic flashed his badge at the ambulance crew, unwilling to be separated from Simon. He was grateful that Camden had a different ambulance. Vic never wanted to see that slimy developer again, unless it was in a courtroom to receive a guilty verdict.

Vic moved out of the team's way as the EMTs started Simon's blood transfusion, and began treating him for shock and exposure. Simon looked so vulnerable, lying pale and still on the gurney, and Vic hated how helpless he felt, unable to do anything except keep Simon company and hope for the best.

Tracey was waiting for them at the hospital. She had Simon's Power of Attorney, something that Vic decided he and Simon might want to discuss at some point. Right now, Vic was just glad that he didn't have to deal with Simon's parents.

"So, here we are again," Tracey said as she and Vic settled in at the waiting room with their cafeteria coffee. Months ago, on Simon and Vic's first case together, a bullet had put Simon in the operating room. Now, while the doctor assured them that the knife wound wasn't life-threatening, Vic felt somehow guilty for not having prevented it.

"Yeah. At least we know not to get coffee out of the vending machine." Vic's weak joke fell flat. He wondered if Tracey blamed him for Simon's injury. After all, before Vic and Simon teamed up, no one had been trying to kill Simon.

"Stop that."

Vic looked up, perplexed. Tracey sighed and shook her head. "You're thinking so loudly, I can practically hear you, and I'm *not* telepathic. It's not your fault. I don't blame you. You didn't put him in danger."

Vic ran a hand back through his hair. "I kinda did, when I came to him about the Slitter on that first case. If I hadn't asked him to do that reading, he'd still be safe, giving ghost tours."

"Huh. That shows what you know." Tracey got a look in her eye that reminded Vic of his mother's expression when she was about to lay down the law. "First, there's nothing to say that the ghosts he was already talking to wouldn't have dragged him into solving crimes. He wouldn't have turned them down, but he'd have been on his own, with no backup."

"Yeah, but—"

"Do I look like I'm done talking?"

Vic shook his head and fell silent.

"If you hadn't gone to his shop, the two of you might have never gotten together. I knew Simon before, and I see him now, and y'all are good for each other. That boy was lonely and didn't know it before he met you."

Vic nodded. "I just don't want anything bad to happen to him. God, Tracey, when I got him off that porch, he was barely breathing, and he was so cold and pale."

"And one of these days, odds are it's going to be Simon sitting here losing his mind, and you under the knife. But unless you toss in your crime-fighting capes and go do something altogether different —like run an antique store like Simon's cousin—I don't think you're going to get away from danger. It goes with the job. And you go with Simon. Period."

Vic rubbed his eyes. The coffee soured in his stomach, and his head throbbed, reminding him it had been too long since he'd eaten. "I know. You're right. I'm not going anywhere. He's it for me. But sometimes that makes it harder, having something to lose."

"You sound like my girl, Shayna," Tracey said. "Always worrying about what's coming down the road. She was in the Army, you know that? So she's got a longer list than most people of horrible things that could happen. And maybe they will. But I keep telling her they haven't happened yet, so we might as well enjoy what we've got while we've got it." She smiled. "So listen up, huh."

Vic managed a weak smile in return. "And you sound like my *nonna*."

Tracey frowned. "Isn't she the one with the evil eye?"

"Yeah. So?"

"Think I could learn that? I'm good at giving the stink eye. I've never tried the evil eye."

"Pretty sure it's something you're born with."

"Huh. Don't go crashing my dreams like that. A person's gotta have goals."

Vic appreciated what Tracey was trying to do, and she looked slyly triumphant when she managed to make him smile. He was grateful for Tracey in the same way he was thankful for a partner like Ross. Good friends were hard to come by.

They both looked up as a figure approached, and Vic recognized Simon's surgeon.

"Ms. Cullen? Lieutenant D'Amato?" Tracey and Vic nodded, anxious for news.

"Simon's injury caused blood loss but didn't do any permanent damage. He came through just fine, although with a deep wound like that, it took us a while to stitch him up. He's on pain medication, and as soon as we move him to his room, you can see him."

"Was he awake at all before you took him in?" Vic pressed.

The surgeon frowned. "No. That's why we required Ms. Cullen to give informed consent. I was given the understanding he'd been attacked?"

It was as good an explanation as any, and not wholly untrue. "Yeah," Vic said. "He stopped a mugging." Camden's attack on Josh counted.

"We gave him a transfusion, and we have him on an IV to keep him from being dehydrated. The scans don't show any brain damage, but we're concerned because we don't know why he hasn't woken up. We'll keep him under observation until we're certain he'll be all right."

"Thank you." Vic felt every minute of his own long hours, first helping with the storm and then sitting vigil. He and Tracey watched the surgeon as he headed down the hallway.

"Go get something to eat," Tracey urged. "You look like you're running on empty. The last thing we need is having you swoon and crack your head."

"Cops don't swoon."

"All right, tough guy. But Shayna's brother, the Marine, gave himself a concussion when he didn't eat and passed out. I'm just sayin'."

"Okay, okay. I'll go get food. You want me to bring something back for you?"

She shook her head. "I'm good. I was safe and dry at home all day, so I ate dinner a while ago. By the time you get back, they'll probably have Simon in a room."

Vic knew anything he ate would sit like lead in his belly, but Tracey wasn't entirely wrong. His headache was likely a combination of stress, the storm, and not having eaten anything since breakfast. Vic managed to choke down a burger in the cafeteria, then hurried back with fresh coffees for both of them.

"Good timing," Tracey said. "They've got him moved in."

Vic thought he was prepared, after the last time, to see Simon in a hospital bed, but it was a sucker punch to the gut even so. It had been so much worse before, touch and go, with far more tubes and wires keeping Simon alive until his body could heal from the bullet wound. Now, a single IV line ran into the back of his left hand, while a few monitor leads fed a bank of screens that showed all his vitals. Still, everything about the room brought back bad memories; the smell of the disinfectant, the beep of the machines, the way Simon looked almost fragile against the stark white sheets.

"I told the nurse that you were his partner and you'd want to stay the night," Tracey said. "I may have also dropped in that you're a cop."

Vic gave her a grateful smile. "Thank you."

Tracey walked over to Simon's bedside and took hold of the hand without the IV. "I'm glad you're going to be okay," she said, looking away from Vic as she tried not to tear up. He knew that beneath Tracey's wisecracking exterior she had a good heart, and she loved Simon like a brother. "Now that the big emergency's over, I'm going home. Vic's gonna stay with you. Don't get up to anything that'll scandalize the nurses," she added, then leaned over to give him a kiss on the forehead.

"Call me when he wakes up," she ordered. "I don't care what time it is."

Vic saluted. Tracey blew raspberries and walked away, leaving Vic alone with Simon and the steady beep of the monitors. He padded over to the right side of the bed and drew up a chair, then took Simon's hand in both of his.

"They fixed you up. You're going to be fine," Vic said quietly, in case no one had bothered to update Simon on his own condition. Vic had been in enough emergency rooms, as a cop and on the receiving end, to know that details tended to get lost in the fray. "But we're all worried that you aren't waking up. I don't know exactly what all happened, and I'm sure it wore you out. So if you need to rest, that's great. Just…I'm counting on you to come back to me, okay?"

Vic brought Simon's hand up to kiss his knuckles. "You scared me. I mean, I'm still scared. Wake up and show me you're really all right." He held Simon's hand against his cheek. "I'm going to be here all night. Not leaving. So you can rest, because you're safe. I, um, borrowed a salt shaker from the cafeteria and put lines down across the door and window. Nurses will have my ass if they notice, but I thought that way maybe there wouldn't be any pesky ghosts bothering you."

He leaned back in his chair, trying to get as comfortable as possible given the thin padding. After a career of stakeouts, he'd slept worse places. "I love you," he murmured. "So you need to wake up and get better."

Hospitals were the worst place to rest. Every few hours, someone always came in to check vital signs. Vic had been a patient enough times to know the drill firsthand. He woke every time someone entered the room, but Simon didn't. The nurses made their rounds, gave him meaningless, encouraging smiles, and left again.

Vic shifted in his chair, leaning forward to rest his head on his folded arms, still keeping one hand clasped with Simon's. His back would ache tomorrow, and his ass was already sore from the chair, but there wasn't really an alternative.

Vic was in the middle of a dream about sleeping hunched over a desk in school when Simon's muttering roused him.

"Hey, Simon. Are you in there? C'mon, wake up. It's lonely out here all by myself."

Simon's eyelids fluttered, and Vic held his breath. Finally, Simon opened his eyes and turned his head toward Vic. "What happened?"

Vic grinned, despite the fact that it was oh-dark-thirty. "You got whammied by a ghost and stabbed by that Camden douchebro. The doc sewed you up, and I've been waiting for you to wake up and join the party."

Simon looked drained. Vic took in the dark circles under his lover's eyes, and the pinched expression that suggested the meds hadn't completely taken the edge off the pain. "I remember…I fought with Dunwood…Josh…shot…Camden with salt. Camden went after me. I…blocked him…Only got my leg. Trevor burned… ledger. Dunwood went away."

Vic went cold. *I blocked him…only got my leg.* Simon had gone after a killer who had a knife. It could have been so much worse. There was a lot more he wanted to ask, but Simon was already asleep again. Vic texted an update to Tracey and then fell back to sleep.

Two hours later, Simon stirred. Vic helped him sit to drink water, and rang for the nurse to bring breakfast.

"Do you remember anything after you got stabbed?" Vic asked once Simon had a chance to eat.

Simon blinked a couple of times, as if he were searching his memories. "Dante…used water magic…made the storm push the *Annabelle* and the *Wilton Stone* away, into deep water." Simon still sounded groggy, and the pain medicine slurred his words. "Beecher's ghost, gone." Simon looked a little confused, and Vic guessed his memory after the final strike was hazy. He didn't want to think too hard about Simon allowing ghosts to possess him, when they'd just seen how that could go very wrong.

"You did it," Vic said, folding Simon's hand between both of his. "You stopped two killers."

"Not by myself. The others—"

"Still, you figured it out, and you used your mojo. I'm so fucking proud of you."

Simon's eyes fluttered shut, and Vic thought he'd fallen asleep. "I didn't think you got my message." Simon's barely-there accent grew thicker the way it did when he was tired or upset. "Was worried."

"Kept losing signal," Vic replied, and one hand went to toy with the hem of the bed sheet. "Then when I did get enough bars, and your text came through, I didn't know how we were going to get there, until I thought of Bret Timmons. He got us through the storm, but I don't want to go on another boat ride for a very long time."

"Deal," Simon promised, and this time he drifted back to sleep. Vic leaned in to kiss his cheek, wondering how he had ever managed to survive without the raw love that tightened his chest and changed his world. Loving someone this much was wonderful, dizzying, and frightening in its vulnerability, but Vic knew he wouldn't want it any other way.

17

SIMON

"So Josh is a null? What does that even mean?" Simon had insisted on coming into the store despite Pete's assurance that he had everything covered. Three days of taking it easy had worn on Simon's last nerve, and he needed to get out of the blue bungalow no matter what Pete—or Vic—thought about it. Fortunately, traffic hadn't picked back up much yet after the storm, so the day promised to be slow.

"It's why you couldn't read anything from him," Gabriella replied. She had made a point of checking in on him, and while her stern demeanor would never be mistaken for motherly, Simon was pleased to know that she cared in her own way. "A null has natural shielding. He might not even know he's doing it. But in the circle, when you and Dante fought Beecher's ghost, Josh grounded us all. That's another thing a null can do—anchor those with power."

"Do you think he realizes?"

Gabriella shrugged. "Hard to say. Nulls aren't common, so he has a special talent. Did you find him restful to be around?"

Simon hadn't really thought about it, but now that he did, he realized that Josh seemed to put him at ease and give him a sense of peace, even in the midst of chaos.

"Yeah. I guess so. I hadn't noticed before."

She nodded. "It's a quiet Gift. Underrated. But as you saw, it brings out the best in other magics."

Simon made a mental note to add Josh to his Skeleton Crew. "What about Reggie? Is he okay?" They had left Reggie protected behind the wardings at Miss Eppie's house the night of the battle, and Simon hadn't thought to ask before this.

Gabriella laughed. "Oh, he's fine. Although I imagine he's got every hoodoo charm Eppie sells somewhere in his house now."

"Thank you again, for everything. You and Miss Eppie were amazing."

Gabriella snorted. "You held your own just fine. Except for the getting stabbed part."

Simon sighed. "Yeah, Vic bought me a Kevlar vest, and so I get stabbed in the leg. He's probably going to buy me a suit of armor next."

"He's okay, for a cop. One of the good ones." She nodded. "He'll do." Gabriella gathered her purse and jacket. "I've got to go. Try not to run across any more ghost murderers for a week or two. My grandchildren are coming to visit, and I'm booked solid." With that, she swept out of the shop, leaving Simon and Pete chuckling.

"She's a force of nature," Pete observed.

Simon shivered, thinking of Dante's water magic. "Yeah. She and Miss Eppie really came through."

The door opened, and Josh Williams walked in. "Simon! Good to see you're up and about. I was down at the station giving another statement, and Vic said you were back to work."

"How's the project going?" Simon wondered how pushing the wreck of the *Annabelle* into deep water and out of reach would affect Josh being able to finish his study.

"Well, the wreck is gone. Everyone says it was the storm, but…" Josh knew the real reason, and he'd handled the truth well when Simon had explained what had happened out at the mansion.

"Yeah. It's easier to just let them fill in the blanks themselves," Simon agreed.

"We've got sonar to show that the *Annabelle* and anything she still carried with her is out of range," Josh said.

"Can you work with what you were able to get from the earlier dives?" As much as Simon was glad to be rid of Beecher's ghost and stop the suicide-murders, he hated to see Josh's grant funding get canceled. He'd spent enough years in academia back when he was a professor to appreciate the dilemma.

"We got enough photos and readings that I have what I need for the research," Josh replied. "And while I never did get a look at Dunwood's ledger, we know it existed. Tragic, being lost in an electrical fire like that." He smiled. That was the cover story Trevor used to explain the smell of smoke in the old manor.

"And now you've got a whole new angle, right? Because you said that some of the old diaries and letters hinted at the Dunwood connection to the *Annabelle*."

Josh nodded. "Yeah. The university's lawyers will have a heyday making sure we can't be sued over it, but everyone involved with the actual smuggling is long dead, so we've got some leeway there."

Simon shifted in his chair, trying to keep his sore leg comfortable. "About what happened out at the house...did you feel anything strange when you were part of the circle, there at the end?"

Josh smiled. "You mean the way I anchored you? Yeah, I felt it."

"So you know you're a null?"

"It goes by a lot of names. My mother had the Sight, and she told me about it early on. Didn't want me to get taken advantage of by an unscrupulous practitioner."

"That's good," Simon agreed. "I know a lot of folks who never got any help with their Gifts."

"I heard you're not just a ghost whisperer, but you're also kind of the psychic shepherd in these parts," Josh said with a grin.

Simon shrugged. "I guess. More like I try to make sure folks who need it get some training and understand what's going on, and know some other people like them, if they ever need to talk to someone."

"And they let you know if there's anything weird going on," Josh finished.

"Yeah, most of the time. It works."

"Got any openings? I make a great anchor."

Simon grinned. "Welcome to the Crew."

Once the storm was over, Myrtle Beach got back to business. Simon's leg didn't allow for him to help un-sandbag the store and the bungalow, so he bought pizza to feed the friends who pitched in. The storm hadn't left as much damage in its wake as it might have, but there were still plenty of downed power lines, broken trees, and electrical outages to keep utility trucks busy for the next few days. Boardwalk merchants swept sand and palm fronds away from their shops, while the city maintenance crews worked overtime blowing sand back where it belonged.

Vic was back to working his usual homicide duties, which meant dealing with Camden's case. As for the men Beecher's ghost had pushed to suicide, even Ross agreed that there was no way to let the truth be known, and nothing to be gained by trying. Beecher and the Wilton Stone were in the depths of the ocean, a rough justice of its own kind. He couldn't hurt anyone again. Privately, Simon debated whether the families of the dead men would feel better if they knew their loved ones hadn't really intended to kill themselves, or worse knowing they were murdered. He was glad it wasn't up to him to decide.

Tonight was Simon's turn to cook dinner. Vic had argued that cooking required too much standing on Simon's bum leg, and Simon countered that he could sit at the table to do all the prep work, and pick a meal that didn't require Simon to be at the stove. He felt vindicated as he hobbled to the oven with his one-pan meal of chicken, potatoes, and vegetables. A frozen Key Lime pie sat defrosting on the counter, next to a bowl of mixed greens from a bag. Mission accomplished.

He sat back and reached for his cup of tea. Gabriella had promised that her special medicinal tea would speed healing without messing with his pain meds, and Simon gave it credit for his rapid progress. The location of the wound—his right thigh—did threaten to put a damper on their love life, although Simon had a few ideas in mind to get around that.

He heard the thrum of Vic's Hayabusa motorcycle in the driveway. Simon already had a Springsteen playlist going—Vic's favorite—and a lit candle in the middle of the table, just because.

"Can you believe it? I'm actually early!" Vic toed out of his shoes in the entranceway, hung up his coat, and slung an arm around Simon's shoulders to bring him in for a kiss. "How's the leg?"

Simon appreciated Vic's protectiveness even if it did go a little over the top. "Pretty good today. Tracey drove me for my check-up, and the doc said it's mending well. No permanent damage. Just need to avoid straining it for a few more weeks."

"Good. That's good. I'm sorry I couldn't take you over myself."

"Don't sweat it. I was barely in the doctor's office half an hour. You're still processing the paperwork from the mess last week."

Vic grabbed a beer out of the fridge, popped off the cap, and headed for the couch. Simon skipped the beer out of respect for his meds, but joined Vic, pleased for moving a bit faster than he did the day before.

"Camden lawyered up—not surprising. The development company dumped him, and they're washing their hands of any connections. We've got his prints on two of the three knives, and witnesses for his attack on you and Josh, as well as his confession about killing the groundskeeper. It's the diver attack that is iffy—prints didn't stick—but if we nail him on one murder and an attempt, the second murder isn't going to make a big difference. And of course he denied any knowledge of the car bombing, but he'll still go away for a long time."

"You think he'll claim it was some kind of psychotic break?"

Vic shrugged. "Probably. And in a way, it was. But he's never going to be able to tell a jury that he was possessed by a ghost without creating even more problems for himself. And with what we've dug up on Camden, murder without being possessed isn't as much of a stretch as you might think."

"He didn't look like the type to get his hands dirty," Simon observed. "I'd have pegged him for outsourcing a hit."

"And you wouldn't be wrong," Vic replied, shaking his head. "There was an incident a few years back where he had a blow-up with a business partner before he started working with his current firm. Big project up for grabs, lots of money at stake. The business partner got in a wreck that took him off the project. He claimed Camden had someone cut his brake line, but he could never prove it."

"Yikes. Will the museum ever get the knives back?"

"That's out of my hands. Maybe, once all the legal wrangling is over. But it could take years."

"They'll be a big draw if they ever get put back on display. Scandal sells, and those knives have it across three centuries!" Simon leaned against Vic, so happy to be home together and safe.

"Trevor said that the renovations are continuing on schedule— losing Camden and being rid of Dunwood's ghost actually is making things go faster," Simon reported. "And Josh got enough of what he needed from the wreck that his project isn't tanked. It sounded to me like he might add some of the Dunwood scandal mystique to his book when it's finished."

"Funny, isn't it?" Vic's fingers massaged Simon's scalp and toyed with his long hair. "Jamie Dunwood's ghost wanted to protect his reputation, but everything he did ended up dragging it through the mud."

"Kind of fitting justice thought." Simon nestled closer. "He lost the thing that mattered the most to him, and he was already dead, so there wasn't really anything else to do to him."

They stayed snuggled on the couch until the timer went off. Simon went to get up, and his leg twinged. Vic caught him around the waist and eased him to standing.

"Thanks. It'll be okay once I get moving. It just gets stiff when I sit for a while."

Vic poured them glasses of sweet tea while Simon took the baking pan with its delicious contents out of the oven and placed it on hot pads. He'd already set the table, so serving the meal was easy.

"This is great," Vic said when they were digging into the food. "Even the vegetables taste good."

Simon grinned. "Coming from you, I'll take that as the compliment it was meant to be."

Vic insisted on cleaning up, so Simon kept him company seated at the table. He watched Vic at the sink, getting a great view of his tight ass and muscular thighs. Now that Simon's pain meds had been tapered off to a low dose and his leg no longer throbbed, other parts of his anatomy were definitely coming back online.

"There are some new movies streaming, if you want to crash on the couch," Vic suggested without turning. "Whatever sounds good to you."

"Whatever?" Simon asked playfully. Vic turned around and froze. Simon had spread his legs and was lazily stroking himself through his jeans, with a noticeably growing bulge to show for it.

"Your leg—"

"Is not the part of my body that wants attention right now," Simon replied. He met Vic's gaze and saw his pupils widen, then did a long, slow head to toe once over, which assured him that Vic's pants had grown tighter, too.

"I don't want to hurt you."

"You won't. I've been thinking about this all day, and I have some ideas."

"All day? Really?"

Simon nodded. "Uh huh. 'Cause it's been *so long*." He said with a little moan. "After all, a man's got *needs*."

Yep, Vic's pants were definitely tighter in the crotch now. Vic ambled toward Simon and stood with one leg between Simon's. He pulled Simon to his feet, slotting them together so Simon's cock rubbed against Vic's thigh. "I might have some needs myself," Vic said, letting his voice drop to a husky growl that sent a shiver through Simon. "Been just as long for me, you know."

"Better be."

"Always," Vic said, bucking a little harder against Simon and getting a thrust of hips in return. "So…what kind of ideas did you have?"

Simon gave him a wicked grin. "Get naked with me, and you'll find out."

Without the injury, that would have been Simon's cue to wrap his legs around Vic's waist to be carried off to the bedroom. Doing that didn't sound like a good idea at the moment, so he settled for kissing Vic long and slow, licking and nipping, until the bulge in Vic's jeans was rock hard.

"Bed. Now." Vic's dark eyes were almost all pupil with arousal, and his face was flushed. Simon kissed Vic's cheek, and couldn't wait to feel his stubble against other parts of his body.

They kissed, groped and fondled their way into the bedroom, but all the while, Simon knew Vic was keenly aware of not hurting him, careful not to bump into his sore leg or make him twist. That protectiveness warmed Simon's heart, making him feel loved and cherished.

They'd gone days without sex before, usually when one of them was sick or injured, or Vic ended up pulling double shifts. That made everything all the hotter when they got down to it. Vic insisted on carefully stripping Simon out of his shirt, then easing his jeans and briefs off carefully over his thighs, and tossing his socks toward the door. When Simon was naked, Vic stood back, appreciating his body like a starving man at a buffet.

"Damn, you're fine," Vic said with a grin.

Simon shimmied his way on the bed until he was stretched out, one leg pulled up and to the side, putting his very hard and leaking cock on full display. He gave himself a shameless tug and met Vic's gaze. "Like what you see?"

"You know I do."

Simon gave a little shrug. "Then how about you get naked and show me?" God, he'd never been such a tease before Vic, but then again, none of his few prior lovers had ever made Simon feel confident and accepted the way Vic did.

Vic took his time, making a show of shedding his clothes. When he wriggled out of his shirt, putting his inked shoulder and arms on display, Simon felt his cock leak, painfully hard. Tracing those tats with his tongue was Simon's new kink, and Vic loved it. The gleam in Vic's eyes told Simon that his lover knew exactly where Simon's mind had gone, and couldn't wait to make those luscious daydreams into reality.

Simon's eyes followed every move of Vic's hands as he undid his belt and popped open his button-flies. With a shimmy of his hips, Vic dropped his jeans, and then toed out of his socks, leaving just his barely-there briefs with a very prominent wet spot where the material strained against his cock. Never breaking eye contact, Vic eased the waistband of his tiny briefs down over his dusky, swollen prick and let them fall to the floor, exposing the infinity symbol tat in the cleft of his groin that he'd added just for Simon.

"I want in you so bad," Vic admitted, as he climbed onto the bed and stalked his way up Simon's body on his hands and knees. Simon could smell Vic's arousal, along with the clean eucalyptus of his favorite soap and a hint of sweat. That just fanned the flames higher. "How can we do this, so you don't get hurt?"

Simon wanted to feel Vic's gorgeous cock deep inside him, filling him up, claiming him. Possessing him, to reassure both of them that no ghost or entity would ever come between them. He ached for that, but Simon knew that no matter how they attempted it, he'd end up putting too much strain on the newly healed stitches. So that reunion would have to wait.

"It all counts as having sex," Simon said, letting his voice drop a bit lower than usual. He always felt a bit silly when he tried for seduction, but from the gleam in Vic's eyes, his lover didn't find him silly at all. "How about you let me suck you—while you're showing me how much you missed me?"

Vic didn't waste any time. He positioned himself on all fours with his cock in easy reach of Simon's mouth, and his own lips perfectly angled to handle Simon's straining erection.

Simon was torn between wanting to savor every sensation—the musk of Vic's pre-come, the warm velvet of his shaft, the weight of his dick on Simon's tongue—and wanting to swallow him down to the back of his throat and suck him senseless. He compromised and licked a stripe up Vic's cock that made Vic shiver and groan, then swiped his tongue over the head, and around again to slip into the slit.

Vic answered by pouncing on Simon's swollen shaft like a wild thing, deep throating him in one move, nuzzling into Simon's dark, wiry thatch and breathing in his scent. That drove all subtlety from Simon's mind, and he wrapped his arms around Vic's trim hips, digging his fingers into the globes of Vic's fine ass and making sure he couldn't get away as Simon feasted on his cock.

Simon wanted to thrust into Vic's hot mouth, but Vic put a hand on Simon's hip, holding him down. Sure, part of it was to keep from straining his stitches, but Simon also knew Vic enjoyed getting to Simon and making him desperate to come. Simon returned the favor, sucking and licking, humming and teasing until he felt Vic tremble. On a lazy weekend, they could edge each other for hours, exploring every inch of skin and sensation, adding fingers and toys for good measure.

But now, even a few days felt like forever, and Simon was torn between wanting to make the pleasure last and giving in to the climax that threatened to roar through him like a wildfire.

Vic made the choice for them. He slipped a spit-slick finger down Simon's crease, teasing at his tight pucker, then pressed inside and angled for his spot, at the same time that he swirled his tongue over the head of Simon's weeping cock and then took him down to the root.

Simon channeled his arousal into owning Vic's straining prick, bobbing up and down as he hollowed his cheeks and flicked his tongue. Vic tensed, then flooded Simon's mouth with his spend, seconds before Simon shot his load and Vic swallowed it down. Simon licked Vic clean, fondling his softening dick with his lips and tongue as Vic pressed a kiss to the inside of Simon's thigh.

Vic rolled to one side, careful not to put any weight on Simon's injured leg. Then he maneuvered himself around until his head was beside Simon's, and leaned in for a kiss, mingling their flavors. Simon raised a hand to cup the back of Vic's head, deepening the kiss, while the other hand caressed the strong muscles of Vic's back. After a few moments, they pulled back, and Simon wondered if his own eyes were as lust-blown as Vic's, who looked like Simon had just rocked his world. That thought made Simon's heart do a crazy little happy dance, to think he could put that look on Vic's face.

"That was…wow," Vic breathed.

"Yeah. Wow." Simon leaned in for another peck, enjoying the feel of Vic's stubble against his cheek and the warmth of his body along his side.

From out in the kitchen, Simon's phone chimed, a reminder to take his bedtime dose of pain medicine. He started to get up, but Vic laid a hand, gently but firmly, on his chest and pushed him back down.

"I'll get it. Need to make sure everything's locked up and turned off. How 'bout you get under the covers and wait for me, so you don't get cold?" Vic kissed his temple as if the journey entailed more than a few dozen steps.

Sleepy and sated, Simon wasn't in a mood to argue. He slid under the sheet and pulled the blanket and comforter up to his chin. Myrtle Beach winter temperatures still got low enough that good blankets were a requirement for a good night's sleep. In minutes, Vic was back. He held out a pill and a glass of water. Simon accepted both gratefully, then sighed as he eased back down onto the pillow.

When Vic returned again, he put both their phones on the nightstand and then joined Simon under the covers. Simon nestled close, resting his head in the crook of Vic's shoulder and slinging an arm around his waist. Vic stroked Simon's hair, while the tip of Simon's tongue lazily traced the closest black swirls of Vic's tattoos. From the way Vic shivered, Simon figured that Vic might have discovered a new kink, too.

"Did we ever decide what to do for Valentine's Day?" Vic sounded tired and totally blissed out.

"We talked about going out for dinner and getting a matching tat. Maybe some kind of protective symbol. Jay always runs a couple's special at the shop."

Vic stroked up and down Simon's back. "Matching tats, huh? You don't have any ink. That's quite a commitment."

Simon chuckled. "No, *this* is quite a commitment," he replied, splaying his fingers wide on Vic's chest. "A tat's just a symbol. I already asked Gabriella for ideas. I mean, if you still want to." Suddenly, Simon felt a little unsure, like he was rushing things. After all, they'd only just moved in together.

Vic reached up to take his hand, twining their fingers together. "Of course I still want to. I want you…this…us…more than I ever thought I'd want anything. It scares me a little how much."

Simon kissed his chest, flicking the nipple with the tip of his tongue for good measure, loving how Vic shivered. "I want you just as much. You're totally stuck with me."

"I can live with that." Vic's voice was warm and sleepy. Simon nuzzled closer, welcoming the way he felt safe and loved in Vic's arms. If he had anything to say about it, they'd both live with that for a long, long time.

AFTERWORD

Myrtle Beach is one of my favorite places, and many of the locations used in this book are real, although I've tweaked them a little for the sake of the story. Once upon a time, pirates were the scourge of the Carolina coast, taking advantage of a shoreline full of coves and inlets that made great places to hide. Major shipping lanes were just offshore, and the depths are littered with the wrecks of unfortunate vessels lost to storms and pirates.

Socastee Manor doesn't exist, but there are plenty of old, historic houses like Hopseewee Plantation and Hobclaw Barony to explore. When you visit the boardwalk, I don't think you'll have any trouble picking a spot where Grand Strand Ghost Tours might have its storefront. If you can see the SkyWheel and the famous Gay Dolphin Gift Shop, you're in the right place.

If you're curious about some of the side characters Simon interacted with, like his cousin Cassidy Kincaide, Teag Logan, and ex-priest Travis Dominick, they have their own series. Cassidy Kincaide is the main character in the Deadly Curiosities series set in Charleston, SC, all about getting cursed and haunted objects out of the wrong hands and saving the world from supernatural threats, and Teag Logan is her best friend. Dante Morris, the privateer ghost, is the star of three prequel Deadly Curiosities short stories set in the 1700s: *Among the Shoals Forever, Steer a Pale Course,* and *The Low Road. The Low Road* tells the story of that cursed set of bagpipes Gabriella mentioned. The stories are available individually in ebook, or in the *Trifles and Folly 2* collection in ebook, print, and now on audiobook. Look for Dante to play a role in the fourth Deadly Curiosities novel, *Inheritance.*

Travis and his partner Brent Lawson are the stars of the Night Vigil books, starting with *Sons of Darkness,* hunting down demonic danger in and around Pittsburgh. And those other hunters who called Simon for advice? That was Mark Wojcik from our Spells, Salt, and Steel series, snarky monster hunting in the wilds of Pennsylvania. (Those are all written under my Gail Z. Martin name.) The other caller was Seth Tanner, the main character of my (Morgan Brice) Witchbane series.

ACKNOWLEDGMENTS

Of course, it takes a village to bring a book to life. Thanks first of all to my husband, Larry N. Martin, for all his editing and work behind the scenes. Also thanks to our editor, Jean Rabe, cover artist Natania Barron, and our beta readers and launch team: Amy, Andrea, Anne, Annmarie, Ashby, Barbara, Carolyn, Carra, Cheryl, Christopher, Darell, Donald, Emma, Jocelyn, Karolina, Kathryn, Kristy, Laurie, Lee, Lisa, Lynn, Manda, Mindy, Renae, and Vickie. Your eagle eyes helped to make this book the best it could be. Thank you also to the bloggers, reviewers, and signal boosters who help others hear about the book. I am deeply grateful to all of you, and I couldn't do it without you. Thank you, most of all, to my readers, who mean the world to me. Because you read, I write.

ABOUT THE AUTHOR

Morgan Brice is the romance pen name of bestselling author Gail Z. Martin. Morgan writes urban fantasy male/male paranormal romance, with plenty of action, adventure, and supernatural thrills to go with the happily ever after.

Gail writes epic fantasy and urban fantasy, and together with co-author hubby Larry N. Martin, steampunk and comedic horror, all of which have less romance, and more explosions.

On the rare occasions Morgan isn't writing, she's either reading, cooking, or spoiling two very pampered dogs.

Watch for additional new series from Morgan Brice, and more books in the Witchbane and Badlands universes coming soon!

Where to find me, and how to stay in touch

On the web at https://morganbrice.com. Sign up for my newsletter and never miss a new release! http://eepurl.com/dy_8oL.

Facebook Group—the place for news about upcoming books, convention appearances, special contests, and giveaways, plus location photos, fantasy casting, and more! Look for http://www.facebook.com/groups/WorldsOfMorganBrice You can also find Morgan on Twitter: @MorganBriceBook and Pinterest (for Morgan and Gail): pinterest.com/Gzmartin.

Support Indie Authors

When you support independent authors, you help influence what kind of books you'll see more of and what types of stories will be available, because the authors themselves decide which books to write, not a big publishing conglomerate. Independent authors are local creators, supporting their families with the books they produce. Thank you for supporting independent authors and small press fiction!